PRAISE FOR *GAME WITHOUT RULES*

"It is hard to say what element is most effective in these tales: the smooth ingenuity of plotting or the manner of telling. These are short thrillers and also short works of art." —**Anthony Boucher, *The New York Times***

"The old Gilbert expertise applies to everything he sets his hand to. *Game Without Rules* gave me great pleasure. Good spies and good stories: rare." —**Eudora Welty**

"Splendidly done." —***The Philadelphia Inquirer***

"There may be readers who can put a Michael Gilbert aside unfinished, but I'm not among them." —***St. Louis Post-Dispatch***

Herald Classics

The Herald Classics series connects adventurous readers to excellent stories and showcases a dynamic and approachable literary canon.

Greatest Hits, by Harlan Ellison

Greatest Hits (Barnes & Noble Exclusive Edition), by Harlan Ellison

Game Without Rules, by Michael Gilbert

GAME WITHOUT RULES

HERALD CLASSICS

GAME WITHOUT RULES

Michael Gilbert
Introduction by Alex Segura

UNION SQUARE & CO.
NEW YORK

UNION
SQUARE
& CO.
NEW YORK

UNION SQUARE & CO. and the distinctive Union Square & Co. logo
are trademarks of Sterling Publishing Co., Inc.

Union Square & Co., LLC, is a subsidiary of Sterling Publishing Co., Inc.

This 2024 edition published by Union Square & Co., LLC.

ISBN 978-1-4549-5426-2

For information about custom editions, special sales, and premium purchases,
please contact specialsales@unionsquareandco.com.

Printed in India

2 4 6 8 10 9 7 5 3 1

unionsquareandco.com

Cover design by Igor Satanovsky
Interior design by Kevin Ullrich

Cover art and spine: Getty Images: ilbusca/DigitalVision Vectors (standing men)
Front and back cover: Shutterstock.com: 4zevar (hats), A7880S (dog),
Nata_Alhontess (watch), save nature and wildlife (body), Simply Amazing (lamp),
VectorVicePhoto (chairs)
Back flap: Shutterstock.com: chempina (tea set)

Contents

Introduction ix

The Road to Damascus 5

On Slay Down 29

The Spoilers 40

The Cat Cracker 85

Trembling's Tours 102

The Headmaster 122

Heilige Nacht 137

"Upon the King . . ." 160

Cross-Over 180

Prometheus Unbound 218

A Prince of Abyssinia 237

Introduction

Alex Segura

I've always been drawn to stories that live in the gray areas of life—that give readers a sense of the complicated, conflicted decisions even the most skilled protagonists must make. Written in the early-to-mid 1960s, perhaps the apex of Cold War paranoia and insecurity, Michael Gilbert's elderly espionage short story collection, *Game Without Rules*, makes for a perfect example of that kind of narrative.

The collection is an oddly prescient rediscovered gem, even at first blush. Constructed as a "novel in stories," a term that's quite du jour of late, *Game Without Rules* features Gilbert's two aging stars, Daniel Joseph Calder and Samuel Behrens (along with Calder's communicative, beloved, and exceedingly large Persian deerhound, Rasselas), who serve as the connective thread between the stories, which were first serialized in *Ellery Queen's Mystery Magazine* in the 1960s. Additionally, Gilbert's far-sighted choice of older, retired protagonists has seen a welcome echo in the recent works of authors like Richard Osman and Deanna Raybourn. Experience is useful. Who knew?

On the surface, Calder and Behrens are your typical, slow-moving retirees settled in a tiny village in Kent. It's immediately made clear to the reader that there is something . . . odd and distant about these two close friends. Both men have a strange habit of disappearing from time to time. There's a secret, buried telephone line between their homes, and there are steel plates concealed in Mr. Calder's window shutters. This is the best kind of opening salvo—one that immediately intrigues, raises questions, but doesn't slow down the story itself. You're buckled in and curious about where the train is going. We soon learn that, in reality, Calder and Behrens are British Intelligence operatives, reporting in regularly to their handler (who is hiding in plain sight as a mild-mannered bank manager), and more than willing to do whatever it takes to protect Queen and Country—even if it means murder.

Gilbert, a Mystery Writers of America Grand Master, beloved by the legendary Anthony Boucher, and recipient of many dazzling accolades, was an author of over thirty novels, almost two hundred short stories, and myriad collections. I'm not here to argue why Gilbert hasn't received the praise he deserves, in life or after. His awards and recognitions are many. But after reading *Game Without Rules*, you may be left wondering why it took so long for this book to return to print, or why you hadn't heard of Gilbert before. I'm just here to tell you, friend, it's okay to feel that.

When it comes to spies and detectives, we tend to favor the flashy James Bond or the haughty Sherlock Holmes to the more dogged George Smiley or Dr. John Watson. Not to begrudge Gilbert at all, but it was quite clear to me that he was workmanlike in his output—and demeanor, I'd wager, much like his memorable creations, Calder and Behrens. Gilbert's daily mission involved writing a set number of words each day on his train ride home from work, where he was a partner at a law firm. This is relevant not because of its trivia value, but because this ethos is clear in Gilbert's work: sparse, lucid prose, while holding close a sense of heart and suspense.

Gilbert's thoughtful, almost subdued wordplay lulls the reader into a state of contentment that makes the darker revelations all the more jarring, like being shaken awake by a stranger. The stories emanate a sense of chill calm, with spikes of emotion and heartfelt resonance reminiscent of the best Scandinavian noir or the mid-period Smiley novels of John le Carré. The reader melts into the world Gilbert is creating, making the twists and turns he injects into the stories with verve and precision all the more surprising and memorable. Gilbert does what the best curators of suspense do, and he makes it look much easier than it really is.

Gilbert's choice to make his characters older is a meaningful one, a lasting decision that runs parallel with le Carré's nebbishy and paper-pushing viper Smiley, and counter to Ian Fleming's debonair and deadly superspy, James Bond. Calder and Behrens serve as prime examples of British manners and decorum, but unlike Smiley, Gilbert's protagonists aren't grizzled, numb Cold Warriors—both have a lightness to them that's unexpected and welcome, but one that can be shut off with an immediacy and speed that will leave you breathless. Whether they're assisting a royal from an undefined African country or retracing the steps of enemy double-agents across the deep geopolitical divisons of Cold War Europe, these are tales of complicated and flawed people forced to dig deep for intelligence. That said, Gilbert's stellar writing—gingerly coated with a dry, comforting wit—creates the perfect backdrop for his layered and memorable heroes.

At the same time, one senses that Gilbert's Calder and Behrens are also echoing the older, even more legendary duo of Sir Arthur Conan Doyle's Holmes and Watson, if not in dynamic then at least in tone, episodic nature, and composed pacing. Gilbert's heroes are systematic and reticent men who have lived life, are set in their ways, and able to toss aside the buzzing of the world around them to execute their tasks—literally and figuratively. As is often the case with great mystery and spy fiction, it's the characters that actualize the plot—and Gilbert created two memorable, enjoyable people you just want to spend time with. The heroes are immediately relatable and likable, and in turn, the saga becomes all the more surprising when Calder and Behrens are revealed to be cold-blooded killers in the service of their government. Gilbert's stories evoke a distance that's almost Vulcan in its detachment, with flourishes of heart and empathy that connect like a roundhouse kick to the chin.

The stories in *Game Without Rules* move at a windswept clip, each serving as a welcome peek into the lives of Calder and Behrens, under the careful supervision of a writer in peak form. But beyond the surface appeal of, arguably, Gilbert's most beloved work, the stories find a way of propelling forward—collecting bits of character and detail to form a greater whole, a moving portrait of an aging male friendship forged in the fires of a complicated, gray, and often confusing post–Cold War world—a world that tees up the hot mess we live in today.

Alex Segura is the acclaimed and bestselling author of the comic book noir novel *Secret Identity*, which won the Los Angeles Times Book Prize in the Mystery/Thriller category and was named an Editor's Choice by the *New York Times*. His next novel, *Alter Ego*, arrives in 2024 from Flatiron Books.

GAME WITHOUT RULES

Samuel Behrens

Born 1910, second son and fourth child of Alfred Behrens and Marie Messenger, of Highgate, London.

Educated:	Shrewsbury (Oldhams House) and London University, and Heidelberg University. Specialized European languages. Taught at Munich High School 1929–32, Baden-Baden 1932–33, Leipzig 1933–35, Berlin 1935–39.

Recruited to MI6, 1933.

Languages:	(A) +Standard-German (A) Standard-French (A) Standard-Greek, Italian, Russian
War service:	Still classified (it has been mentioned in *Reminiscences* of Franz Mulbach, Bonn, 1963, that S. B. was in Germany for two months prior to the first attempt on Hitler's life and supplied the sabotage device which failed to detonate in the Fuehrer's plane).

Joined JSSIC(E) 1956.

Special interests:	Beekeeping, chess.
Club:	Dons-in-London.
Residence:	The Old Rectory, Lamperdown, Kent. Tel: Lamperdown 272
Blood group:	O.Rh +

Daniel Joseph Calder

Born 1913, only son of Rev. Joseph Calder (Canon of Salisbury) and Sandra Kisfaludy (Hungarian).

Educated: Bishop Wordsworth's School, Salisbury and Università di Perugia.

Reuters Foreign Correspondent, Athens, 1932; Budapest, 1934; Baghdad, 1937; Bucharest, Head Office, 1938.

Recruited to MI6, 1935.

Languages: (A) Standard-Albanian and Hungarian
(B) Standard-Greek, Italian, Arabic, Russian

War service: Partly still classified. 1939–41 at Blenheim and Hatfield Special Interrogation Centers. Member of British Military Mission to Albania, 1944.

Joined JSSIC(E) June, 1958.

Special interests: Small arms; cello; history of the Peninsular War.

Club: R.A.C.

Residence: The Cottage, Hyde Hill, near Lamperdown, Kent. Tel: (ex-directory)

Blood Group: AB. Rh+

MICHAEL GILBERT

Rasselas

Persian deerhound; by Shah Jehan out of Galietta.

Height:	32 inches. Weight: 128 pounds.
Color:	Golden with darker patches. Eyes amber. Nose blue-black. Hair rough, with distinctive coxcomb between ears. Neck, long. Quarters exceptionally powerful. Legs, broad and flat.
Club:	Kennel Club.
Blood group:	(canine classification) A5

The Road to Damascus

Everyone in Lamperdown knew that Mr. Behrens, who lived with his aunt at the Old Rectory and kept bees, and Mr. Calder, who lived in a cottage on the hilltop outside the village and was the owner of a deerhound called Rasselas, were the closest of close friends. They knew, too, that there was something out of the ordinary about both of them.

Both had a habit of disappearing. When Mr. Calder went he left the great dog in charge of the cottage; and Mr. Behrens would plod up the hill once a day to talk to the dog and see to his requirements. If both men happened to be away at the same time, Rasselas would be brought down to the Old Rectory where, according to Flossie, who did for the Behrenses, he would sit for hour after hour in one red plush armchair, staring silently at Mr. Behrens' aunt in the other.

There were other things. There was known to be a buried telephone line connecting the Old Rectory and the cottage; both houses had an elaborate system of burglar alarms; and Mr. Calder's cottage, according to Ken who had helped to build it, had steel plates inside the window shutters.

The villagers knew all this and, being countrymen, talked very little about it, except occasionally among themselves toward closing time. To strangers, of course, they said nothing.

That fine autumn morning Rasselas was lying, chin on ground, watching Mr. Calder creosote the sharp end of a wooden spile. He sat up suddenly and rumbled out a warning.

"It's only Arthur," said Mr. Calder. "We know him."

The dog subsided with a windy sigh.

Arthur was Mr. Calder's nearest neighbor. He lived in a converted railway-carriage in the company of a cat and two owls, and worked in the woods which cap the North Downs from Wrotham Hill to the Medway—Brimstone Wood, Molehill Wood, Long Gorse Shaw, Whitehorse Wood, Tom Lofts Wood and Leg of Mutton Wood. It was a very old part of the country and, like all old things, it was full of ghosts. Mr. Calder could not see them, but he knew they were there. Sometimes when he was walking with Rasselas in the woods, the dog would stop, cock his head on one side and rumble deep in his throat, his yellow eyes speculative as he followed some shape flitting down the ride ahead of them.

"Good morning, Arthur," said Mr. Calder.

"Working, I see," said Arthur. He was a small, thick man, of great strength, said to have an irresistible attraction for women.

"The old fence is on its last legs. I'm putting this in until I can get it done properly."

Arthur examined the spile with an expert eye and said, "Chestnut. That should hold her for a season. Oak'd be better. You working too hard to come and look at something I found?"

"Never too busy for that," said Mr. Calder.

"Let's go in your car, it'll be quicker," said Arthur. "Bring a torch, too."

Half a mile along a rutted track they left the car, climbed a gate and walked down a broad ride, forking off it onto a smaller one. After a few minutes the trees thinned, and Mr. Calder saw that they were coming to a clearing where wooding had been going on. The trunks had been dragged away and the slope was a litter of scattered cordwood.

"These big contractors," said Arthur. "They've got no idea. They come and cut down the trees, and lug 'em off, and think they've finished the job. Then I have to clear it up. Stack the cordwood. Pull out the stumps where they're an obstruction to traffic."

What traffic had passed, or would ever pass again through the heart of this secret place, Mr. Calder could hardly imagine. But he saw that the workmen had cleared a rough path which followed the contour of the hill and disappeared down the other side, presumably joining the track they had come by somewhere down in the valley. At that moment the ground was a mess of tractor marks and turned earth. In a year the raw places would be skimmed over with grass and nettles and bluebells and kingcups and wild garlic. In five years there would be no trace of the intruders.

"In the old days," said Arthur, "we done it with horses. Now we do it with machinery. I'm not saying it isn't quicker and handier, but it don't seem altogether right." He nodded at his bulldozer, askew on the side of a hummock. Rasselas went over and sneered at it, disapproving of the oily smell.

"I was shifting this stump," said Arthur, "when the old cow slipped and came down sideways. She hit t'other tree a proper dunt. I thought I bitched up the works, but all I done was shift the tree a piece. See?"

Mr. Calder walked across to look. The tree which Arthur had hit was no more than a hollow ring of elm, very old and less than three feet high. His first thought was that it was curious that a heavy bulldozer crashing down onto it from above should not have shattered its frail shell altogether.

"Ah! You have a look inside," said Arthur.

The interior of the stump was solid concrete.

"Why on earth," said Mr. Calder, "would anyone bother—?"

"Just have a look at this."

The stump was at a curious angle, half uprooted so that one side lay much higher than the other.

"When I hit it," said Arthur, "I felt something give. Truth to tell, I thought I'd cracked her shaft. Then I took another look. See?"

Mr. Calder looked. And he saw.

The whole block—wooden ring, cement center and all—had been pierced by an iron bar. The end of it was visible, thick with rust, sticking out of the broken earth. He scraped away the soil with his fingers and presently found the U-shaped socket he was looking for. He sat back on his heels and stared at Arthur, who stared back, solemn as one of his own owls.

"Someone," said Mr. Calder slowly, "—God knows why—took the trouble to cut out this tree stump and stick a damned great iron bar right through the middle of it, fixed to open on a pivot."

"It would have been Dan Owtram who fixed the bar for 'em, I don't doubt," said Arthur. "He's been dead ten years now."

"Who'd Dan fix it for?"

"Why, for the military."

"I see," said Mr. Calder. It was beginning to make a little more sense.

"You'll see when you get inside."

"Is there something inside?"

"Surely," said Arthur. "I wouldn't bring you out all this way just to look at an old tree stump, now would I? Come around here."

Mr. Calder moved round to the far side and saw, for the first time, that when the stump had shifted it had left a gap on the underside. It was not much bigger than a badger's hole.

"Are you suggesting I go down *that?*"

"It's not so bad, once you're in," said Arthur.

The entrance sloped down at about forty-five degrees and was only really narrow at the start, where the earth had caved in. After a short slide Mr. Calder's feet touched the top of a ladder. It was a long ladder. He counted twenty rungs before his feet were on firm ground. He got out his torch and switched it on.

He was in a fair-sized chamber, cut out of the chalk. He saw two recesses, each containing a spring bed on a wooden frame;

two or three empty packing cases, upended as table and seats; a wooden cupboard, several racks, and a heap of disintegrating blankets. The place smelled of lime and dampness and, very faintly, of something else.

A scrabbling noise announced the arrival of Arthur.

"Like something outer one of them last war films," he said.

"Journey's End!" said Mr. Calder. "All it needs is a candle in an empty beer bottle and a couple of gas masks hanging up on the wall."

"It was journey's end for him all right." Arthur jerked his head toward the far corner, and Mr. Calder swung his torch round.

The first thing he saw was a pair of boots, then the mildewy remains of a pair of flannel trousers, through gaps in which the leg bones showed white. The man was lying on his back. He could hardly have fallen like that; it was not a natural position. Someone had taken the trouble to straighten the legs and fold the arms over the chest after death.

The light from Mr. Calder's torch moved upward to the head, where it stayed for a long minute. Then he straightened up. "I don't think you'd better say much about this. Not for the moment."

"That hole in his forehead," said Arthur. "It's a bullet hole, ennit?"

"Yes. The bullet went through the middle of his forehead and out at the back. There's a second hole there."

"I guessed it was more up your street than mine," said Arthur. "What'll we do? Tell the police?"

"We'll have to tell them sometime. Just for the moment, do you think you could cover the hole up? Put some sticks and turf across?"

"I could do that all right. 'Twon't really be necessary, though. Now the wooding's finished you won't get anyone else through here. It's all preserved. The people who do the shooting, they stay on the outside of the covers."

"One of them didn't," said Mr. Calder, looking down at the floor and showing his teeth in a grin.

Mr. Behrens edged his way through the crowd in the drawing room of Colonel Mark Bessendine's Chatham quarters. He wanted to look at one of the photographs on the mantelpiece.

"That's the *Otrango*," said a girl near his left elbow. "It was Grandfather's ship. He proposed to Granny in the Red Sea. On the deck-tennis court, actually. Romantic, don't you think?"

Mr. Behrens removed his gaze from the photograph to study his informant. She had brown hair and a friendly face and was just leaving the puppy-fat stage. Fifteen or sixteen he guessed. "You must be Julia Bessendine," he said.

"And you're Mr. Behrens. Daddy says you're doing something very clever in our workshops. Of course, he wouldn't say what."

"That was his natural discretion," said Mr. Behrens. "As a matter of fact, it isn't hush-hush at all. I'm writing a paper for the Molecular Society on Underwater Torque Reactions and the Navy offered to lend me its big test tank."

"Gracious!" said Julia.

Colonel Bessendine surged across.

"Julia, you're in dereliction of your duties. I can see that Mr. Behrens' glass is empty."

"Excellent sherry," said Mr. Behrens.

"Tradition," said Colonel Bessendine, "associates the Navy with rum. In fact, the two drinks that it really understands are gin and sherry. I hope our technical people are looking after you?"

"The Navy have been helpfulness personified. It's been particularly convenient for me, being allowed to do this work at Chatham. Only twenty minutes' run from Lamperdown, you see."

Colonel Bessendine said, "My last station was Devonport. A ghastly place. When I was posted back here I felt I was coming home. The whole of my youth is tied up with this part of the country. I was born and bred not far from Tilbury and I went to school at Rochester."

His face, thought Mr. Behrens, was like a waxwork. A clever waxwork, but one which you could never quite mistake for human flesh. Only the eyes were truly alive.

"I sometimes spent a holiday down here when I was a boy," said Mr. Behrens. "My aunt and uncle—he's dead now—bought the Old Rectory at Lamperdown after the First World War. Thank you, my dear, that was very nicely managed." This was to Julia, who had fought her way back to him with most of the sherry still in the glass. "In those days your school," he said to the girl, "was a private house. One of the great houses of the county."

"It must have been totally impracticable," said Julia Bessendine severely. "Fancy trying to *live* in it. What sort of staff did it need to keep it up?"

"They scraped along with twenty or thirty indoor servants, a few dozen gardeners and gamekeepers, and a cricket pro."

"Daddy told me that when he was a boy he used to walk out from school, on half holidays, and watch cricket on their private cricket ground. That's right, isn't it, Daddy?"

"That's right, my dear. I think, Julia—"

"He used to crawl up alongside the hedge from the railway and squeeze through a gap in the iron railings at the top and lie in the bushes. And once the old lord walked across and found him, and instead of booting him out, he gave him money to buy sweets with."

"Major Furlong looks as if he could do with another drink," said Colonel Bessendine.

"Colonel Bessendine's father," said Mr. Behrens to Mr. Calder later that evening, "came from New Zealand. He ran away to sea at the age of thirteen, and got himself a job with the Anzac Shipping Line. He rose to be head purser on their biggest ship, the *Otrango.* Then he married. An Irish colleen, I believe. Her father was a landowner from Cork. That part of the story's a bit obscure, because her family promptly disowned her. They didn't approve of the marriage at all. They were poor but proud. Old Bessendine had the drawback of being twice as rich as they were."

"Rich? A purser?"

"He was a shrewd old boy. He bought up land in Tilbury and Grays and leased it to builders. When he died, his estate was declared for probate at £85,000. I expect it was really worth a lot more. His three sons were all well educated and well behaved. It was the sort of home where the boys called their father 'sir,' and got up when he came into the room."

"We could do with more homes like that," said Mr. Calder. "Gone much too far the other way. What happened to the other two sons?"

"Both dead. The eldest went into the Army: he was killed at Dunkirk. The second boy was a flight lieutenant. He was shot down over Germany, picked up and put into a prison camp. He was involved in some sort of trouble there. Shot, trying to escape."

"Bad luck," said Mr. Calder. He was working something out with paper and pencil. "Go away." This was to Rasselas, who had his paws on the table and was trying to help him. "What happened to young Mark?"

"Mark was in the Marines. He was blown sky high in the autumn of 1940—the first heavy raid on Gravesend and Tilbury."

"But I gather he came down in one piece."

"Just about. He was in hospital for six months. The plastic surgeons did a wonderful job on his face. The only thing they couldn't put back was the animation."

"Since you've dug up such a lot of his family history, do I gather that he's in some sort of a spot?"

"He's in a spot all right," said Mr. Behrens. "He's been spying for the Russians for a long time and we've just tumbled to it."

"You're sure?"

"I'm afraid there's no doubt about it at all. Fortescue has had him under observation for the last three months."

"Why hasn't he been put away?"

"The stuff he's passing out is important, but it's not vital. Bessendine isn't a scientist. He's held security and administrative jobs in different naval stations, so he's been able to give details of the progress and success of various jobs—where a project has run smoothly, or where it got behind time, or flopped. There's nothing the other side likes more than a flop."

"How does he get the information out?"

"That's exactly what I'm trying to find out. It's some sort of post-office system, no doubt. When we've sorted that out, we'll pull him in."

"Has he got any family?"

"A standard pattern Army-type wife. And a rather nice daughter."

"It's the family who suffer in these cases," said Mr. Calder. He scratched Rasselas' tufted head, and the big dog yawned. "By the way, *we* had rather an interesting day, too. We found a body."

He told Mr. Behrens about this, and Mr. Behrens said, "What are you going to do about it?"

"I've telephoned Fortescue. He was quite interested. He's put me on to a Colonel Cawston, who was in charge of Irregular Forces in this area in 1940. He thinks he might be able to help us."

Colonel Cawston's room was littered with catalogs, feeding charts, invoices, paid bills and unpaid bills, seed samples, gift calendars, local newspapers, boxes of cartridges, and buff forms from the Ministry of Agriculture, Fisheries and Food.

Mr. Calder said, "It's really very good of you to spare the time to talk to me, Colonel. You're a pretty busy man, I can see that."

"We shall get on famously," said the old man, "if you'll remember two things. The first is that I'm deaf in my left ear. The second, that I'm no longer a colonel. I stopped being that in 1945."

"Both points shall be borne in mind," said Mr. Calder, easing himself round onto his host's right-hand side.

"Fortescue told me you were coming. If that old bandit's involved, I suppose it's Security stuff?"

"I'm not at all sure," said Mr. Calder. "I'd better tell you about it . . ."

"Interesting," said the old man, when he had done so. "Fascinating, in fact."

He went across to a big corner cupboard, dug into its cluttered interior and surfaced with two faded khaki-colored canvas folders, which he laid on the table. From one of them he turned out a thick wad of papers, from the other a set of quarter- and one-inch military maps.

"I kept all this stuff," he said. "At one time, I was thinking of writing a history of Special Operations during the first two years of the war. I never got round to it, though. Too much like hard work." He unfolded the maps, and smoothed out the papers with his bent and arthritic fingers.

"Fortescue told me," said Mr. Calder, "that you were in charge of what he called 'Stay-put Parties.'"

"It was really a very sound idea," said the old man. His frosty blue eyes sparkled for a moment, with the light of unfought battles. "They did the same thing in Burma. When you knew that you might have to retreat, you dug-in small resistance groups, with arms and food and wireless sets. They'd let themselves be overrun, you see, and operate behind the enemy lines. We had a couple of dozen posts like that in Kent and Sussex. The one you found would have been—Whitehorse Wood you said?—here it is, Post Six. That was a very good one. They converted an existing dene-hole—you know what a dene-hole is?"

"As far as I can gather," said Mr. Calder, "the original inhabitants of this part of the country dug them to hide in when *they* were overrun by the Angles and Saxons and such. A sort of pre-Aryan Stay-put Party."

"Never thought of it that way." The old man chuckled. "You're quite right, of course. That's exactly what it was. Now then. Post Six. We had three men in each—an officer and two NCOs." He ran his gnarled finger up the paper in front of him. "Sergeant Brewer. A fine chap that. Killed in North Africa. Corporal Stubbs. He's dead, too. Killed in a motor crash, a week after VE-day. So your unknown corpse couldn't be either of *them*."

There was a splendid inevitability about it all, thought Mr. Calder. It was like the unfolding of a Greek tragedy; or the final chord of a well-built symphony. You waited for it. You knew it was coming. But you were still surprised when it did.

"Bessendine," said the old man. "Lieutenant Mark Bessendine. Perhaps the most tragic of the lot, really. He was a natural choice for our work. Spoke Spanish, French and German. Young and fit. Front-line experience with the Reds in Spain."

"What exactly happened to him?"

"It was the first week in November 1940. Our masters in Whitehall had concluded that the invasion wasn't on. I was told to seal up all my posts and send the men back to their units. I remember sending Mark out that afternoon to Post Six—it hadn't been occupied for some weeks—told him to bring back any loose stores. That was the last time I saw him—in the flesh, as you might say. You heard what happened?"

"He got caught in the German blitz on Tilbury and Gravesend."

"That's right. Must have been actually on his way back to our HQ. The explosion picked him up and pushed him through a plate-glass window. He was damned lucky to be alive at all. Next time I saw him he was swaddled up like a mummy. Couldn't talk or move."

"Did you see him again?"

"I was posted abroad in the spring. Spent the rest of the war in Africa and Italy . . . Now you happen to mention it, though, I thought I did bump into him once—at the big reception center at Calais. I went through there on my way home in 1945."

"Did he recognize you?"

"It was a long time ago. I can't really remember." The old man looked up sharply. "Is it important?"

"It might be," said Mr. Calder.

"If you're selling anything," said the old lady to Mr. Behrens, "you're out of luck."

"I am neither selling nor buying," said Mr. Behrens.

"And if you're the new curate, I'd better warn you that I'm a Baptist."

"I'm a practicing agnostic."

The old lady looked at him curiously, and then said, "Whatever it is you want to talk about, we shall be more comfortable inside, shan't we?"

She led the way across the hall, narrow and bare as a coffin, into a surprisingly bright and cheerful sitting room.

"You don't look to me," she said, "like the sort of man who knocks old ladies on the head and grabs their life's savings. I keep mine in the bank, such as they are."

"I must confess to you," said Mr. Behrens, "that I'm probably wasting your time. I'm in Tilbury on a sentimental errand. I spent a year of the war in an Air Force prison camp in Germany. One of my greatest friends there was Jeremy Bessendine. He was a lot younger than I was, of course, but we had a common interest in bees."

"I don't know what you were doing up in an airplane, at your time of life. I expect you dyed your hair. People used to do that in the 1914 war. I'm sorry, I interrupted you. Mr.—?"

"Behrens."

"My name's Galloway. You said Jeremy Bessendine."

"Yes. Did you know him?"

"I knew *all* the Bessendines. Father and mother, and all three sons. The mother was the sweetest thing, from the bogs of Ireland. The father, well, let's be charitable and say he was old-fashioned. Their house was on the other side of the road to mine. There's nothing left of it now. Can you see? Not a stick nor a stone."

Mr. Behrens looked out of the window. The opposite side of the road was an open space containing one row of prefabricated huts.

"Terrible things," said Mrs. Galloway. "They put them up after the war as a temporary measure. Temporary!"

"So that's where the Bessendines' house was," said Mr. Behrens, sadly. "Jeremy often described it to me. He was so looking forward to living in it again when the war was over."

"Jeremy was my favorite," said Mrs. Galloway. "I'll admit I cried when I heard he'd been killed. Trying to escape, they said."

She looked back twenty-five years, and sighed at what she saw. "If we're going to be sentimental," she said, "we shall do it better over a cup of tea. The kettle's on the boil." She went out into the kitchen but left the door open, so that she could continue to talk.

"John, the eldest, I never knew well. He went straight into the Army. He was killed early on. The youngest was Mark. He was a wild character, if you like."

"Wild? In what way?" said Mr. Behrens.

Mrs. Galloway arranged the teapot, cups, and milk jug on a tray and collected her thoughts. Then she said, "He was a rebel. Strong or weak?"

"Just as it comes," said Mr. Behrens.

"His two brothers, they accepted the discipline at home. Mark didn't. Jeremy told me that when Mark ran away from school—the second time—and his father tried to send him back, they had a real set-to, the father shouting, the boy screaming. That was when he went off to Spain to fight for the Reds. Milk and sugar?"

"Both," said Mr. Behrens. He thought of Mark Bessendine as he had seen him two days before. An ultracorrect, poker-backed, poker-faced regular soldier. How deep had the rebel been buried?

"He's quite a different sort of person now," he said.

"Of course, he would be," said Mrs. Galloway. "You can't be blown to bits and put together again and still be the same person, can you?"

"Why, no," said Mr. Behrens. "I suppose you can't."

"I felt very strange myself for a week or so, after it happened. And I was only blown across the kitchen and cracked my head on the stove."

"You remember that raid, then?"

"I most certainly do. It must have been about five o'clock. Just getting dark, and a bit misty. They came in low, and the next moment—*crump, bump*—we were right in the middle of it. It was the first raid we'd had—and the worst. You could hear the bombs coming closer and closer. I thought, I wish I'd stayed in Saffron Walden—where I'd been evacuated, you see—I'm for it now, I thought. And it's all my own fault for coming back like the posters told me not to. And the next moment I was lying on the floor, with my head against the stove, and a lot of warm red stuff running over my face. It was tomato soup."

"And that was the bomb that destroyed the Bessendines' house—and killed old Mr. and Mrs. Bessendine?"

"That's right. And it was the same raid that nearly killed Mark. My goodness!"

The last exclamation was nothing to do with what had gone before. Mrs. Galloway was staring at Mr. Behrens. Her face had gone pale. She said, "Jeremy! I've just remembered! When it happened they sent him home, on compassionate leave. He *knew* his house had been blown up. Why would he tell you he was looking forward to living in it after the war—when he must have known it wasn't there?"

Mr. Behrens could think of nothing to say.

"You've been lying, haven't you? Who are you? What's it all about?"

Mr. Behrens put down his teacup, and said, gently, "I'm sorry I had to tell you a lot of lies, Mrs. Galloway. Please don't worry about it too much. I promise you that nothing you told me is going to hurt anyone."

The old lady gulped down her own tea. The color came back slowly to her cheeks. She said, "Whatever it is, I don't want to know about it." She stared out of the window at the place where a big house had once stood, inhabited by a bullying father and a sweet Irish mother, and three boys. She said, "It's all dead and done with, anyway."

As Mr. Behrens drove home in the dusk, his tires on the road hummed the words back at him. *Dead and done with. Dead and done with.*

Mr. Fortescue, who was the manager of the Westminster branch of the London and Home Counties Bank, and a number of other things besides, glared across his broad mahogany desk at Mr.

Calder and Mr. Behrens and said, "I have never encountered such an irritating and frustrating case."

He made it sound as if they, and not the facts, were the cause of his irritation.

Mr. Behrens said, "I don't think people quite realize how heavily the scales are weighted in favor of a spy who's learned his job and keeps his head. All the stuff that Colonel Bessendine is passing out is stuff he's officially entitled to know. Progress of existing work, projects for new work, personnel to be employed, Security arrangements. It all comes into his field. Suppose he *does* keep notes of it. Suppose we searched his house, found those notes in his safe. Would it prove anything?"

"Of course it wouldn't," said Mr. Fortescue, sourly. "That's why you've got to catch him actually handing it over. I've had three men—apart from you—watching him for months. He behaves normally—goes up to town once or twice a week, goes to the cinema with his family, goes to local drink parties, has his friends in to dinner. All absolutely above suspicion."

"Quite so," said Mr. Behrens. "He goes up to London in the morning rush-hour. He gets into a crowded Underground train. Your man can't get too close to him. Bessendine's wedged up against another man who happens to be carrying a briefcase identical with his own . . ."

"Do you think that's how it's done?"

"I've no idea," said Mr. Behrens. "But I wager I could invent half a dozen other methods just as simple and just as impossible to detect."

Mr. Calder said, "When exactly did Mark Bessendine start betraying his country's secrets to the Russians?"

"We can't be absolutely certain. But it's been going on for a very long time. Back to the Cold War which nearly turned into a hot war—1947, perhaps."

"Not before that?"

"Perhaps you had forgotten," said Mr. Fortescue, "that until 1945 the Russians were on our side."

"I wondered," said Mr. Calder, "if before that he might have been spying for the Germans. Have you looked at the 'Hessel' file lately?"

Both Mr. Fortescue and Mr. Behrens stared at Mr. Calder, who looked blandly back at them.

Mr. Behrens said, "We never found out who Hessel was, did we? He was just a code name to us."

"But the Russians found out," said Mr. Calder. "The first thing they did when they got to Berlin was to grab all Admiral Canaris' records. If they found the Hessel dossier there—if they found out that he had been posing successfully for more than four years as an officer in the Royal Marines—"

"Posing?" said Mr. Fortescue, sharply.

"It occurred to me as a possibility."

"If Hessel is posing as Bessendine, where's Bessendine?" said Mr. Fortescue.

"At the bottom of a pre-Aryan chalk pit in Whitehorse Wood, above Lamperdown," said Mr. Calder, "with a bullet through his head."

Mr. Fortescue looked at Mr. Behrens, who said, "Yes, it's possible. I had thought of that."

"Lieutenant Mark Bessendine," said Mr. Calder, slowly, as if he was seeing it all as he spoke, "set off alone one November afternoon, with orders to close down and seal up Post Six. He'd have been in battle dress and carrying his Army pay book and identity papers with him, because in 1940 everyone did that. As he was climbing out of the post, he heard, or saw, a strange figure. A civilian, lurking in the woods, where no civilian should have been. He challenged him. And the answer was a bullet, from Hessel's gun.

Hessel had landed that day, or the day before, on the South Coast, from a submarine. Most of the spies who were landed that autumn lasted less than a week. Right?"

"They were a poor bunch," said Mr. Fortescue. "Badly equipped, and with the feeblest cover stories. I sometimes wondered if they were people Canaris wanted to get rid of."

"Exactly," said Mr. Calder. "But Hessel was a tougher proposition. He spoke excellent English—his mother was English, and he'd been to an English public school. And here was a God-sent chance to improve his equipment and cover. Bessendine was the same size and build. All he had to do was to change clothes and instead of being a phony civilian, liable to be questioned by the first constable he met, he was a properly dressed, fully documented Army officer. Provided he kept on the move, he could go anywhere in England. No one would question him. It wasn't the sort of cover that would last forever. But that didn't matter. His pickup was probably fixed for four weeks ahead—in the next no-moon period. So he put on Bessendine's uniform, and started out for Gravesend. Not, I need hardly say, with any intention of going back to Headquarters. All he wanted to do was to catch a train to London."

"But the Luftwaffe caught him."

"They did indeed," said Mr. Calder. "They caught him—and they set him free. Free of all possible suspicion. When he came out of that hospital six months later, he had a new face. More. He was a new man. If anyone asked him anything about his past, all he had to say was—'Oh, that was before I got blown up. I don't remember very much about that.'"

"But surely," said Mr. Fortescue, "it wasn't quite as easy as that. Bessendine's family—" He stopped.

"You've seen it too, haven't you?" said Mr. Calder. "He had no family. No one at all. One brother was dead, the other was in a prison camp in Germany. I wonder if it was a pure coincidence that he should later have been shot when trying to escape. Or did Himmler send a secret instruction to the camp authorities? Maybe it was just another bit of luck. Like Mark's parents being killed in the same raid. His mother's family lived in Ireland—and had disowned her. His father's family—if it existed—was in New Zealand. Mark Bessendine was completely and absolutely alone."

"The first Hessel messages went out to Germany at the end of 1941," said Mr. Fortescue. "How did he manage to send them?"

"No difficulty there," said Mr. Calder. "The German shortwave transmitters were very efficient. You only had to renew the batteries. He'd have buried his in the wood. He only had to dig it up again. He had all the call signals and codes."

Mr. Behrens had listened to this in silence, with a half-smile on his face.

Now he cleared his throat and said, "If this—um—ingenious theory is true, it does—um—suggest a way of drawing out the gentleman concerned, does it not . . . ?"

"I was very interested when you told me about this dene-hole," said Colonel Bessendine to Mr. Behrens. "I had heard about them as a boy, of course, but I've never actually seen one."

"I hope we shan't be too late," said Mr. Behrens. "It'll be dark in an hour. You'd better park your car here. We'll have to do the rest of the trip on foot."

"I'm sorry I was late," said Colonel Bessendine. "I had a job I had to finish before I go off tomorrow."

"Off?"

"A short holiday. I'm taking my wife and daughter to France."

"I envy you," said Mr. Behrens. "Over the stile here and stright up the hill. I hope I can find it from this side. When I came here before I approached it from the other side. Fork right here, I think."

They moved up through the silent woods, each occupied with his own, very different, thoughts.

Mr. Behrens said, "I'm sure this was the clearing. Look. You can see the marks of the workmen's tractors. And this—I think—was the stump."

He stopped, and kicked at the foot of the elm bole. The loose covering pieces of turf on sticks, laid there by Arthur, collapsed, showing the dark entrance.

"Good Lord!" said Colonel Bessendine. He was standing, hands in raincoat pockets, shoulders hunched. "Don't tell me that people used to live in a place like that?"

"It's quite snug inside."

"Inside? You mean you've actually been inside it?" He shifted his weight so that it rested on his left foot and his right hand came out of his pocket and hung loose.

"Oh, certainly," said Mr. Behrens. "I found the body, too."

There was a long silence. That's the advantage of having a false face, thought Mr. Behrens. It's unfair. You can do your thinking behind it, and no one can watch you actually doing it.

The lips cracked into a smile.

"You're an odd card," said Colonel Bessendine. "Did you bring me all the way here to tell me that?"

"I brought you here," said Mr. Behrens, "so that you could explain one or two things that have been puzzling me." He had seated himself on the thick side of the stump. "For instance, you must have known about this hideout, since you and Sergeant Brewer and Corporal Stubbs built it in 1940. Why didn't you tell me that when I started describing it to you?"

"I wasn't quite sure then," said Colonel Bessendine. "I wanted to make sure."

As he spoke his right hand moved with a smooth unhurried gesture into the open front of his coat and out again. It was now holding a flat blue-black weapon which Mr. Behrens, who was a connoisseur in such matters, recognized as a *Zyanidpistole* or cyanide gun.

"Where did they teach you that draw?" he said. "In the *Marineamt*?"

For the first time he thought that the colonel was genuinely surprised. His face still revealed nothing, but there was a note of curiosity in his voice.

"I learned in Spain to carry a gun under my arm and draw it quickly," he said. "There were quite a few occasions on which you had to shoot people before they shot you. Your own side, sometimes. It was rather a confused war in some ways."

"I imagine so," said Mr. Behrens. He was sitting like a Buddha in the third attitude of repose, his feet crossed, the palms of his hands pressed flat, one on each knee. "I only mentioned it because some of my colleagues had a theory that you were a German agent called Hessel."

In the colonel's eyes a glint of genuine amusement appeared for a moment, like a face at a window, and ducked out of sight again.

"I gather that you were not convinced by this theory?"

"As a matter of fact, I wasn't."

"Oh. Why?"

"I remembered what your daughter told me. That you used to crawl up alongside a hedge running from the railway line to the private cricket ground at the big house. I went along and had a look. You couldn't crawl up along the hedge now. It's too overgrown. But there *is* a place at the top—it's hidden by the hedge, and I scratched myself damnably getting into it—where two bars are bent apart. A boy could have got through them easily."

"You're very, thorough," said the colonel. "Is there anything you *haven't* found out about me?"

"I would be interested to know exactly when you started betraying your country. And why. Did you mean to do it all along and falling in with Hessel and killing him gave you an opportunity—the wireless and the codes and the call signs—?"

"I can clearly see," said the colonel, "that you have never been blown up. Really blown to pieces, I mean. If you had been, you'd know that it's quite impossible to predict what sort of man will come down again. You can be turned inside out, or upside down. You can be born again. Things you didn't know were inside you can be shaken to the top."

"Saul becoming Paul, on the road to Damascus."

"You *are* an intelligent man," said the colonel. "It's a pleasure to talk to you. The analogy had not occurred to me, but it is perfectly apt. My father was a great man for disciplining youth, for regimentation, and the New Order. Because he was my father, I rebelled against it. That's natural enough. Because I rebelled against it, I fought for the Russians against the Germans in Spain. I saw how those young Nazis behaved. It was simply a rehearsal for them, you know. A rehearsal for the struggle they had dedicated their lives to. A knightly vigil, if you like. I saw them fight, and I saw them die. Any that were captured were usually tortured. I tortured them myself. If you torture a man and fail to break him, it becomes like a love affair. Did you know that?"

"I, too, have read the work of the Marquis de Sade," said Mr. Behrens. "Go on."

"When I lay in hospital in the darkness with my eyes bandaged, my hands strapped to my sides, coming slowly back to life, I had the strangest feeling. I *was* Hessel, I *was* the man I had left lying in the darkness at the bottom of the pit. I had closed his eyes and folded his hands, and now I was him. His work was my work.

Where he had left it off, I would take it up. My father had been right and Hitler had been right and I had been wrong. And now I had been shown a way to repair the mistakes and follies of my former life. Does that sound mad to you?"

"Quite mad," said Mr. Behrens. "But I find it easier to believe than the rival theory—that the accident of having a new face enabled you to fool everyone for twenty-five years. You may have had no family, but there were school friends and Army friends and neighbors. But I interrupt you. When you got out of hospital and decided to carry on Hessel's work, I suppose you used his wireless set and his codes?"

"Until the end of the war, yes. Then I destroyed them. When I was forced to work for the Russians I began to use other methods. I'm afraid I can't discuss them, even with you. They involve too many other people."

In spite of the peril of his position, Mr. Behrens could not suppress a feeling of deep satisfaction. Not many of his plans had worked out so exactly. Colonel Bessendine was not a man given to confidences. A mixture of carefully devised forces was now driving him to talk. The time and the place; the fact that Mr. Behrens had established a certain intellectual supremacy over him; the fact that he must have been unable, for so many years, to speak freely to anyone; the fact that silence was no longer important, since he had made up his mind to liquidate his audience. On this last point Mr. Behrens was under no illusions. Colonel Bessendine was on his way out. France was only the first station on a line which led to eastern Germany and Moscow.

"One thing puzzles me," said the colonel, breaking into his thoughts. "During all the time we have been talking here—and I cannot tell you how much I have enjoyed our conversation—I couldn't help noticing that you have hardly moved. Your hands, for instance, have been lying cupped, one on each knee. When a fly annoyed you just now, instead of raising your hand to brush it off you shook your head violently."

Mr. Behrens said, raising his voice a little, "If I were to lift my right hand a very well-trained dog, who has been approaching you quietly from the rear while we were talking, would have jumped for your throat."

The colonel smiled. "Your imagination does you credit. What happens if you lift your left hand? Does a genie appear from a bottle and carry me off?"

"If I raise my left hand," said Mr. Behrens, "you will be shot dead."

And so saying, he raised it.

The two men and the big dog stared down at the crumpled body. Rasselas sniffed at it, once, and turned away. It was carrion and no longer interesting.

"I'd have liked to try to pull him down alive," said Mr. Behrens. "But with that foul weapon in his hand I dared not chance it."

"It will solve a lot of Mr. Fortescue's problems," said Mr. Calder. He was unscrewing the telescopic sight from the rifle he was carrying.

"We'll put him down beside Hessel. I've brought two crowbars along with me. We ought to be able to shift the stump back into its original position. With any luck, they'll lie there, undisturbed, for a very long time."

Side by side in the dark earth, thought Mr. Behrens. Until the Day of Judgment, when all hearts are opened and all thoughts known.

"We'd better hurry, too," said Mr. Calder. "It's getting dark, and I want to get back in time for tea."

On Slay Down

"The young man of today," said Mr. Behrens, "is physically stronger and fitter than his father. He can run a mile quicker—"

"A useful accomplishment," agreed Mr. Calder.

"He can put a weight farther, can jump higher and will probably live longer."

"Not as long as the young lady of today," said Mr. Calder. "*They* have a look of awful vitality."

"Nevertheless," said Mr. Behrens—he and Mr. Calder, being very old friends, did not so much answer as override each other; frequently they both spoke at once—"nevertheless he is, in one important way, inferior to the older generation. He is mentally softer—"

"Morally, too."

"The two things go together. He has the weaknesses which go with his strength. He is tolerant—but he is flabby. He is intelligent—but he is timid. He is made out of cast iron, not steel."

"Stop generalizing," said Mr. Calder. "What's worrying you?"

"The future of our Service," said Mr. Behrens.

Mr. Calder considered the matter, at the same time softly scratching the head of his deerhound, Rasselas, who lay on the carpet beside his chair.

Mr. Behrens, who lived down in the valley, had walked up, as he did regularly on Tuesday afternoons, to take tea with Mr. Calder in his cottage on the hilltop.

"You're not often right," said Mr. Calder, at last.

"Thank you."

"You could be on this occasion. I saw Fortescue yesterday."

"Yes," said Mr. Behrens. "He told me you had been to see him. I meant to ask you about that. What did he want?"

"There's a woman. She has to be killed."

Rasselas flicked his right ear at an intrusive fly; then, when this proved ineffective, growled softly and shook his head.

"Anyone I know?" said Mr. Behrens.

"I'm not sure. Her name, at the moment, is Lipper—Maria Lipper. She lives in Woking and is known there as Mrs. Lipper, although I don't *think* she has ever been married. She has worked as a typist and filing clerk at the Air Ministry since—oh, since well before the last war."

"And how long has she been working for them?"

"Certainly for ten years, possibly more. Security got on to her in the end by selective coding, and that, as you know, is a very slow process."

"And not one which a jury would understand or accept."

"Oh, certainly not," said Mr. Calder. "Certainly not. There could be no question here of judicial process. Maria is a season ticket holder, not a commuter."

By this Mr. Calder meant that Maria Lipper was an agent who collected, piecemeal, all information which came her way and passed it on at long intervals of months or even years. No messengers came to her. When she had sufficient to interest her master, she would take it to a collecting point and leave it. Occasional sums of money would come to her through the post.

"It is a thousand pities," added Mr. Calder, "that they did not get on to her a little sooner—before Operation Prometheus Unbound came off the drawing board."

"Do you think she knows about *that*?"

"I'm afraid so," said Mr. Calder. "I wasn't directly concerned. Buchanan was in charge. But it was her section that did the Prometheus typing, and when he found out that she had asked for an urgent contact, I think—I really think—he was justified in getting worried."

"What is he going to do about it?"

"The contact has been short-circuited. I am taking his place. Two days from now Mrs. Lipper is driving down to Portsmouth for a short holiday. She plans to leave Woking very early—she likes clear roads to drive on—and she will be crossing Salisbury Plain at six o'clock. Outside Upavon she turns off the main road. The meeting place is a barn at the top of the track. She has stipulated for a payment of five hundred pounds in one-pound notes. Incidentally, she has never before been paid more than fifty."

"You must be right," said Mr. Behrens, "I imagine that I am to cover you here. Fortunately my aunt is taking the waters at Harrogate."

"If you would."

"The same arrangements as usual."

"The key will be on the ledge over the woodshed door."

"You'd better warn Rasselas to expect me. Last time he got it into his head that I was a burglar."

The great hound looked up at the mention of his name and grinned, showing his long white incisors.

"You needn't worry about Rasselas," said Mr. Calder. "I'll take him with me. He enjoys an expedition. All the same, it *is* a sad commentary on the younger generation that a man of my age has to be sent out on a trip like this."

"Exactly what I was saying. Where did you put the backgammon board?"

Mr. Calder left his cotttage at dusk on the following evening. He drove off in the direction of Gravesend, crossed the river by the Dartford underpass and made a circle round London, recrossing the Thames at Reading. He drove his inconspicuous car easily and efficiently. Rasselas lay across the back seat, between a sleeping bag and a portmanteau. He was used to road travel, and slept most of the way.

At midnight the car rolled down the broad High Street of Marlborough and out onto the Pewsey Road. A soft golden moon made a mockery of its headlights.

A mile from Upavon, Mr. Calder pulled up at the side of the road and studied the 1/25,000-range map with which he had been supplied. The track leading to the barn was clearly shown. But he had marked a different and roundabout way by which the rendezvous could be approached. This involved taking the next road to the right, following it for a quarter of a mile, then finding a field track—it was no more than a dotted line even on his large-scale map—which would take him up a small re-entrant. The track appeared to stop just short of the circular contour which marked the top of the down. Across it, as Mr. Calder had seen when he examined the map, ran, in straggling gothic lettering, the words SLAY DOWN.

The entrance to the track had been shut off by a gate and was indistinguishable from the entrance to a field. The gate was padlocked, too, but Mr. Calder dealt with this by lifting it off its hinges. It was a heavy gate, but he shifted it with little apparent effort. There were surprising reserves of strength in his barrel-shaped body, thick arms, and plump hands.

After a month of fine weather the track, though rutted, was rock-hard. Mr. Calder ran up it until the banks on either side had leveled out and he guessed that he was approaching the top of the rise. There he backed his car into a thicket. For the last part of the journey he had been traveling without lights.

Now he switched off the engine, opened the car door and sat listening.

At first the silence seemed complete. Then, as the singing of the engine died in his ears, the sounds of the night reasserted themselves. A nightjar screamed; an owl hooted. The creatures of the dark, momentarily frozen by the arrival among them of this great palpitating steel-and-glass animal, started to move again. A mile away across the valley, where farms stood and people lived, a dog barked.

Mr. Calder took his sleeping bag out of the back of the car and unrolled it. He took off his coat and shoes, loosened his tie and wriggled down into the bag. Rasselas lay down too, his nose a few inches from Mr. Calder's head.

In five minutes the man was asleep. When he woke he knew what had roused him. Rasselas had growled, very softly, a little rumbling, grumbling noise which meant that something had disturbed him. It was not the growl of imminent danger. It was a tentative alert.

Mr. Calder raised his head. During the time he had been asleep the wind had risen a little, and was blowing up dark clouds and sending them scudding across the face of the moon; the shadows on the bare down were horsemen, warriors with horned helmets riding horses with flying manes and tails. Rasselas was following them with his eyes, head cocked. It was as if, behind the piping of the wind, he could hear, pitched too high for human ears, the shrill note of a trumpet.

"They're ghosts," said Mr. Calder calmly. "They won't hurt us." He lay down, and was soon asleep again.

It was five o'clock, and light was coming back into the sky when he woke. It took him five minutes to dress himself and roll up his sleeping bag. His movements seemed unhurried, but he lost no time.

From the back of the car he took a Greener 25 caliber rifle, and clipped on a telescopic sight, which he took from a leather case. A handful of nickel-capped ammunition went into his jacket pocket. Tucking the rifle under his arm, he walked cautiously toward the brow of the hill. From the brow a long thin line of trees, based in scrub, led down to the barn, whose red-brown roof could now just be seen over the convex slope of the hill.

Mr. Calder thought that the arrangement was excellent. "Made to measure," was the expression he used. The scrub was thickest round the end tree of the windbreak, and here he propped up the rifle, and then walked the remaining distance to the wall of the barn. He noted that the distance was thirty-three yards.

In front of the barn the path, coming up from the main road, opened out into a flat space, originally a cattle yard but now missing one wall.

She'll drive in here, thought Mr. Calder. And she'll turn the car, ready to get away. They always do that. After a bit she'll get out of the car and she'll stand, watching for me to come up the road.

When he got level with the barn he saw something that was not marked on the map. It was another track which came across the down, and had been made quite recently by Army vehicles from the Gunnery School. A litter of ammunition boxes, empty cigarette cartons and a rusty brew can suggested that the Army had taken over the barn as a staging point for their maneuvers. It was an additional fact. Something to be noted. Mr. Calder didn't think that it affected his plans. A civilian car coming from the road would be most unlikely to take this track, a rough affair seamed with the marks of Bren carriers and light tanks.

Mr. Calder returned to the end of the trees and spent some minutes piling a few large stones and a log into a small breastwork. He picked up the rifle and set the sights carefully to thirty-five yards. Then he sat down with his back to the tree and lit a cigarette. Rasselas lay down beside him.

Mrs. Lipper arrived at ten to six.

She drove up the track from the road, and Mr. Calder was interested to see that she behaved almost exactly as he had predicted. She drove her car into the yard, switched off the engine and sat for a few minutes. Then she opened the car door and got out.

Mr. Calder snuggled down behind the barrier, moved his rifle forward a little and centered the sight on Mrs. Lipper's left breast.

It was at this moment that he heard the truck coming. It was, he thought, a fifteen-hundredweight truck, and it was coming quite slowly along the rough track toward the barn.

Mr. Calder laid down the rifle and rose to his knees. The truck engine had stopped. From his position of vantage he could see, although Mrs. Lipper could not, a figure in battle dress getting out of the truck. It was, he thought, an officer. He was carrying a light rifle, and it was clear that he was after rabbits. Indeed, as Mr. Calder watched, the young man raised his rifle, then lowered it again.

Mr. Calder was interested, even in the middle of his extreme irritation, to see that the officer had aimed at a thicket almost directly in line with the barn.

Three minutes passed in silence. Mrs. Lipper looked twice at her watch. Mr. Calder lay down again in a firing position. He had decided to wait. It was a close decision, but he was used to making close decisions and he felt certain that this one was right.

The hidden rifle spoke; and Mr. Calder squeezed the trigger of his own. So rapid was his reaction that it sounded like a shot and an echo. In front of his eyes, Mrs. Lipper folded onto the ground. She did not fall. It was quite a different movement. It was as though a puppet master who had previously held the strings taut had let them drop and a puppet had tumbled to the ground, arms, legs and head disjointed.

A moment later the hidden rifle spoke again. Mr. Calder smiled to himself. The timing, he thought, had been perfect. He was quietly packing away the telescopic sight, dismantling the small redoubt he had created, and obliterating all signs of his presence. Five minutes later he was back in his car. He had left it facing outward and downhill, and all he had to do was take off the hand brake and start rolling down the track. This was the trickiest moment in the whole operation. It took three minutes to lift the gate, drive the car through and replace the gate. During the whole of that time no one appeared on the road in either direction.

"And that," said Mr. Calder, some three days later, to Mr. Fortescue, "was that." No one seeing Mr. Fortescue a square, sagacious-looking man, would have mistaken him for anything but a bank manager, although, in fact, he had certain other, quite important, functions.

"I was sorry, in a way, to saddle the boy with it, but I hadn't any choice."

"He took your shot as the echo of his?"

"Apparently. Anyway, he went on shooting."

"You contemplated that he would find the body—either then, or later."

"Certainly."

"And would assume that he had been responsible—accidentally, of course."

"I think that he should receive a good deal of sympathy. He had a perfect right to shoot rabbits. The rough shooting belongs to the School of Artillery. The woman was trespassing on War Department property. Indeed, the police will be in some difficulty in concluding why she was there at all."

"I expect they would have been," said Mr. Fortescue, "if her body had been discovered."

Mr. Calder looked at him.

"You mean," he said at last, "that no one has been near the barn since it happened?"

"On the contrary. One of the troops of the Seventeenth Field Regiment, to which your intrusive subaltern belongs, visited the barn two days later. It was their gun position. The barn itself was the troop command post."

"Either," said Mr. Calder, "they were very unobservant soldiers, or one is driven to the concluson that the body had been moved."

"I was able," said Mr. Fortescue, "through my influence with the Army, to attend the firing as an additional umpire, in uniform. I had plenty of time on my hands, and was able to make a thorough search of the area."

"I see," said Mr. Calder. "Yes. It opens up an interesting field of speculation, doesn't it?"

"Very interesting," said Mr. Fortescue. "In—er—one or two different directions."

"Have you discovered the name of the officer who was out shooting?"

"He is a National Service boy. A Lieutenant Blaikie. He is in temporary command of C Troop of A Battery—it would normally be a captain, but they are short of officers. His colonel thinks very highly of him. He says that he is a boy of great initiative."

"There I agree with you," said Mr. Calder. "I wonder if the Army could find *me* a suit of battle dress."

"I see you as a major," said Mr. Fortescue. "With a France and Germany Star and a 1939 Defence Medal."

"The Africa Star," said Mr. Calder, firmly . . .

Approximately a week later Mr. Calder, wearing a Service dress hat half a size too large for him and a battle-dress blouse which met with some difficulty round the waist, was walking up the path which led to the barn. It was ten o'clock, dusk had just fallen, and around the farm there was a scene of considerable activity as C Troop, A Battery, of the Seventeenth Field Regiment settled down for the night.

Four guns were in position, two in front of and two behind the barn. The gun teams were digging slit trenches. Two storm lanterns hung in the barn. A sentry on the path saluted Mr. Calder, who inquired where he would find the troop commander.

"He's got his bivvy up there, sir," said the sentry.

Peering through the dusk Mr. Calder saw a truck parked on a flat space, beyond the barn, and enclosed by scattered bushes. Attached to the back of the truck, and forming an extension of it, was a sheet of canvas pegged down in the form of a tent. He circled the site cautiously.

It seemed to him to be just the right distance from the barn, and to have the right amount of cover. It was the place he would have chosen himself.

He edged up to the opening of the tent and peered inside. A young subaltern was seated on his bedroll examining a map. His webbing equipment was hanging on a hook on the back of the truck.

Mr. Calder stooped and entered. The young man frowned, drawing his thick eyebrows together, then recognized Mr. Calder and smiled.

"You're one of our umpires, aren't you, sir," he said. "Come in."

"Thank you," said Mr. Calder. "Can I squat on the bedroll?"

"I expect you've been round the gun position, sir. I was a bit uncertain about the AA defenses myself. I've put the sentry on top of Slay Down. He's a bit out of touch."

"I must confess," said Mr. Calder, "that I haven't examined your dispositions. It was something—rather more personal I wanted a little chat about."

"Yes, sir?"

"When you buried her—" Mr. Calder scraped the turf with his heel—"how deep did you put her?"

* * *

There was silence in the tiny tent, lit by a single bulb from the dashboard of the truck. The two men might have been on a raft, alone, in the middle of the ocean.

The thing which occurred next did not surprise Mr. Calder. Lieutenant Blaikie's right hand made a very slight movement outward, checked and fell to his side again.

"Four foot, into the chalk," he said.

"How long did it take you?"

"Two hours."

"Quick work," said Mr. Calder. "It must have been a shock to you when a night exercise was ordered exactly on this spot, with special emphasis on the digging of slit trenches and gun pits."

"It would have worried me more if I hadn't been in command of the exercise," said Lieutenant Blaikie. "I reckoned if I pitched my own tent exactly here, no one would dig a trench or a gun pit inside it. By the way—who are you?"

Mr. Calder was particularly pleased to notice that Lieutenant Blaikie's voice was under firm control.

He told him who he was, and made a proposal to him.

"He was due out of the Army in a couple of months' time," said Mr. Calder to Mr. Behrens, when the latter came up for a game of backgammon. "Fortescue saw him, and thought him very promising. I was very pleased with his behavior in the tent that night. When I sprang it on him, his first reaction was to reach for the revolver in his webbing holster. It was hanging on the back of his truck. He realized that he wouldn't be able to get it out in time, and decided to come clean. I think that showed decision and balance, don't you?"

"Decision and balance are *most* important," agreed Mr. Behrens. "Your throw."

The Spoilers

On Friday night Colonel Geoffrey Bax went down alone for a last visit to his week-end cottage in Sussex. It was a last visit, because the cottage had been put up for sale. He was alone because his wife was escorting her mother on her summer pilgrimage to Torquay.

On Saturday morning the farmer drove up with milk and eggs, and discovered the colonel. He was seated in the chair at the head of the kitchen table, under the still-burning electric light. It was a hot June morning, and the flies were already gathering round the pool of blackening blood on the table top. The gun which had killed the colonel was in his right hand.

Mr. Behrens had known Colonel Bax. He read the news in his Sunday paper, and walked up the hill to discuss it with his old friend, Mr. Calder.

"It's in my paper too," said Mr. Calder. "But I didn't really know Bax. Wasn't he working for DI5?"

"Yes. He got a job with them when he retired from the Army. It wasn't anything hush-hush, you know. He did a lot of their positive vetting."

"I'd rather pick oakum," said Mr. Calder.

(Positive vetting was a palliative devised by the government in 1952 after a series of Security scandals. It meant, in practice, that any government servant who attained a certain degree of seniority had to supply the name of a referee; and it then became the duty of the positive vetter to interview the referee and inquire of him whether the officer concerned was reliable. The answer was predictable.)

"Most of those jobs went to officers who had been axed," said Mr. Behrens. "They got quite well paid for it. Add the salary to their service pensions and they could get by."

Mr. Calder looked up sharply. He had known Mr. Behrens long enough to ignore the plain meaning of what he said and jump to the thought behind it.

"Do you think there was some sort of pressure on Bax?"

"It's not impossible. The material was there. In his case it was a girl. Her parents were Poles. Geoffrey did them a good turn just after the war, and was godfather to their little daughter."

"Daddy Longlegs," said Mr. Calder, scratching the head of his deerhound Rasselas, who was stretched out under the breakfast table.

"It's all very well for you to sneer," said Mr. Behrens. "I've met the girl. She's very beautiful."

"Did Bax's wife know about her?"

"If she had, she'd have started divorce proceedings at once. She was that sort of woman."

"If she was that sort of woman, Bax would have been well rid of her."

"He'd have lost his job."

Mr. Calder, considering the matter, was inclined to agree. He knew that in certain branches of the Security Services sexual irregularity was considered a good deal worse than crime and nearly as bad as ideological deviation.

"He could have lived on his pension."

"*And* paid alimony to his wife?"

"He wouldn't have starved," said Mr. Calder. "There was no need to blow his brains out. *That* didn't help."

"That cottage of his," said Mr. Behrens. "He was very fond of it. He often talked about it. He was going to retire there."

"So?"

"I wondered why he had to sell it."

"You're making my flesh creep," said Mr. Calder. And from under the table Rasselas gave a rumbling snarl, just as if he had been following the whole conversation.

Her Majesty's Secretary of State for Education, Dermot Nicholson, read the news in his elegant flat on Campden Hill.

He said to his sister Norah—who had retired from the vice-principalship of an Oxford college to keep house and write his speeches for him—"Colonel Geoffrey Bax. Do we know a Geoffrey Bax? The name seems familiar."

"Wasn't that the name of the man who was round here a few weeks ago, asking you a lot of questions?"

"Oh, was that the chap? I thought I'd seen the name somewhere."

"What *did* he want? Did you ever find out?"

"It was some sort of routine check."

"We're getting so Security-minded," said Miss Nicholson, "that we might as well be living in a totalitarian state, under the control of the Gestapo."

Miss Nicholson, who was an intellectual liberal, often said things like this in letters to the Press and at public meetings, possibly because she had never lived in a totalitarian state and had no experience of the Gestapo . . .

Professor Julius Gottlieb, a citzen of Czechoslovakia by birth, and of Great Britain by naturalizaton, read the news in his service flat in Northumberland Court. He took eight different Sunday papers and he found the story, with minor differences and embellishments, in all of them. It was clearly based on an official handout.

As he finished reading, the telephone rang. He hesitated for a long moment before answering it, but when he did so it was only his daughter Paula. She had gone down to Henley for the weekend.

"It's lovely," she said. "You ought to have come."

"I wanted to," said the professor. "But I had too much work."

"You'd be better off bathing and lying in the sun, than worrying about that silly paper. Fritz is enjoying it like anything. He had a fight with another dog. And he fell into the river and was hissed at by a swan."

"Good," said the professor. "Good." He spoke absently. When his daughter had rung off he seemed to be in no hurry to get on with the urgent work which was keeping him in London that fine June week end. He sat in the window seat, watching the traffic swirl up Northumberland Avenue and turn down Whitehall Place. The telephone rang again . . .

On the Thursday afternoon a coroner's jury came, without difficulty, to the conclusion that Colonel Geoffrey Bax had taken his own life while the balance of his mind was disturbed. Sympathy was expressed for his widow.

On Sunday morning the Prime Minister took breakfast at Chequers with the prime ministers of five of the newly independent African States. He thought that they looked politely surprised at the modest bacon and eggs and toast and marmalade.

"What the devil did they expect me to eat," he said to his private secretary when the last of his guests had gone, "boar's head and ambrosia?"

"I imagine Nwambe's idea of a suitable breakfast would be the head of the leader of the opposition, seethed in milk," said the private secretary. "Your next appointment's in five minutes. They've all arrived. I've put them in the small library."

The Prime Minister switched his mind to a problem which was worrying him a lot more than the growing pains of the new African States. He said, "I want those papers. Particularly that rather odd letter that Gottlieb wrote me."

He found four men waiting for him. Ian Maver, the head of DI5, Air Vice-Marshal Pulleyne, the acting head of DI6—his boss was in America, engaged on one of their interminable wrangles with the CIA—and Commander Elfe, of the Special Branch. All of these the Prime Minister knew personally. The face of the fourth man was unfamiliar, and even when Maver introduced Mr. Fortescue it took him a moment to place him. Then he remembered that this sedate and respectable-looking man was ostensibly a bank manager, and in fact the controller and paymaster of a bunch of middle-aged cutthroats known as the "E" (or External) Branch of the Joint Services Standing Intelligence Committee. When the Prime Minister, on taking office, had shouldered, among other unwanted burdens, the supreme responsibility for all Security matters, his predecessor had explained to him, "If there's a job which is so disreputable that none of the departments will handle it, we give it to the 'E' Branch."

The Prime Minister looked a second time at Mr. Fortescue, who looked back at him kindly but firmly, as if preparing to refuse him an overdraft. An interesting face, thought the Prime Minister. Not unlike Arthur Balfour, in middle age.

"You're busy men," he said, "and I apologize for disrupting Sunday for all four of you. If I'd had a more accurate idea of what this trouble was, I could probably have let three of you off." He smiled the boyish smile which had won the hearts of so many of his constituents in the old days and was now collecting high TAM ratings on television. "But the fact of the matter is that, although I'm worried, I'm not at all sure which of you gentlemen is going to have to shoulder my worries for me. I'll put the problem to you in a nutshell. Certain key men in my government are being got at. You've got to find out who's doing it. And you've got to stop it."

Mr. Fortescue, who was himself an adept in the handling of conferences, found himself admiring the Prime Minister's technique. First the gentle introduction. Then the sharp slap.

"*Got* at, Prime Minister?" said Maver.

"That was the word I used. I can't be more specific, until you gentlemen find out more about it. They are being got at. Not by the opposition, which would be natural, or by the Press, which would be understandable, but by some private agency or group of persons who seem to be determined to get this government out of office."

The Prime Minister saw the quick look which Maver shot Pulleyne, but gave no sign of having done so. He chalked it up as one more item on the debit account of the head of DI5. He had liked Maver's predecessor, a garrulous, drunken, inefficient Irishman, a great deal more than the cold, self-contained, unquestionably efficient Scot.

"I think," the Prime Minister continued, "that when you hear the facts you will agree that I have some grounds for disquiet. A few months ago, Sir William Hamson, one of the most senior Revenue officials, and the man who did most of the work on last year's budget, came to me and told me that he wished to retire. He had eight years to go before his normal retirement. It was extremely inconvenient though not, as it turned out, disastrous because he had a deputy who was capable of doing his job. But it might have upset the whole of our financial plans. Sir William gave me no reason, apart from saying that he was tired. I pointed out that he would lose a good slice of his pension. Since he had private means, that didn't worry him. We had to let him go, of course. He's now in the south of France, and seems to have recovered his health and spirits. By itself, such an incident meant nothing.

Two months ago Dermot Nicholson who, as you know, is Minister of Education, and is therefore in charge of the most important measure of this Session—a measure whose success might make the difference between defeat and victory—came to see me. I was at once reminded of Hamson. There was the same request—to be relieved of office. The same lack of any plausible reason. The same . . . I find it difficult to hit on the right word . . . it was something a great deal stronger than depression. There was an edge of fear to it. And a background of hopelessness." The Prime Minister paused, and then added, "If his doctor had told him that morning that he was suffering from inoperable cancer, I should have expected much the same sort of reactions."

The four men stirred uncomfortably in their chairs.

"I suppose," said Elfe, "that he wasn't—"

"I happen to know that there is nothing wrong with Nicholson's health at all. Let me finish. A fortnight ago I had to send for Professor Julius Gottlieb. You all know roughly what his job is, I expect? He is the leading town-planning expert in the world. Even the Americans admit it. Some months ago, at my request, he completed the first rough draft of a White Paper on Planning. It wasn't perfect, but believe me, it was two decades in advance of anything this country has yet seen. The departments concerned—particularly the Treasury and the Ministry of Agriculture—picked a few holes in it but they couldn't shoot it down. When all the criticisms had been collected, Gottlieb was to draw up the final version. He now says—" the Prime Minister paused again, not for effect this time Mr. Fortescue thought, but because he was really worried and angry—"he now says that he doesn't feel up to the job. He is thinking of retiring. He has a holiday chalet in Switzerland, in the Upper Vaud. I believe it's famous for its wild flowers. He has decided to retire and make it his permanent home."

Commander Elfe said, "It's disturbing, Prime Minister. But is it necessarily political?"

"When Education and Planning are the two cornerstones of this Session? What are people going to say—more to the point, what is the Press going to say—if we have to tell them that the chief architect of the new Education Bill has thrown in the sponge—and the government's principal adviser on planning has refused to finish his own White Paper, and is retiring to Switzerland to pick wild flowers?"

"It was six months ago," said Pulleyne, in his precise voice, "when Hamson walked out. Two months ago when you first got worried about Nicholson. A fortnight ago when Gottlieb threatened to throw in his hand. Have no steps been taken?"

"Yes," said Maver. "It looked like a Home Security matter, so it was handed to us. We put one of our most reliable men onto it. He talked to Nicholson and Gottlieb."

"Did he come to any conclusion as a result of these talks?"

"We don't know. He committed suicide a week ago."

"Then you're talking about Colonel Bax?"

"Yes."

"And has he himself been investigated?"

Maver flushed and said, "Of course. And there *was* a background story, which could have accounted for it. We haven't got very far with it yet. But it's quite possible that he was being blackmailed, and had been driven too far."

"Well, that's the position, gentlemen," said the Prime Minister. "It could be organized pressure from an unscrupulous group in this country. I don't mean the official opposition. But there are plenty of extremist groups who wouldn't stop short of it. It could be foreign-inspired. I can think of four countries at this moment which would give a great deal to have the present government discredited. Or it may be simple blackmail. I leave you, gentlemen, to sort out the departmental priorities amongst yourselves. *I just want it stopped.*"

To his secretary when they had all gone away, he said, "Do you realize that all prime ministers have to live out the enthusiasms of their predecessors? Because of Lloyd George's lower-middle-class habits I have to entertain official guests to breakfast. Because of Winston's boyish enthusiasm for cops and robbers I have to pretend to be personally responsible for Security. Do you remember that thing he wrote—?"

The private secretary didn't remember, but being a good private secretary he was able to put his hand on the reference his employer required. He fetched down a battered olive-green volume from the library shelf, found the place and read out: "'. . . plot and counterplot, ruse and treachery, cross and double-cross, true agent, false agent, gold and steel, the bomb, the dagger and the firing-party, interwoven in a texture so intricate as to be incredible, yet true, the high officers of the Secret Service revelled in these subterranean labyrinths, and pursued their task with cold and silent passion.'"

"I didn't notice them reveling," said the Prime Minister. "Did you?"

Ian Maver and Mr. Fortescue traveled back in the official car together. Maver said nothing until they were approaching the outskirts of London. Then he closed the glass panel to shut off the driver and said, "The PM mentioned three possible explanations. There are at least two more that he omitted."

"Yes," said Mr. Fortescue.

"The whole thing could be a coincidence. People crack up pretty quickly in government service these days. And all three of the people he mentioned had private means. There was no reason for them to kill themselves by going on doing a job which had got beyond them."

"No," said Mr. Fortescue. "And your other explanation?"

"The other possible explanation is that the Prime Minister has greatly exaggerated the whole thing as an excuse for getting rid of me. I'm afraid he doesn't like me very much."

Mr. Fortescue did not make any comment on this.

On the following Monday Dermont Nicholson got back to his flat at Campden Hill at just after midnight. A threatened all-night sitting of the House had failed to develop. He was looking forward to a nightcap and bed.

His key went into the lock but he was unable to turn it, and when he tried to get it out again he found it was stuck. He rang the bell. Nothing happened. His sister very rarely went to bed before midnight and was most unlikely to be asleep.

Someone, or something, moved in the flat.

There was an indeterminate shuffling noise and, as he bent his head to listen, he thought he heard a faint moan.

In a sudden panic he rattled the door, shouted, put his shoulder to it, then turned and raced downstairs. There was a night porter, who had a master key.

"If your key's stuck in the lock, sir," he said, "it's no good trying to use my master key. We shall have to break the door down, and the police'll do that quicker than we will."

"Hurry," said Nicholson. "Hurry. Something's happened to my sister. She may have had a stroke."

Detective Sergeant Hallows, who was night duty officer at Notting Hill Gate, arrived inside five minutes. He and the police driver went up, carrying between them an assortment of housebreaking implements. It took them a further three minutes to deal with the front door. Nicholson pushed past them, and went straight to his sister's bedroom. She had been tied to the end of the bed with sheets, and gagged with a towel. The knots had been so savagely tightened that Nicholson was unable to do anything with them. He picked a pair of scissors from the dressing table, but his hands were shaking and he dropped them. The sergeant cut through the sheets with a knife; as soon as the gag was out of her mouth Miss Nicholson started to scream . . .

"I have to announce," said the Prime Minister to the House, on Wednesday, "the news—to me, personally, it is very sad news—that the Right Honourable Member for Burnham Heath has had to offer me his resignation as Minister for Education. He has done this on the advice of his doctors. I have not yet finally decided on a successor, but I can assure the House that there will be no change in the government's education policy."

An opposition back-bencher said, "While we sympathize with the Prime Minister for having lost yet another of his already depleted team, we should be interested to know exactly what the late Minister of Education was suffering from? Could it be that he was sick of the Education Bill—"

The rest was lost in a roar of government protest and opposition laughter.

On the same Wednesday, Mr. Calder and Mr. Behrens both received telephone calls at home. Mr. Behrens said to his aunt, "I've some business in town. I'll probably stay at the Club for a few nights."

His aunt said, "You know that I don't like being left here alone."

"Why don't you visit Millicent?"

"It's tiresome you couldn't have given me more notice."

Mr. Calder got his old car out of the woodshed. To Rasselas, who was sunning himself in his favorite spot behind the woodpile, he said, "Back tonight." The big dog sighed windily, in exactly the same way that Miss Behrens had done.

Mr. Fortescue normally operated from the Westminster branch of the London and Home Counties Bank. But he had other offices. The one which he used on official occasions was in Richmond Terrace Mews, and it was here that Mr. Calder and Mr. Behrens found him.

When he had finished talking, Mr. Calder said, "Mightn't there be some danger of getting our wires crossed over this? Most of it sounds like ordinary police work."

"I agree that there's a police angle to it," said Mr. Fortescue. "Since it involves the security of Ministers, it's the Special Branch which is involved. Elfe will be in charge of that side of it. DI5 and the police. Generally speaking, however, it's agreed that you're to have a free hand."

Mr. Behrens said, "I knew Gottlieb slightly. I met him in the 'forties, when he first came to England. I could have a word with him."

"Then I'll start with Nicholson," said Mr. Calder . . .

"It was a pigsty," said the detective sergeant. "They did everything filthy they could think of. Over the floor, in the beds, everywhere. We've cleared up as best we could, but there's some things—well, come and have a look."

He led the way into the living room. Someone had broken the glass in each of the half-dozen pictures on the wall and smeared filth over them. They were flower pictures, originals from Montessor's great folio. Looking closer, Mr. Calder saw that not only had the glass been smashed. The name of each plant was inscribed in copperplate at the foot of each picture. Someone had scored these through with an indelible pencil, and printed the word, PANSY.

"It's not only the pictures," said Hallows. "It's the books too. Someone took a lot of trouble over this little job."

There were a couple of hundred books in the fitted bookshelves between the windows. The back had been ripped out of each book, with a knife.

"We don't know just what they did to his sister," said Hallows. "She's in a private nursing home. Maybe she'll be able to tell us something when she gets her wits back."

"Did they take anything?"

"Nicholson says they took some money out of the desk, but it wasn't money they were after. It was a grudge job."

"I agree," said Mr. Calder. He phrased his next question delicately, aware that it might give offense. "Seeing that he was a senior cabinet minister, I wondered if any special arrangements might have been made. I know the police can't keep a twenty-four hour watch on all these people—"

"He was guarded," said Hallows. "A private outfit was doing the job."

"Private?"

"That's right. We're so short of policemen that government departments have started using private outfits lately. As a matter of fact, some of them are ex-policemen."

"They seem to have slipped up on this occasion."

The doorbell rang.

Hallows said, as he went to open it, "They didn't slip. They were ditched. I asked the head of the firm to come round. This is probably him now. He can tell you about it."

Mr. Cotter, the managing director and founder of Cotter's Detectives, was a thickset, red-faced man with a brigade mustache. He shook hands with Mr. Calder and said, "Bad business. I've had to give Romilly his cards. No alternative. I don't know that it was one hundred percent his fault. He's never let me down before, anyway."

"What happened?"

"Someone telephoned the night porter, said he was Nicholson's secretary. The Minister had been detained at a meeting out at Finchley. Could Romilly pick up his car from the forecourt of the House, drive it out to Finchley, pick the old man up and bring him back to Westminster. It was plausible. After all, his main job's to look after the Minister."

"When this man telephoned," said Mr. Calder, "did he actually say *Romilly*?"

Mr. Cotter thought for a moment, and then said, "Yes. I think he did. Why?"

"It would argue a pretty close knowledge of your setup if he knew the name of the man on duty at any given time. How many men do you have on a job like this?"

"It's a team of three. They do ten-hour stretches. That gives them a sort of dogwatch."

"Who are the other two?"

Mr. Cotter shot a glance at Sergeant Hallows, who said, "That's all right. Mr. Calder is from the Security Executive. He's helping us."

"I see," said Mr. Cotter. "My other two men on this assignment were Angel and Lawrie." He added stiffly, "They're both reliable men."

"Frank Angel," said Mr. Calder. "Small, dark, thick and Welsh?"

"That's him. Do you know him?"

"I worked with him on one or two jobs at Blenheim," said Mr. Calder. The atmosphere seemed to have become easier.

Mr. Behrens knew the Head of Records personally, and was thus able to get in to see this most closely guarded of all Home Office and Ministry of Defence officials. He said, "I want your full record on Gottlieb. The X *and* the Y file, please."

"You know as well as I do," said the Head of Records, "that you can't see the Y file without Cabinet authority."

Mr. Behrens laid his authority on the desk. The Head of Records read it through carefully and made a telephone call.

To the plump, serious young man with the middle-aged face who arrived in answer to it, he said, "This is Mr. Behrens, Smythe. Will you show him the X *and* Y files on Professor Julius Gottlieb."

Smythe said, in the manner of Jeeves, "If you would kindly step this way, sir," and conducted Mr. Behrens to the room in the basement of the building which contained, in numbered filing cabinets, enough high explosive to blow up both sides of Whitehall. He unlocked one of the cabinets, drew out two folders, one thick and one thin, placed a table and chair and said, "I'll leave you to it, sir."

As Mr. Behrens leafed through the folders he was smiling to himself. He was aware of the principles upon which this particular room was constructed, and he knew that anyone having access to a Y file was not only watched but normally photographed as well.

When he had finished he touched the bell. As he did so, he smiled again. He knew that all he had to do was to say, without raising his voice, "Oh, Smythe—" and the guardian of the papers would have reappeared. By doing this he would have demonstrated that he knew that not only was every one of his movements being watched, but the room was wired for sound as well.

Mr. Behrens did no such thing. He had long outgrown any desire to give pointless exhibitions of his own expertise.

After a decent interval, Mr. Smythe reappeared.

"A lot of this Y file," said Mr. Behrens, "is in summary and précis. I imagine that the original documents—verbatim records of interrogations, and so on—were too bulky to file. Where would they be kept?"

"If they *were* kept," said Smythe, "I imagine they'd be at Brooklands. Or perhaps at Staines."

Mr. Behrens thanked him. Since it was then a quarter to one, he thought he would have lunch before tackling Gottlieb.

* * *

The girl who opened the door of the flat in Northumberland Court was, as Mr. Behrens saw even in the poor light of the front hall, pretty. When she had shown him into the drawing room, he changed his mind. Pretty was all wrong. A stupid word in any human context. She was attractive, with the attractions of dark hair, bright eyes, a good figure and youth.

She chased a dachshund off the sofa. "We call all our dachshunds Fritz," she said. "After the dog in that strip they used to have in the *Daily Mirror.* Do you remember? This one is Fritz the Third. He's the nicest and naughtiest of the lot. Daddy's mad about him."

She departed to summon her father. Mr. Behrens was not himself a susceptible man, but he made a mental note of the charm of Miss Gottlieb, since an attractive girl could be a relevant factor in any equation.

Professor Gottlieb who came in at that moment turned out to be a small man, with a suggestion of a humpback, a brown face and a mop of snowy white hair. He, like his daughter, was friendly. But it was clear to Mr. Behrens that he was on the defensive. They talked a little about the war. The professor had left Czechoslovakia in the summer of 1940 and had reached England in the autumn of that year by a roundabout route, through Greece and Turkey. After being screened, he had been allowed to work on deep penetration bombs where his theoretical knowledge of electronics had been valuable. He had also done some work on DZ fuses, and, at the end of the war, on guided missiles.

"It is curious when you come to think of it," said the professor. "For the first twelve or fifteen years of my professional life, I worked on planning projects—in my own country, in Sweden and Denmark and America. I was hoping to contrive new and better towns for people to live in. Then for six whole years I worked at destruction. I helped to knock down whole cities—I was sorry for the people in them, of course. But even while I was doing it—yes, even when the bombs were falling on me in London—I could not help saying to myself, We are clearing the way for a gigantic reconstruction, a reconstruction such as the world has never seen before." For a moment, the professor's eyes were alight with an old enthusiasm. The glow died down. "The chance has been missed," he said. "And it will never come again."

"If it is missed," said Mr. Behrens, "it won't be your fault. When your paper is published—"

"Ah, my paper," said the professor, "I am afraid that too much reliance has been placed on that. You cannot change human nature with a piece of paper."

"You can't if it isn't published."

The professor looked up sharply. "I trust," he said, "that you are not going to turn what has been a very pleasant conversation into the channels of politics."

"I'm not a politician," said Mr. Behrens. "I'm a policeman. Of a sort. I can show you my credentials if you like."

"Don't bother," said the professor. "I was warned that you might be coming. It was not made clear to me how you could help, though."

"I can only help," he said, "if you tell me what's been happening."

"Silly things. Stupid things. Things one hardly wants to talk about." He hesitated. "Letters. Telephone calls. We had a word for it in my country. Nadelstich. You would translate it as pin-prickery."

"When did it start?"

"About six months ago."

"Did you report it at once?"

"Not until it became—unpleasant. Not until it started to involve my family as well as me. Paula, my daughter, was sent these one morning. They made her sick."

The professor, as he was speaking, had moved across and unlocked a drawer in his desk. Now he handed Mr. Behrens a postcard-sized folder. On the outside was printed: "A present for a nice girl." It opened out into a string of connected photographs. They were so revolting that even Mr. Behrens' lips wrinkled.

He said, "Have the police tried to trace the origin of these?"

"I have shown them to no one. Paula forbade it. The thought of having to give evidence—"

"It wouldn't be nice," agreed Mr. Behrens. "Can I keep them for the moment?"

"Please," said the professor. "I never wish to see them again."

Mr. Behrens paused before framing his next question. He said, "These letters and messages. Have they been just general stuff? Or has there been anything specific?"

"The police have the letters. I cannot remember what was said on the telephone."

"Of course not. But what line did they take? Pure xenophobia? 'Go home Czechoslovak.' That sort of thing." He paused invitingly.

"It was that sort of thing," agreed the professor.

He's lying, thought Mr. Behrens. And he's going to go right on lying. Because he's been frightened. I shan't get anything more out of him at the moment.

He said, "I'll leave you this telephone number. It's on the London Code. Someone there will be able to contact me at once if I should be wanted." He took his leave . . .

Richard Redmayne finished his whisky, accepted a second one, and said to Mr. Calder, "It's a bloody shame. The old man's the best prospect as Minister of Education this country has had this century. You think I'm prejudiced because I'm his secretary. Perhaps I am. But I can tell you this. Without Nicholson we're never going to get this Bill through."

"The PM said he had an able deputy, who would carry on with the same policy."

“Able deputy, my foot. Morris is an old woman.”

They were in a public house near St. James’ Park underground station, much patronized by the junior staffs from Whitehall.

Mr. Calder said, “I suppose there’s no chance he’ll change his mind.”

“None at all. He’s made all his plans. As soon as his sister’s fit to move, they’re both going out to Canada.”

“Why Canada?”

“That’s where his family came from. He says they’ve got a really efficient Security Service out there, too. If *they* say they’re going to look after you, they do it.”

“We bought that one,” said Mr. Calder. “Look here—you knew Nicholson as well as anyone. Better than most. Have you got any idea why—or, more to the point, how—anyone could have been getting at him?”

“Apart from politics, you mean?”

“Apart from politics. This wasn’t the first attack, was it?”

“He’d had letters. And telephone calls. The sort of thing every public man gets.”

“General abuse? Or specific?”

“I don’t follow you.”

Mr. Calder said, patiently, “There are two ways of attacking a public man. You can pick on some large, popularly believed sort of lie. If the man’s a Jew, he’s financially crooked. If he went to the London School of Economics and wears a red tie, he’s a Communist. If he’s a bachelor, he’s homosexual. If you go on repeating the lie long and loud enough, someone will believe it in the end. The other method is to pick up some incident in their past life. It may be something quite silly, which wouldn’t matter twopence if it were you or me—but which can be magnified out of all proportion if you’re a public figure. You know what I mean?”

"Yes," said Redmayne. "I know exactly what you mean." He sat staring into his glass, and then said, "Well, he was a bachelor—"

The disposal of paper is a recurrent headache in government departments. Some of it can be destroyed and some of it must clearly be kept handy, but the bulk of it falls into that middle class of documents which no one can see any immediate use for, but which may conceivably be wanted some day. Having filled an abandoned motorcar factory near Staines Bridge, the Records Department has now taken over an airplane hangar at Brooklands and is fast filling that up too.

"Five cubic yards of paper a week," said the custodian to Mr. Behrens. "And it's getting worse. I haven't the staff to cope with it."

Mr. Behrens sympathized. He had found that a little sympathy went a long way with minor officials. "I'll do the searching myself," he said, "if you could just put me on the right track. For instance, I imagine that you index this stuff by departments. The papers I want would have come from the old MI5."

"The worst of the lot," said the custodian.

"I can tell you the approximate year of origin too. This would have originated at Blenheim in late 1940."

"When would it have been filed?"

"Probably after the end of the war."

"We got a lot of stuff from Blenheim in 1946. That's all at Staines, though."

Mr. Behrens went to Staines.

Late that afternoon he unearthed a bundle of yellow dockets. They were labeled: "Routine interrogation reports: Nov.–Dec. 1940. A-L." They appeared to be curiously incomplete.

He read them through, and then pressed the bell. When the official shuffled up, Mr. Behrens said to him, "Has anyone else been having a look at these particular records lately?"

The official said that he really couldn't say. All sorts of people came down every day to see papers. All *he* had to do was to be satisfied about their credentials. *He* couldn't keep a record of what papers they looked at.

Mr. Behrens reflected that if you paid people as little as they probably paid this particular civil servant it was idle to expect any enthusiastic or efficient service. He went back to London.

He had booked himself a room at Dons-in-London (or the "Dilly" Club), which occupies two large houses north of Lord's Cricket Ground and has the worst food and the best wine in London. It also has a unique library of classical pornography and several complete sets of the works of Dickens, Trollope and Thackeray. Mr. Behrens always used the D-I-L when he could, since he could rely on meeting a number of his cronies there.

"I understand that Sand-Douglas is up in London," he said to Mr. Calder. "I wanted to have a word with him—he was at Blenheim in 1940. You probably remember him. Why don't you join us at dinner?"

"*After* dinner," said Mr. Calder firmly.

At seven o'clock, Mr. Behrens alighted from the Bakerloo tube at Marlborough Road station and started up toward the street. The evening rush was over, and the long escalator was nearly empty. Mr. Behrens sailed sedately upward, rapt in meditation. At the top he gave up his ticket and dawdled out into the street.

There were very few people about in the Finchley Road. Mr. Behrens noticed a policeman, strolling along the opposite pavement in a purposeful way which suggested that he was coming off duty and heading for home. Mr. Behrens crossed the road. When he reached the pavement, he stopped so abruptly that the man who had been crossing behind him bumped into him.

Mr. Behrens whirled round, glared at him and said, "Why are you following me?"

"What chew talking about," said the man. He was stout, bald and unremarkable except for a twisted upper lip which seemed to give him some difficulty in enunciating.

"You've been following me for more than an hour," said Mr. Behrens. "And doing it very badly."

"You're making a nerror there," said the man. Mr. Behrens was blocking his way, and he dodged to one side to get past him.

Mr. Behrens whipped up his umbrella and thrust the metal tip, hard, into the man's crutch. The man let out a scream.

"Now then," said the policeman. "What's all this?"

The man was doubled up, speechless. Mr. Behrens said, "This gentleman has been making a nuisance of himself. He accosted me, and tried to sell me some most unpleasant pictures."

"Thass a lie," said the man. But his eyes were flickering from side to side. "I never did anything to him. He poked me with his umbrella."

"*Did* you offer to sell anything to this gentleman?"

"Course I didn't."

"He's got them in his coat pocket," said Mr. Behrens.

"Thass a lie too." The man clapped a hand into his pocket, and his expression changed. He drew out the postcard-sized folder. As he did so, it fell open disclosing the photographs inside it.

"Do you mind if I have a look at those?" said the constable.

"It's a plant," said the man. "I never—"

He handed off the constable, dodged past Mr. Behrens and started off up the pavement. Mr. Behrens, reversing his umbrella, caught him round one ankle with the handle. The man crossed his legs and fell heavily.

"You'll have to come along to the station," said the constable. "I take it you'll be preferring a charge, sir."

"I shall certainly do so," said Mr. Behrens. "Here is my card. I think it disgraceful if one cannot pay a visit to London without being subjected to the attention of men like that."

Harry Sand-Douglas was a very large man, with a pink face, a mop of iron-gray hair, and eyes the color of forget-me-nots. He finished his helping of marmalade pudding, pushed back his plate and lit a pipe.

"I think you did quite right," he said. "I hope you can make the charge stick."

"It might be difficult actually to charge him," said Mr. Behrens. "All I really hoped to do was to get rid of him. He was annoying me."

"They'll hold him overnight," said Mr. Calder. He had joined them at the port stage. "If you go round to the police station and withdraw the charge, they'll probably let him go. Then we could put a tail on him and see who's employing him. That really would be useful."

"It's an idea," said Mr. Behrens. "I'll telephone Elfe tonight. The interrogation originals at Staines were incomplete. Someone's been through them. But Harry tells me that duplicates *were* kept."

"They were microfilmed," said Sand-Douglas. "They were too bulky to be kept in any other way. When I think of the amount of paper we filled up questioning perfectly harmless people!"

"Where are the microfilm stored?"

"I've an idea it's somewhere at Oxford. I can find out. I'll ask Happold. He was in charge of that side of it."

"Good heavens," said Behrens. "Is Happold still alive? He must be ninety."

"Ninety-one," said Sand-Douglas. "And bathes in the Cherwell every morning."

At half-past ten Mr. Behrens said to Mr. Calder, "Why don't you stay the night here? I'm sure they can find you a bed."

"It's kind of you," said Mr. Calder, "but I told Rasselas I'd be back. He'll be worried if I don't turn up."

He caught the last train from Victoria to Swanly, picked up his car which he had left there and drove back to Lamperdown under a half moon, through the quiet lanes which smelled of tar and honeysuckle. A question about Mr. Behrens' assailant was teasing him. It was a matter of timing. The morning would probably solve it. He put it out of his mind.

Half a mile from the cottage a gray shape loomed. Mr. Calder braked sharply, and pulled the car up before a field gate. The great dog ran up to him and stopped, head cocked.

"All right," said Mr. Calder. "Message received and understood." He opened the gate, and manhandled his car in. It was a slight slope, and it was not a light car, but there was a surprising strength in Mr. Calder's barrel chest and stocky legs. When the car had been hidden, he started to walk home.

The dog ran ahead, silent as a cloud.

Two hundred yards from the cottage a roughly metaled track forked to the left. It led to a field, which was rented to a farmer. Rasselas went forward slowly. At a bend in the track he stopped again.

A van was parked, facing toward him. The offside door was open and there was a man standing beside it. Mr. Calder turned softly and went back the way he had come. Fifty yards down the track there was a gap in the hedge. He wriggled through it on hands and knees, and crept up the inside of the hedge until he could see the top of the van. Then, very gently, an inch at a time, he edged forward until he could see the whole van.

The man was standing beside the open door of the cab, one foot on the step. He was watching the track, and had one hand in his pocket. He looked remarkably wide-awake. Mr. Calder didn't like it. A van suggested numbers.

Half an hour passed slowly. Then there came the clink of shod feet against stone, and three other forms loomed.

Rasselas, who was lying almost on top of Mr. Calder inside the hedge, stiffened, and his lips drew back from his long white teeth. Mr. Calder clamped a hand firmly down on his head.

Two of the newcomers were carrying something heavy between them. It looked like an ammunition box. They opened the back of the van, pushed it in and climbed in beside it. The third man got up beside the driver. Under its own momentum the van rolled quietly down the track. As it reached the road, Mr. Calder heard the engine start up.

Not being a man who believed in taking chances against professional opposition, Mr. Calder spent the remaining hours of darkness in the ditch.

At a quarter to four, as the sky was whitening and the birds were starting to talk, he walked up the track and approached his cottage with caution. Rasselas moved beside him. They avoided the doors and went in by one of the side windows, which Mr. Calder opened with a long flat knife. Then, together, they made a very careful search. They both worked by sight but Rasselas had the additional faculty of smell to help him. And it was he who unearthed both of the booby traps. One was under the gas cooker, operated by the gas switch. The other was in the cistern of the lavatory, operated by the plug. Neither was exactly original but both, as Mr. Calder noted, had been very neatly and professionally done.

He telephoned Mr. Fortescue at his home in Leatherhead and gave him the registration number of the van, and a brief account of what had happened.

Mr. Fortescue, who sounded very wide-awake although it was still short of six in the morning, said, "Someone's got on to you very quickly, haven't they?"

"I thought the same," said Mr. Calder. "And another thing—they were trained men, working under discipline."

There was a long silence. Then Mr. Fortescue said, "When you come up to town you'd better come to the bank."

After breakfast Mr. Calder recevored his car and drove it back to the cottage. He was nearly out of petrol, but there was a can in his garage. When he pulled at the door it stuck, as it very often did. He gave it a sharp jerk. As he did so, the garage disintegrated and the door came out to meet him.

When Mr. Behrens arrived at Swiss Cottage police station, he sensed that something had happened. The station sergeant showed him straight up to the CID room where he found Detective Inspector Larrymore in conference with a red-faced detective sergeant and a youngish, black-haired superintendent from the Special Branch.

"What's gone wrong," said Mr. Behrens, pleasantly.

"You've heard?" said Larrymore.

"I've heard nothing," said Mr. Behrens, "but you've all got faces like a wet Monday morning, and I've never known a station sergeant be affable before, so I guessed—"

"I'm afraid," said the Special Branch man, "that they've pulled a fast one on us. I got instructions from Commander Elfe late last night that a man might be released from here in the course of the morning, and that he was to be followed. I've got a two-car team wating outside."

"Then—?"

"He was released at ten o'clock last night."

"What!"

Larrymore said, "Two men turned up, with a car. They had full DI5 credentials. They took over the prisoner. The man in charge ought to have checked back—"

The red-faced detective sergeant went even redder, and Mr. Behrens guessed that he had been the man in charge and felt sorry for him.

"It's easy to be wise after the event," he said. "Exactly what credentials did they produce?"

"They had identity cards with photographs, sir. As far as I could see they were properly signed and had the official stamp on them. And a letter on official notepaper to the officer in charge here, authorizing the handover. But it wasn't only that, sir—"

The Special Branch man looked up sharply and said, "What else, then?"

"Well, sir, it's difficult to say—but they *looked* right. When I was a recruit we did a three weeks' course with the Security people. As a matter of fact, I thought I recognized one of them as an instructor on the course. It was some time ago, of course, and I must have been mistaken—"

An uncomfortable silence was broken by the ringing of the telephone. Larrymore took the call and said, "It's for you, Mr. Behrens."

It was Mr. Fortescue. He said, "Would you come round to the bank at once. Use a police car. It can drop you at the Abbey, and you can use the back way. Don't waste any time."

"Has something happened?"

"Yes," said Mr. Fortescue. "Calder's in Gravesend Hospital. He's not dead, but he's quite far down the danger list."

"I got the message at my Whitehall office, when I got there this morning," said Mr. Fortescue. "Calder must have been conscious, because he gave the number to the senior houseman at Gravesend and it was he who rang me. It must have happened between six and nine in the morning. Because Calder had already telephoned me . . ."

He told Mr. Behrens about it.

"I see," said Mr. Behrens. "He must have missed a third trap. They're very thorough, these people, aren't they? Were you able to trace the van?"

"The police traced it. It was stolen in the Borough yesterday."

"At about what time? Do they know?"

"Before two o'clock. Between one and two." Before Mr. Behrens could say anything, Mr. Fortescue stopped him. "I hadn't missed the point," he said. "Take it with the business at Swiss Cottage police station last night, and it adds up to something I'm not at all keen on thinking about. I gather that I'm to see the Prime Minister this afternoon. And I've gathered something else, too. Maver is *not* being invited to the meeting."

From Mr. Fortescue's office you could hear Big Ben quite clearly. First, the four sets of warning notes, then the ten strokes of the hour. It wasn't until the last of them had died away that either of them spoke again. It was Mr. Behrens who broke the silence. He said, "Of course, it was always on the cards that something like that might happen. It's happened often enough in other countries. We've never had it here. I think I'd better go down to Gravesend. If Calder can still talk, he'll find it easier to talk to me than anyone else."

"Very well," said Mr. Fortescue. "I don't need to tell you to be careful."

"I shall be extremely careful," Mr. Behrens assured him.

He was so careful that it took him three hours to reach Gravesend, and he entered the hospital by the tradesmen's entrance. He found a policeman standing in the corridor that led to the private wards, identified himself and was allowed into an anteroom. Here he found a grim-faced Sister seated at a table, guarding the inner door. She said, "No one can go in without Dr. Henfry's permission."

"Then perhaps," said Mr. Behrens, "you would be kind enough to send for Dr. Henfry."

This was clearly a breach of protocol. Sisters in hospitals do not run errands for visitors. She rang a bell, summoning a porter. The porter disappeared and silence fell.

Dr. Henfry, when he arrived five minutes later, was large and red-headed, the sort of man who would be a welcome addition to the pack in any hospital rugger team. He said, "If your name's Behrens, you can come in for five minutes."

"Thank you," said Mr. Behrens.

"Will you want the blood transfusions, doctor?"

"I'll let you know," said Dr. Henfry. "Come along, Mr. Behrens. And very quiet, please."

The bed in the room was entirely hidden by screens. Dr. Henfry closed the door carefully and bolted it. Then he moved the nearest screen and Mr. Behrens saw Mr. Calder. He was sitting up in bed reading the *Times.* On the table by his bed were the remains of a pork pie and two bottles of beer.

"It's not what we like to give our invalids for breakfast," said Dr. Henfry with a grin. "Particularly when they're at death's door. But it's all I could manage. I had to buy it myself and smuggle it in in my instrument case."

"Do I gather," said Mr. Behrens, "that you are *not* dying?"

"That's right," said Mr. Calder. "But you and Dr. Henfry are the only people who know it, and it's going to stay that way for a bit. The deputation who called at my cottage last night left a third visiting card, in the form of a few pounds of gelignite controlled by a trembler fuse and a detonator. They left it in the inspection pit in my garage. If I'd driven the car over it, I'd have been blown to Jericho. Luckily I set it off from outside by banging the door. The door hit me and knocked me cold. But it also protected me. I was still unconscious when the milkman came along. He put me straight into his van, bless him, and brought me down here. I'd come round by that time, and I realized what a stroke of luck the whole thing was. I put Dr. Henfry wise, and he's done the rest."

"I've had a gaggle of reporters round here already," said Dr. Henfry. "I told them you might recover—with luck and devoted nursing. You'd had three blood transfusions already."

"Excellent," said Mr. Calder.

"I'd better take Mr. Behrens out now, or Sister will start worrying. I'll show him the back way in along the balcony."

When they were alone together, Mr. Calder said, "You can tell Fortescue, of course. But no one else. I'm going to clear out as soon as it's dark. Dr. Henfry is fetching me."

"I assume you're going under cover?"

"We both are. We'll use Mrs. Palfrey's."

"Is this just general caution . . . or something special?"

Mr. Calder was busy pouring out the second bottle of beer and did not answer for a moment. Then he said, "That fuse on the plastic explosive under the grill was micrometer set. I shouldn't have needed to turn the gas on. The lightest touch on the switch would have set it off. When I'd immobilized it, I took some photographs. The whole thing had been beautifully concealed. Even if you stooped down you could hardly see a thing. All the wires were taped, and the tapes themselves had been fish-tailed and folded under at the end. Do you remember that sergeant at the demolition school? 'Five minutes' extra work, gentlemen. But it may well make the difference between success and failure.' *He* always fish-tailed the ends of *his* tapes. It was when I saw those tapes that I decided to go under cover."

"I have on my books at this moment," said Mr. Fortescue to the Prime Minister, "twenty men and four women, any two of whom—they usually work in pairs—I *might* have allotted to this particular assignment. I selected Calder and Behrens, and I telephoned both of them on Wednesday evening. The line which I used is, I can assure you, secure. They both saw me on Thursday morning. It is true that they came quite openly, and my office in Richmond Terrace might be watched—although, as Commander Elfe will tell you, the Security precautions are such that it would be very difficult for anyone to do so without themselves being observed."

Commander Elfe, who was the only other person present, nodded and said, "Not impossible, but so difficult that I think we might rule it out."

"In any event," went on Mr. Fortescue, "Calder and Behrens were not the only people who saw me that morning. I had routine matters to discuss with at least six other members of my department."

"So," said the Prime Minister, "up to that time, no one would have any reason to connect them with this particular job. What did they do next?"

"Behrens visited the Records Department in the new Defence building and went from there to call on Professor Gottlieb. Calder went to Campden Hill to talk to the inspector in charge of the Nicholson inquiry."

"At either of which points they could have been picked up and followed."

"Oh, certainly," said Mr. Fortescue. "Only Mr. Behrens did not reach the Gottlieb flat until a quarter past two, and Mr. Calder went to Campden Hill even later—at three o'clock. The van which was used for the visit to Mr. Calder's cottage was stolen between one and two. It was clearly stolen for that job, and was abandoned when it had been done."

The Prime Minister looked at Elfe, who looked at Mr. Fortescue, and said, "What it amounts to is this: the only people who could have known by midday that Behrens was on this job were the staff of the Defence Ministry. If they knew Behrens was on it, they would have assumed Calder was involved as well."

"I'm afraid that's right," said Mr. Fortescue.

"Gentlemen," said the Prime Minister, "I am not an alarmist. And thirty years in politics has taught me not to jump to conclusions. But if you add that last fact to certain others—the way in which Behrens' assailant was liberated; the method and execution of the attack on Calder—I'm afraid that a very distasteful possibility emerges."

"You mean," said Commander Elfe bluntly, "that Security Executive are playing politics."

In a comfortable bed-sitting room, in that area of bed-sitting rooms which lies between the station and the Rugby football ground at Twickenham, Mr. Behrens poured out a cup of tea for Mr. Calder and said, "How many so far?"

"Seventeen near certainties," said Mr. Calder. "Seventeen cases of public servants driven out. Nine of them have gone to live abroad. Two are in institutions. Six, including Bax, have taken their own lives. And, if those are the ones we know about, you can be certain that the true total is twice or three times as great."

Mr. Behrens said, "It was the technique which convinced me, much more than all that working out of times and places. It was such an exact reproduction of the interrogation techniques which both sides brought to horrible perfection during the war. If you wanted to break a man down, what did you do? First you made him uncomfortable. It was far more demoralizing for a man to be cold, or filthy, or sleepless, or thirsty than actually to be hurt. Discomfort weakens. Torture builds up a resistance. The Russians discovered that long ago. The interrogator's second weapon was to find something—it didn't matter what—but something which his victim was ashamed of. Some weakness, some slip. If he harped on it skillfully he could take the man to pieces."

Mr. Calder stirred his tea, and looked round the comfortable, lower-middle-class sitting room. Mrs. Palfrey's grandfather and grandmother stared back at him from fading brown oleographs over the mantelpiece. He found reassurance in their Victorian rigidity. He said, "Public servants are sitting ducks. They loathe fuss. They eschew scandal. And they can't run away. That's the point. They're nailed to their jobs. Take a man like Nicholson. He had to be within reach of Westminster and Whitehall. The only way to go out was to go right out. I wonder what they had on him. And how many times he paid up."

The arrival of Mrs. Palfrey, with a kettle of hot water and the evening paper, saved Mr. Behrens from having to reply. He found an item at the foot of the front page which seemed to interest him. He read it out: "A party of birdwatchers on the Cooling Marshes yesterday discovered, in one of the saltwater dikes, the body of a man. He has not yet been identified. The following description has been issued. Age, about forty-five. Height, five foot six. Stoutly built. A marked malformation of the upper lip."

"Do we know him?" said Mr. Calder.

"My acquaintance with him," said Mr. Behrens, "was limited to poking him with my umbrella. I cannot regard him as a great loss."

"Quick work, all the same," said Mr. Calder. "They don't believe in leaving loose ends about, do they? I wonder what they'll do next . . ."

Richard Redmayne and Paula Gottlieb sitting on the seat in Green Park made a handsome couple. His conventional dress could not conceal a certain long-limbed, coordinated strength, the product of a school which was unfashionable enough to think athletic prowess important; the girl, dark, lively and very young.

She said, "Have you heard from Mr. Nicholson?"

"He's arrived in Canada," said Richard. "I had a short letter. He and his sister have got a flat in Toronto. He says they're settling down very happily."

"'We that had loved him so, followed him, honoured him, lived in his mild and magnificent eye, learned his great language, caught his clear accents, made him our pattern to live and to die.'"

"That's poetry," said Richard suspiciously.

"Robert Browning. 'The Lost Leader.' You remember? 'Just for a handful of silver he left us.'"

"It wasn't money in his case," said Richard. "It was fear. How's your father?"

This change of subject did not appear to surprise Paula. She had reached a stage of intimacy with Richard when such sudden jumps were part of the fun. She said, "If only he'd make up his mind. It's the uncertainty which is so horrible. If he'd only tell me—tell someone—what it's all about. He just sits at home. He hardly goes out at all. I had a job to persuade him to go out this morning and get his hair cut."

"That's two o'clock striking now," said Richard. "I've got to get back. But I'll walk home with you first."

As soon as Paula opened the door of the flat, she knew something was wrong.

"Whats up?" said Richard.

"Where's Fritz?" There was panic in the girl's voice. "We left him to guard the house . . . he always runs out to meet me."

Through the open door of the drawing room they could glimpse the chaos within. Overturned chairs, broken glass, something seeping under the door and staining the hall carpet.

Richard said urgently, "Don't go in there—stop." But he found himself unable to hold her. She burst past him and threw herself into the room. As he grabbed the telephone, he heard her give a single choked scream.

When the police and her father arrived together five minutes later, she was still on her knees, sobbing uncontrollably, with a brown and black head cradled on her lap . . .

In the hot blacked-out room, half laboratory, half office, two men pored over the microfilm reader. "It's here if it's anywhere," said Sand-Douglas. "November 2nd, 1940. That was the day he arrived. The main interrogation would have started the day after. We usually gave them a night's rest."

Old Mr. Happold, as thin and as indestructible as dried seaweed, fed a second roll of microfilm into the reader and adjusted the reading glass. He was unaffected by the heat and closeness of the room. "This looks like the one," he said. "Do you know exactly what it is we're looking for?"

"We're looking for a name," said Sand-Douglas. "A name out of the past. And I do believe"—he wiped a hand across to clear the sweat out of his eyes—"yes, that's it. I'll have to use your telephone. I think we'll risk an open line this time."

Professor Gottlieb looked round the table. There were four men there. Commander Elfe of the Special Branch he knew; and he had met Mr. Fortescue once, and was aware that he was connected with Security. The other two were a thickset man whom they called Mr. Calder, and Mr. Behrens.

"I don't think," said the professor, "that they could do anything more horrible than they did this morning. It was a mistake. Since there is nothing worse they can do, I have no motive not to speak. When I came to this country in 1940, I brought with me a secret of which I was bitterly ashamed. I am not a man of action. I could never have arranged my own escape from Prague. I should not have known how to start. It was arranged for me. When I told my story to your interrogators, I said that it was arranged by the Czech underground. That was a lie. It was arranged by the Germans. They bartered my escape with me for some information I was able to give them. I didn't know why they wanted it—that's no excuse. It led to the execution of two of my colleagues in

Prague University. I thought, for a long time, the secret had died with them. I still have no idea how anyone could have found out."

"The man who interrogated you," said Mr. Fortescue, "also dealt with other compatriots of yours. He heard a rumor from them, and was able to verify it after the war from German sources. But please go on."

"There is no more. Seven years ago, when I began to be well known here, and well paid—the blackmail started. For seven years I have paid away about a third of all my income. Lately the demands were increased. I dug in my toes. Different forms of pressure were applied. I could do nothing to stop them. I was afraid that if I complained the whole truth would come out. I see now that I have been stupid. I should have spoken at once. But it is difficult to see these things when you are on your own."

"Have you any idea at all who the blackmailers were?" asked Commander Elfe.

"None at all. I never saw them, or spoke to them except on the telephone. I drew the money every month in notes and sent it to what I imagine was an accommodation address." He paused, and looked round the table at the four men. Mr. Calder and Mr. Behrens were looking impassive. The burly Commander Elfe had a scowl on his face. Mr. Fortescue was looking out of the window. He had a cold and clinical glint in his eye. It reminded Professor Gottlieb of a surgeon he had once watched, weighing up the chances of a delicate and critical operation. "And that's really all I can tell you," he said. "Do you think there is any chance of catching these men?"

Mr. Fortescue swiveled his head round so that he was looking directly at the professor. He said, "Oh, yes. We have found out who these men are, and where they operate from. It would be comparatively simple to render them harmless. But if we are actually to catch and convict them, we shall need a lot of luck—and your help . . ."

"I am glad that my worst suspicions were wrong," said the Prime Minister, "and I apologize for them." He had invited Ian Maver, the head of DI5, to dinner and they were sitting together over their brandy.

"Not so far wrong," said Maver. The apology and the brandy were working on him. "Most of them are either ex-MI5 or ex-policemen. The leader is a man called Cotter. I knew him quite well. A guardsman. A very able officer, an excellent linguist and a good organizer. A bit ruthless for peacetime operations. He left us in the mid-'fifties. I think he was disappointed over promotion. Then he set up this private inquiry organization, Cotter's Detectives. We've been using him quite a bit lately ourselves. Guarding VIPs and that sort of thing."

"And it was his men who were put in charge of Nicholson?"

"That wasn't very clever," said Maver, "but if they keep us short of policemen it's bound to happen. Businesses use private gunmen to look after their payrolls now. Private watchmen patrol building estates. Private guards for VIPs? It was a logical step."

"How did you find out about him?"

"We went right back to the record of Gottlieb's first interrogation. Cotter was the man who conducted it. We got a cross-reference when we found out that Cotter and one of his men, Lawrie, had been the two 'referees' given by Smythe when he got his job in our Records Department. That was a bad slip, and it was entirely my fault."

The Prime Minister was aware that the head of DI5 was offering him his resignation if he chose to take it. He rejected the offering. His opinion of Ian Maver had changed in the course of the evening.

He said, "Everyone's allowed one mistake. Even in politics. What are you doing about Smythe?"

"For the moment, we're leaving him where he is. He happens to form rather a useful channel of communication. One of his jobs is to monitor the Records room. If we want to get a piece of information across to Cotter, without appearing to do so, all that's necessary is a little calculated indiscretion between two of our men when searching the files."

"Do I gather from that," said the Prime Minister, "that some definite action is contemplated?"

"Mr. Fortescue has the matter in hand," said Maver.

"It's not going to be at all easy," said Mr. Fortescue, "but we have three points in our favor." He ticked them off with one finger of his right hand.

"First, they have no reason at all to think that we suspect them. And of course they must continue in this happy state of ignorance. Secondly, we can, if we are careful, leak information to them through Smythe. Third, and most important, I think they are bound to react to Professor Gottlieb. Like all bullies, if one of their victims rebels and they do nothing about it, other victims will follow suit. I am arranging for Professor Gottlieb to show fight."

"They might go for his daughter," said Elfe.

"I had thought of that myself," said Mr. Fortescue, and Elfe looked up sharply.

"Do I understand that you're going to use the girl as bait?"

"It seems to me the simplest of a number of possible methods," said Mr. Fortescue. "We'll keep the professor in town, and put such a ring fence of guards round him that they can't touch him. As a preliminary precaution, the girl will be sent into the country. Not too far. I had in mind the Thetford area in Norfolk. The army used it at a battle school during the war, and parts of it are still quite deserted."

"And you're going to let them know she's there?"

"It will come to their ears in about a week's time."

"I don't like it," said Elfe. "It's too risky."

"Any plan will be risky," said Mr. Fortescue. "This plan will, I think, have less risk than most. I always prefer to play a match on ground of my own choosing."

"Who are you going to send with her? Calder—or Behrens?"

"If I sent either of them, it would be stupid of Cotter to go near her and Cotter is not a stupid man. No. I had in mind that Nicholson's secretary, young Redmayne, would be the man for the job. They know each other and are, I believe, good friends. They'll be suitably chaperoned, of course."

Harwood Farm lay at the end of mile of lane. It was a pleasant, rambling, yellow-brick building with two vast barns. It had been empty for some months, since the last tenant-farmer had moved out. Its fields were now farmed by a man who came over occasionally from Tunstock.

One of the pleasantest features of their stay, thought Richard Redmayne, had been the efforts they had made to bring the place back to life. For a fortnight he and Paula and the dour Mrs. Mason had washed and scrubbed and scoured and sandpapered and painted. Paula had revealed several unexpected skills. First she had dismantled and cleaned the engine and dynamo which supplied them with electricity. Then, with the aid of a carload of technical stores from Norwich, she had stepped up the output, so that bulbs which had previously shone dimly now glowed as brightly as though they were on mains.

"My father taught me not to be afraid of electricity," she said. "It's just like water. You see water coming out of a tap. A nice steady flow. Halve the outlet, and you double the power. Like this." She was holding a length of hosepipe in her hand, swilling down the choked gutters in the yard. As she pinched the end of the hose, a thin jet of water hissed out.

"All right," said Richard, ducking. "You needn't demonstrate it. I understand the principle. I didn't know it applied to electricity, that's all."

"Tomorrow," said Paula, "I'm going to get Mrs. Mason to stoke up the boiler, and I'm going to run a hose into the big barn. I'll use a proper stopcock, and we'll build up the pressure. Then you'll see what steam can do. Did you know that if you got a fine enough jet and sufficient pressure you could cut metal with steam?"

"For goodness' sake, don't try it," said Richard. "We shall blow ourselves up."

"You're a coward," said Paula. "By the way, did you see the *Times* this morning? It's got something about Daddy in it."

It was a paragraph on the Home News page. It said that Professor Gottlieb was confident of finishing his final revision of the White Paper on Planning before the end of the month. The professor had held a news conference, in which he had said that certain minor technical difficulties which had been holding him up had been satisfactorily disposed of.

"He's trailing his coat," said Paula.

"What do you mean?"

"You must think me an idiot if you imagine I don't know what's going on. He's provoking those people to attack him, isn't he? And that's why I've been stowed away here, to be out of harm's way."

"Well—" said Richard.

"And you're my guard. There's no need to apologize. I'm enjoying it—when I stop worrying about Daddy."

"He'll be well looked after," said Richard.

Better looked after, he couldn't help thinking, than Paula herself. He recalled the single afternoon of instruction he had been given—on the range in Wellington Barracks—with the automatic pistol which he now carried tucked under his left armpit by day and placed under his pillow each night. It was comforting to have a gun, but he was still far from certain that he could hit anything with it. Mrs. Mason, he knew, was connected with Fortescue's organization, but if real trouble developed . . .

"What are *you* looking so serious about?" said Paula.

"Nothing," said Richard. "I was working out what we had to do to the barn now that we've got the house in order."

Visitors to the farm were few but regular, and already their visits had fallen into a pattern. The grocer from East Harling delivered on Tuesday and Friday. The fishmonger and butcher came out from Diss on Thursday. Twice every day the little red post van came bowling down the lane with letters and newspapers. And on Friday the dustcart arrived to carry away the week's rubbish.

Mrs. Mason, doubtless acting on orders, allowed none of them near the house but went out to the gate to collect their offerings herself. To Richard they were blurred faces seen behind a windshield, except for the rubbish collectors, whose names were Ernest and Leonard and with whom he had exchanged local gossip.

The postman was a plump cheerful man. He operated from Diss, and had taken over the round which included Harwood Farm on the day before Richard and Paula arrived. He lodged in a back street and, although apparently a temporary, carried out his work in an efficient manner.

Indeed, so conscientious was he that in the evenings, after his rounds were completed, he would often take the van and tour the district, memorizing roads and lanes, houses and farms, and the position of telephone kiosks and AA boxes.

That Thursday night, when he returned to his lodging, he found a postcard propped up on the mantelpiece. The front showed a stout lady in a bathing dress, whose toe was being eaten by a crab. On the back was written: "Uncle Tom and the three boys planning to start for country tomorrow." It was signed "Edna," and the name was underlined three times.

"Three-line whip," said the postman to himself. He went across to the cupboard and took out a violin case. But what he took out of it was certainly not a violin . . .

Friday was a perfect day. The sun rose through a cloak of early-morning mist, scattered it and sailed in majesty across the heavens. Life at Harwood Farm pursued its unexciting course. The grocer came with groceries, and the postman on his morning round stopped for a gossip with Mrs. Mason. He seemed to do most of the talking. Mrs. Mason contented herself with nodding. She was a woman of few words. Her only relaxation was the *Times* crossword puzzle which she regularly finished in the kitchen when they had given it up in the drawing room. In the afternoon Paula rigged her steam hose, a fearsome contraption of plastic pipe and chromium fitting, and cleaned out the cowstalls at the end of the barn. The thin scalding jet stripped the filth of ages from the floors and wooden walls with the speed of a rotary plane.

It was five o'clock in the afternoon when the dustcart drove up. The driver reversed the lumbering vehicle in the space in front of the gate. He did it clumsily, crashing his gears, as if he was unused to driving it. Three men got out of the back. They walked quickly through the yard, ignoring the two dustbins, and pushed into the kitchen.

Mrs. Mason jumped up, saw the gun in the hand of the leading man and said, calmly, "What do you want?"

"Take it easy," said the man, "and you won't get hurt." As he said this the second man walked round behind her and smacked her across the back of the neck with a leather-covered cosh. The third man caught her as she fell forward.

"Put her in that cupboard," said the leader. "There's a bolt on the outside."

Mr. Calder, turning the post van in at the top of the lane, saw signs of the ambush. The surface of the road was broken where the heavy dustcart had lurched to a halt, and the hedge was broken too. Mr. Calder jumped out to investigate, and found Ernest and Leonard in the ditch, their elbows and ankles strapped and their heads in paper dust sacks. He undid them and they sat up, swearing. Mr. Calder cut them short.

"There's a public telephone three hundred yards down the main road," he said. "Get there as quick as you can—ask for this number—and just say the word '*Action*.'"

Leonard, who was the younger and more spirited of the two, said, "Couldn't we get after those bastards first?"

"No," said Mr. Calder. "You'd be in the way. Just do what I told you. And quick."

As they lumbered off down the road, he got back into his van. He could be heard coming, but that couldn't be helped. Speed was now more important than surprise. Anyway, he had no intention of driving up to the house. He had long ago located a field track, usable in dry weather, which led off the lane to a point behind the barn . . .

The farmhouse being old and its walls thick, Richard, who was writing in the drawing room, had heard nothing of the goings-on in the kitchen. He did, however, hear heavy footsteps coming along the stone-floored passage, footsteps which could not belong to Mrs. Mason or Paula. He had time to get his gun out. It wasn't a bad shot for a first attempt. He missed Cotter who led the rush through the door, but hit the man behind him in the knee.

Cotter, steadying himself, shot Richard through the right shoulder, knocking him off his chair onto the floor. Then he picked up his gun and took no further notice of him.

"We'll look after Lawrie in a moment," he said. "We've got to grab the girl before she runs for it.

It was unfortunate for them that, being in a hurry, they came out of the door and into the yard together. Cotter realized their mistake when he heard the girl's voice from behind them. She said, "This gun's loaded, both barrels. Even I couldn't miss you from here."

The two men turned. Cotter's gun was back in its shoulder holster. The other man had not drawn his. And the girl was holding a twelve-bore, double-barreled sporting rifle.

"Into the barn," she said.

They moved slowly ahead of her. Cotter looked at the door as he went through to see if he could slam it, but it was too heavy and had been firmly wedged open with a stake.

"Down that end," she said. "Now. Take your guns out slowly and drop them on the ground."

The two men had spread themselves out. It was a deliberate movement. They knew very well that the odds were still on their side. As Cotter pulled his gun and dropped it onto the flooor in front of him, he let it fall even farther to one side, and shuffled after it. The other man did the same. The gun barrel wavered. They were now so far apart that one shot could not hit both of them.

"What are you planning to do?" said Cotter, edging over a little farther. He was now almost up against the side wall of the barn. "Keep us here till it's dark?" He had seen the side door of the barn move and guessed that it was the fourth man, the driver of the van, coming to lend a hand. Keep her attention, and the driver could jump her from behind. No point in shooting her.

Paula saw the danger out of the corner of her eye. She swung round and fired both barrels. The first missed altogether. The second hit the driver full in the chest. As she fired, she dropped the gun, put out a hand without hurry, laid hold of the steam hosepipe and flicked open the faucet.

A jet of scalding steam, thin and sharp as a needle, hissed from the nozzle and seemed to hang in the air for a moment, then hit Cotter full in the face as he stooped for his gun. He went forward onto his knees. The hose followed him down, searing and stripping.

The second man got hold of his gun. Mr. Calder, standing square in the doorway of the barn, shot his legs from under him with his tommy gun.

When the carload of Special Branch men arrived they found Mr. Calder in the barn. The officer in charge was the same dark-haired young man whom Mr. Behrens had encountered at the police station. He introduced himself to Mr. Calder as Superintendent Patrick Petrella.

"We got your message," he said, "and passed it on to London. Behrens will have rounded up Smythe and the others by now. I don't think they're going to give us much trouble. Cotter was the mainspring of the whole thing."

"He's a busted mainspring now," said Mr. Calder. "There's going to be a lot of clearing up to do. I've got three wounded men for you. And two dead."

"I've yet to learn," said Petrella, "that it's a crime to resist an armed attempt at kidnaping. She'll get a vote of thanks." He moved across to the other end of the barn where two shapes lay, covered by sacks. "Which is Cotter?"

"This one," said Mr. Calder. "He isn't a very nice sight."

"Good God," said Petrella, shaken out of his phlegm. "What did she do that with?"

"She used a high-pressure steam hose," said Mr. Calder. "Cotter made a mistake. He killed her dog and mutilated it. I know just how she felt. I've got a dog myself."

The Cat Cracker

Mr. Behrens adjusted his glasses, aligned his left foot against the telltale, raised the heavy brass dart until it was level with his eye and flipped it. As it left his hand the door of the public bar of the Lamb opened and a man came in.

Mr. Behrens' opponents said, "Double four. Nice shot." The newcomer said, "Good God, if it isn't Mr. Behrens."

Mr. Behrens came out of the trance which affects a dart player trying for his final double, blinked and said, "I've got a feeling I ought to know your face."

"No reason you should," said the newcomer. He was a man in his early forties with hair already thinning and graying, a long thick nose and shrewd brown eyes. "When you last saw me I was fifteen and spotty."

"Now wait a minute," said Mr. Behrens. "Wait a minute. Talbot. No. Tabor."

"Right, sir. Alan Tabor. And I hope I didn't put you off your throw."

"Not half you didn't," said his opponent. "If a bomb went off in the next room *he'd* still get his double four."

He put down the half pint of beer which was his tribute to Mr. Behrens' skill. He didn't really feel sour about it. But he was the local champion and for a week now he had been trying, with little success, to win a beer from Mr. Behrens. "I must be off. See you this evening, I hope."

"You shall have your revenge this evening," said Mr. Behrens. And then to Tabor, "Have you come in here for a drink, or to eat? If you're going to have lunch, perhaps you'd care to join me? Or you may have people with you? I take it you're motoring."

"I'm alone," said Tabor. "I'd love to have lunch with you. And I haven't a car, I walked."

"Then you must have walked a long way," said Mr. Behrens. "Because there are few lonelier pubs in England than this one. That's one of the things I like about it."

"I come out here quite a lot from Ravenshoe," said Tabor. "It's a bit bleak now in winter. But you ought to see it in spring and summer."

"I've seen it in spring *and* in summer," said Mr. Behrens. "I'm one of Ruby's most regular customers. Isn't that right, Ruby?"

"That's right," said Ruby. "Spring and autumn. Like the rates. What'll it be? There's hot steak-and-kidney pie or cold beef."

Resident guests were a rare occurrence at the Lamb, so Mr. Behrens and Mr. Tabor had the coffee room to themselves.

"You're at the refinery, of course," said Mr. Behrens. "When you mentioned Ravenshoe the penny ought to have dropped. After I had failed to teach you the rudiments of Latin, you went off and specialized in science, didn't you? And got a science scholarship at Oxford?"

"They didn't call it a scholarship," said Tabor. There was an edge of bitterness in his voice. "Words like 'scholarship' are reserved for respectable subjects like Latin and Greek. But it came to the same thing—other people paid for my education. The odd thing was that the further I got, the more money people seemed willing to splash out."

"Invest," said Mr. Behrens with a crinkled smile. "Invest. Where did you go after Oxford?"

"Back to Leipzig. After that I *was* going to Moscow—but Fate willed otherwise."

"Of course. That would have been 1939. A pity." Mr. Behrens toyed with the idea of asking him what he had done during the war, but decided that it might be tactless. Instead he said, "I've always heard that Ravenshoe was an interesting place. You produce more than oil and petrol, don't you?"

"Oil and petrol are almost a side line. We sell enough to pay our overhead. I suppose you wouldn't care to look over it? You were always rather scornful of science, as I remember."

"That was when I was twenty-five and you were seventeen," said Mr. Behrens. "Our respective outlooks may have developed in the interim."

"It really is rather a wonderful place," said Tabor. "We can turn out end products which even five years ago no one would have associated with crude oil. Plastics, nylon stockings, paint, explosives."

"I am prepared to admit," said Mr. Behrens, "that modern science is capable of almost anything. But it has *not* turned out anything quite like Ruby's, or her mother's, steak-and-kidney pie."

He regarded with a shade more than avuncular approval the trim but well-developed figure of the eighteen-year-old daughter of the house, who was approaching them with a loaded and steaming tray.

"That's the Primary Distillation Unit," said Tabor, pointing to something which looked like a church tower under repair. "We could climb the scaffolding if you want, but you won't see any more from the top. The temperature's kept constant at one thousand degrees—that's nothing out of the way, of course, but it's quite hot as refining processes go."

He raked open one of the boilerplate hatches and Mr. Behrens peered into an antechamber of the inferno. Gas, distilled from the oil, was carried around through pipes and ignited in a brick-kiln oven. The flames glowed white at the center of the heat, tawny-red and orange around the outer edges. The roaring was still in his ears as he moved away.

"So you don't call that hot?" he said.

"Chemically, no. We can produce ten times that heat. But, as a matter of fact, in a lot of ways it's *too* hot. You see—look here, how much of this are you really understanding?"

"I'm with you so far, I think," said Mr. Behrens. "You heat up the crude oil and distill off different products with different boiling points. Gas at the top, then petrol, after that paraffin and diesel—and asphalt at the bottom. And the whole process is commonly known as 'cracking.' Right?"

"Correct," said Tabor. "But the trouble is that you can do a lot of harm to the crude oil if you have to heat it as high as one thousand degrees centigrade. On the other hand—it won't crack at less."

Mr. Behrens said, though whether jocularly or not it was hard to detect, "The Nazis had just the same problem, I believe. When interrogating prisoners, I mean. With some of them they had to use so much force to crack them that the prisoner disintegrated in the process."

They were walking away from the distillation unit toward an affair shaped like a lopsided hourglass, with trimmings. Tabor checked for a moment in his stride, looked sideways at Mr. Behrens and said, with a shade of hesitancy in his voice, "That's an odd analogy." They walked for a few steps in silence, and Tabor added, "Chemically, we overcome the difficulty in rather an ingenious way. We mix a catalyst with the fuel—usually china clay—then the mixture can be cracked at much lower temperatures. That's the machine that does it."

Mr. Behrens stared at the squat appartus. It had, he thought, an evil look. "I've heard oilmen talk about a 'cat cracker,'" he said. "I'd no idea that was what it was."

"There's not a lot to see," said Tabor. "No moving parts. No action. No excitement. It's rather an efficient piece of apparatus, all the same."

"It has a sort of feminine, yet feline, look about it, hasn't it?" said Mr. Behrens. "I wasn't only referring to its shape—although there's something in that too. I meant its general appearance of dangerous docility. One has the feeling that inside those deceptive curves processes of unsuspected ferocity are taking place."

"You're an odd chap," said Tabor. But there was an undercurrent of affection in his voice.

"I should never have made a scientist," agreed Mr. Behrens. "I am far too fanciful."

A week later Mr. Behrens and Mr. Tabor both happened to go up to London. Mr. Behrens went by train. He had an appointment with his bank manager. Tabor went by car. He also had an appointment.

Tabor parked his car in a side street near Paddington Station, walked back down the Harrow Road and turned into Saint Mary's Terrace. This runs up to the canal, sometimes hopefully referred to as London's Little Venice; on this bleak winter's day Saint Mary's Terrace was an empty stretch of road beside a dirty reach of water.

There was only one human being in sight. He was a huge man, further enlarged by a tentlike overcoat, with a red face and a corona of white hair which ruffled in the breeze. Tabor hurried toward him, both hands outstretched. The big man awaited him impassively.

"Paulus!"

"My dear Alan."

They shook hands warmly, Tabor looking into the older man's eyes as if there was some reassurance he hoped to find there.

"I remember this place from my youth in London," said Professor Paulus Mann. "When I suggested meeting you here, I visualized us sitting side by side on a bench watching the ducks in the canal, and the pretty barges going up and down. I had forgotten the time of year and the weather."

"There's a pub down there," said Tabor. "Or there was ten years ago. They used to have an open fire in the saloon bar too."

"Splendid," said the professor. "We will sit all afternoon and talk."

"Not in an English pub you won't," said Tabor.

At about the same moment, Mr. Behrens was seated in the private office of Mr. Fortescue, the manager of the Westminster branch of the London and Home Counties Bank. The room was, in Mr. Behrens' considered opinion, one of the most appalling in London. It seemed to have been designed by a sanitary engineer, being paneled—if such was the correct word—in three shades of brown porcelain. An elaborate chandelier sprouted from a coffee-colored porcelain rosette; flowers in golden porcelain patterned the walls; and an enormous chocolate-colored porcelain overmantel lowered above a tiny fire.

In front of the fire stood an old, plain, brown desk, and on the desk stood a photograph of Mrs. Fortescue in Court dress, and two telephones, neither of which was connected with a public line. Mr. Behrens had once heard Mr. Fortescue keep the Home Secretary waiting on one while he spoke to the Foreign Secretary on the other.

Fortescue now placed the tips of his fingers together in a manner much approved by bank managers of the old school, and said, "It's an extremely delicate situation. You do see that, don't you?"

"Oh, I do," said Mr. Behrens.

"It is not a case in which direct or forceful methods are likely to achieve anything but disaster. It is not a problem which would appeal to Mr. Calder. That is why we have turned to you."

Mr. Behrens was not sure whether to take this as a compliment or not. He contented himself with merely saying, "Yes."

"Was Tabor at all suspicious?"

"I don't think so. No. Fortunately *he* recognized *me* first. That was a great help. He was in my class at Leipzig High School in 1934. I taught him Latin actually. Not Science."

"And he would find out, if he chose to inquire, that you were an habitué of the Lamb."

"I have been using it for over a year. And so, incidentally, has he. We might have met at any time. It just happened to be last Saturday."

"We can only hope," said Mr. Fortescue, "that we are not too late." There was a touch of genuine sadness in his voice. "Professor Mann is in London. He arrived last night. Tabor motored up to town this morning. I have no doubt they are deep in talk now, even as we are."

"Did you have the professor followed?" asked Mr. Behrens.

"Certainly not," said Mr. Fortescue. "Certainly not. As I told you, this situation is extremely delicate. There is, on the face of it, nothing at all—apart, one would hope, from a certain natural patriotism—to prevent Tabor leaving this country and working for our enemies. We are not at war. And Tabor is not in government employment. Nor is he subject to the Official Secrets Act. Even his patriotism might work either way. His mother was English, but his father was German."

"But he is too good a scientist for us to lose him."

Mr. Fortescue was not a man given to extravagant statement. So when he said, "He is one of the ablest scientists in the world," the words conveyed more to Mr. Behrens than an elaborate eulogy.

"He has specialized in cosmoelectronics, which is the electronics of the universe. It is a study which bears the same relationship to electronics as electronics does to old-fashioned electricity. It is almost more a logic than a science. There are no blueprints. The handful of men whose minds are capable of understanding and studying it make up their own rules, draw their own charts and speak their own language."

"And Professor Paulus Mann is one of them?"

"He was a pioneer. Tabor studied under him at Leipzig. I do not suppose that the professor would claim to be in the front rank now. Nevertheless it was a very astute move sending him over here. Tabor will listen to him if he will listen to no one else."

"I remember Tabor at school," said Mr. Behrens. "A very withdrawn boy. I used to imagine that he was bullied, but in retrospect I doubt it. He was too self-contained to make a good subject for bullies. A natural enemy of the Establishment. Do you think we have any chance of keeping him?"

"By force, no chance at all. If we keep him, it will have to be by conviction."

"Are you suggesting," said Mr. Behrens, "that I should corner the poor young man and lecture him on the Western way of life?"

"It may come to that," said Mr. Fortescue seriously. "Much will depend on what success Professor Mann is having with him now. I must ask you to stay within reach of a telephone for a while."

On his way out Mr. Behrens paused for a moment in the anteroom to admire the Landseer painting which hung on the wall. It was an allegorical study showing Thrift conducting a tug of war with Extravagance. Thrift seemed to be winning, but only just.

It was almost exactly three weeks later, at four o'clock in the afternoon, that the call came.

"He has thrown up his job at the refinery," said the thin voice of Mr. Fortescue. "He did not even offer notice. He told them he was going, and he simply walked out."

"That's bad. Where is he now?"

"He's taken his stuff out to that public house—the one you mentioned."

"The Lamb. Yes. Is there any reason to think that he's actually contemplating leaving the country?"

"No direct evidence. But Professor Mann is flying back to Düsseldorf on Monday. And he has booked two seats."

"If Tabor *is* at the Lamb," said Mr. Behrens, looking out of the window at the snow, which had started to fall again, "he might not get to London Airport all that easily on Monday."

"We can't rely on his being snowbound. You'll have to go over and talk to him."

Mr. Behrens had received some steep instruction from Mr. Fortescue from time to time, but this seemed to him to be nearly the steepest. He opened his mouth to protest, but shut it again. All the objections which were occurring to him would already have occurred to all superiors. If this really was the only possible course, slight though the chance of success might be, it would have to be pursued to the end.

He said, "I shall have to tell some story to account for my arrival."

"Tell no story at all. Explain exactly who you are, and what you are doing."

"You think that is wise?"

"Certainly. The other side are not fools. They will have warned him against you already."

"Of course," said Mr. Behrens. "Very well. I'll see what I can do."

His aunt, with whom he shared the Old Rectory at Lamperdown, said crossly, "You can't be thinking of going out in weather like this."

"The call of duty," said Mr. Behrens. "One of my pupils in difficulties."

"Fiddlesticks," said the old lady, who was no fool. "It's one of your jobs. I suppose Mr. Calder's in it with you. And that dog of his."

"No," said Mr. Behrens sadly. "I fear this is something I have to do on my own."

It was not a pleasant drive. As dusk fell, the snow thickened, crusting the windshield and collecting on the blades of the wiper. After a few miles Mr. Behrens had to stop his car and get out with a cloth to clear away the accumulation. On the first occasion he was incautious enough to do this on a slight upgradient, and found when he tried to restart that his wheels were unable to grip the road, which had frozen under fresh-fallen snow. He succeeded eventually in sliding backward onto a level patch, and finally got going with a wild scurry. After that he chose his stopping places more carefully.

It was nearly eight o'clock when he saw the welcoming lights of the Lamb. The last hour had been a nightmare of crawling along frozen humpbacked roads which dropped on either side into black ditches. There was nothing amiss with Mr. Behrens' nerves, and he had unexpected reserves of stamina in his thin body, but he could not refrain from a sigh of relief as he climbed out of the driving seat.

Ruby was in the empty public bar, polishing glasses. "Not that we'll get any customers on a night like this," she said. "We got your telephone message. I put a hot bottle in your bed."

"Good girl," said Mr. Behrens. "Is Mr. Tabor here?"

"He's in the coffee room. I told him you were coming."

"Did he seem to be surprised?"

"No. He said he'd been expecting you'd be over."

"I'll join him in a moment. And make us up a good fire. We may be sitting up late tonight. We've got a lot to talk about."

For a moment Ruby's brown eyes rested on him shrewdly. He wondered if she had any idea what was going on. Tabor had been alone in the place for some days, and a man who is unhappy and undecided would confide in any sympathetic listener.

"Don't you go keeping him up late," said Ruby. "He's got a lot on his mind."

"So have I," said Mr. Behrens sadly. "So have I."

"Can you honestly, and in all conscience," said Tabor, "give me a single reason why I shouldn't go?"

Mr. Behrens got up, selected three more lumps of coal from the nearly empty scuttle and placed them on the fire.

"I've spent the best part of four hours giving you reasons," he said. He had forced himself to keep any traces of weariness, any touch of exasperation, out of his voice. The fact that Tabor had been willing to argue at all must in itself be a hopeful sign. His mind was not yet closed.

"And what do they amount to? That the world is divided into two halves, the West and the East. The rights and the wrongs. The Goods and the Bads—like a film."

"It's not quite as simple as that—"

"You're arguing a prepared case, like a barrister who's been briefed. I accept that you've got your job to do—you're acting on orders. You've been very frank with me about that. But it doesn't make your case any stronger."

"If I didn't believe what I've been telling you," said Mr. Behrens flatly, "I shouldn't have bothered to come out on a night like this."

"All right," said Tabor. "I take that back. I'll accept that you, personally, believe what you're saying. But that's because you've been conditioned to believe it. Very few people in the West are capable of thinking internationally any more. But if you could only get outside your traditional English skin for a moment, shake off the moss, clear away the cobwebs, you'd see what everyone else has been seeing for a long time now—that you're finished. You're dying on your feet. Every symptom of degeneracy is there. Softness, selfishness, fear. The sort of softness that's bringing up a whole generation to think that it can do what it likes, without facing unpleasant consequences. For God's sake, what sort of mess do you think they'll make of the world after an education like that!"

He paused as if inviting comment, but Mr. Behrens found nothing to say. He wasn't particularly hopeful himself of the generation which was growing up around him.

"And for selfishness—read your newspaper. Fatuous go-slow strikes, when now's the moment, if ever, to be going fast. Mad industrial disputes, which not only do neither side any good, but which both sides *know* in advance will do nothing but harm. Do you think they're working according to the rule in China today?"

"I think they probably are," said Mr. Behrens. "Only it happens to be rather a different sort of rule."

Tabor ignored this. His knuckles showed white as he gripped the arms of the chair.

"And fear," he said. "The smell of fear is everywhere. It rises like the steam off their backs, where they squat in the rain in Trafalgar Square. Squat like aborigines, rocking and moaning, in front of some juju they are trying to propitiate."

Mr. Behrens thought, he's arguing with himself. And the real trouble is, he doesn't know whether he wants to win or lose. Half of him's on my side. One good pull, and I'll have him.

He said, "Aren't you overlooking one thing? And isn't it the one thing that matters? I'll take your own example. I haven't much to say for the way we bring up children. We used to be a lot too strict with them, and nowadays we're a great deal too easy. We're about due for a swing of the pendulum in the other direction. But as for strikes and antinuclear demonstrations—we could, in theory, stop them if we wanted to. The Executive has the power. It could break strikes with troops and break up demonstrations with mounted policemen. But in practice it can't and it doesn't, because we value freedom above expediency. It's taken us four hundred years to get there, and I'm not prepared to abandon the position just because another country has tried a new system and found that it paid quick dividends."

"Freedom," said Tabor. "You're prepared to accept inefficiency, selfishness, slackness, lack of purpose, timidity and greed—provided you have on the other side of the scales a fictitious thing called freedom."

"Certainly," said Mr. Behrens. "And it isn't fictitious. If *you'd* ever lived in a police state, you'd know that."

"What do you mean by a police state?"

Mr. Behrens was desperately tired. But he could feel that Tabor was even more tired. If he had not been, he would not perhaps have presented him with such an opening.

"In Belgrade last year," Behrens said, "a meeting was called. Not a political meeting. The question to be discussed was the formation of a new national theater. The government objected. They did not ban the meeting; they simply gave it out that they did not approve. Some hundreds of people came. Many because they had not heard of the ban. Some from idle curiosity, or even by mistake, because they happened to be passing and stopped to listen. As soon as the meeting started, the police blocked all exits. No one was allowed to leave until his name and address had been taken and confirmed. For some days nothing happened. Then the police visited every house on the list—every house—there were hundreds, so it took time—and broke every window in every house. No one of course dared to stop them, but one or two people did ask them why they were doing it, and the police said, 'You make trouble for us, we make trouble for you.' It was mid-winter, so it wasn't amusing. That's what I mean by a police state."

There was a long silence. Then Tabor said, "That's just a story you've heard. It may not be true."

"I assure you it is true," said Mr. Behrens. "I was at the meeting myself."

Tabor started to pace up and down the room. Mr. Behrens said to himself, "I believe that's fixed him." It was at this moment that he heard the telephone ringing out in the hall. Such was his preoccupation that it could have been ringing for some time. Tabor seemed to be unconscious of it, too.

The ringing stopped. There was a pause. Then the door opened and Ruby came in. She was wearing a quilted dressing gown and a gray woolen scarf around her neck, on which her tousled head rested like a single cut flower. She looked indignant.

"If you're going to sit up nattering till three in the morning you might take your own telephone calls."

They both stared at her. Mr. Behrens had the irrelevant thought that when girls displayed their figures they often looked absurd. It was when they hid them that they always became attractive.

"It's for you," she said to Tabor. "Someone from London."

Tabor followed her out into the hall. Mr. Behrens put the last of the coal onto the fire and tried to shake off a sense of impending disaster.

It was a long five minutes before Tabor came back into the room. When he did so, Mr. Behrens knew before he even opened his mouth, that something of decisive importance had happened.

Tabor said, "This evening your police, your trustworthy, non-political, judicially controlled police, arrested Professor Mann on a trumped-up charge of smuggling. He's in a cell in Cannon Row police station now."

Mr. Behrens could think of nothing to say.

"It looks as if I shall have a busy day tomorrow. I'm going to bed." Tabor went out again, shutting the door quietly but firmly behind him.

Mr. Behrens sat for a long time by the dying fire. He had no idea how it had been worked, but it seemed to him that the opposition was still a step ahead of them.

Presently he heard the sound which he had been unconsciously waiting for. The telephone was ringing. It was Mr. Fortescue.

"Has Tabor heard the news?"

"About Professor Mann? Yes."

"Somebody telephoned him?"

"About half an hour ago. It came at a most unfortunate moment."

"It was a clever piece of timing," said Mr. Fortescue. He sounded as if he were discussing the French defense to an attack on the Queen's rook side.

"It was certainly effective," said Mr. Behrens. "How did they do it?"

"Someone from their embassy telephoned Scotland Yard and told them that Professor Mann had offered one of their embassy servants eight ounces of cocaine, for payment in dollars. And that he was leaving England by air tomorrow. They had to do something, of course. The professor was uncooperative. I believe he spat in the superintendent's eye. So they pulled him in. He'll be released first thing tomorrow morning—with an apology, of course."

"I'm afraid the harm will have been done," said Mr. Behrens. He was tired, more tired than he could ever remember feeling in his life before, and something of this must have reached Mr. Fortescue. "I am sure you have done all that anyone could have done," he said and then, as if embarrassed by this unusual display of sentiment, rang off.

Mr. Behrens crept upstairs to bed. There were only two guest rooms. He had to pass Tabor's door to get to his own. The door was ajar, and Mr. Behrens could not help seeing, in the bright moonlight which was streaming through the window, that Tabor's bed was empty and unused.

"He can't have gone already," he thought. "Or if he has, he won't get very far in this snow."

But he was too tired to worry any further about it. He fell into bed and to sleep . . .

When Mr. Behrens woke next morning the sun was shining. He crept out of bed and hobbled to the window. He felt as stiff as if the long struggle he had engaged in the night before had been physical.

Outside he looked at a white world. Five miles away the Ravenshoe Refinery stood out black and sharp against the snowy hillside. He could even see, in clear silhouette, the curious outline of the catalytic cracker. It seemed to be grinning at him.

As he turned away, there was a knock at the door. Behrens snatched up a dressing gown and shouted, "Come in."

It was Ruby.

"It's nearly ten o'clock," she said. "Dad sent me up to see if you wanted any breakfast."

"I'll be down in five minutes," said Mr. Behrens. "Is Mr. Tabor up yet?"

When Ruby failed to answer, Mr. Behrens looked up and saw that her face was scarlet.

He said, "I'm afraid we sat up very late last night. I'm sorry if we kept you up as well."

Ruby sat down on the bed and started to cry, softly. Mr. Behrens, being a sensible man, said nothing. He sat down beside her, and put his arms around her.

* * *

"Extraordinary," said Mr. Fortescue.

"It was the catalytic process," said Mr. Behrens. "Tabor explained it all to me that day at the refinery. A substance will stand up to any amount of heat and pressure by itself. But add one simple outside ingredient and it will dissolve at once. In an oil refinery, I understand, the thing they use is china clay."

"And in this case, it was Ruby."

"She's a very nice girl," said Mr. Behrens. "They're getting married next week, and I've promised to be best man. He's taking back his job at the refinery until he can get some research work."

"And he's entirely changed his mind about leaving us?"

"Oh, entirely. Ruby doesn't approve of Europe."

"I see," said Mr. Fortescue.

Trembling's Tours

"You can book straight through to Heidelberg," said Mr. Leonard Caversham, "but it's a long and tiring journey, and I'd suggest that you break it at Cologne. You can go on next morning."

"I've never been to Germany before," said the man. "Matter of fact, I dropped quite a few bombs on it during the war."

"It might perhaps be wiser not to mention that when you get there," said Mr. Caversham with a smile.

"Could you book me a room in a hotel at Cologne?"

"Certainly. It will take a couple of days to arrange. If you come back at the end of the week, I should have the tickets and reservations all ready for you."

"And if I am going to stop the night at Cologne, I suppose I ought to notify the hotel in Heidelberg that I shall be a day late."

"We could do that for you, too," said Mr. Caversham.

Before he had come to work at Trembling's Tours, Mr. Caversham sometimes wondered why anyone should employ someone else to do a simple job like booking a ticket or making a reservation. Now he was beginning to understand that such a simple assignment could be stretched to include quite a number of other services. He had spent the previous afternoon telephoning four different hotels in Amsterdam in one of which a lady was certain she had left her jewel case. (It was found later in the bottom of her husband's suitcase.)

As the ex-bomber pilot departed, Roger Roche came through from the back office. He looked dusty, disorganized and depressed. In the last two respects, as Mr. Caversham knew, appearances were deceptive. Roger had shown himself, in the short time he had been with Trembling's Tours, a competent and irrepressibly cheerful courier.

"What a crowd," he said, running his stubby fingers through his mop of light hair. "What a bleeding marvelous collection."

"Were they worse than the last lot, Roger?"

"Compared with this crowd, the last lot were a school treat. We had a dipsomaniac, a kleptomaniac, five ordinary maniacs, and two old women who never stopped quarreling. What bothered 'em most was who sat next to the window. 'On my right,' I said, 'you will hobserve the magnificent Tyrolean panner-rammer of the Salzkammergut.' 'I *told* you it was going to be extra-special today, Gertrude. I can't think why I let you have the window. We'll change at lunchtime.' 'You had it all yesterday.' '*Yesterday* was just forests.'"

Mr. Caversham laughed. He noticed that when Roger was reporting his own remarks he lapsed into exaggerated cockney, while the observations of his passengers were reproduced in accurate suburbanese.

"You get well tipped for your pains," he said. "The last lot were mad about you."

"Ah! There was a girl on the last lot—and when I say a girl, I mean a girl. Nothing in this bunch under ninety."

The bell sounded behind the counter.

"I'm wanted," said Mr. Caversham. "You'll have to hold the fort."

"I was going to have lunch."

"It'll only be five minutes."

Mr. Caversham went through the door behind the counter and along the passage. He was of average height, and he moved with deliberation.

The room at the end of the passage was still known as the Founder's Room, having belonged to Mr. Walcott Trembling, who had organized and accompanied tours at a time when a visit to the continent was an adventure, when a tourist expected to be swindled from the moment he arrived at Calais, and a careful family carried its drinking water with it.

Arthur Trembling, his great-grandson, rarely found time to visit the continent himself, being, as he told his friends, "snowed under" with the work of the agency, the largest in Southampton and still one of the best-known in the country.

Mr. Caversham looked at him inquiringly.

Mr. Trembling said, "I believe you've got a car here, haven't you?"

"Yes," said Mr. Caversham. He drove into Southampton every day from the furnished cottage he had rented on the fringes of the New Forest.

"I wouldn't bother you, but my car's tied up at the garage. I wondered if you could run a parcel round to my brother Henry's shop."

"No trouble at all," said Mr. Caversham. "The only thing is that it'll leave the front office empty. Mr. Snow is away this week, and Mr. Belton's having lunch."

"Who's there now?"

"I left Roger holding the fort."

"He can go on holding it. It won't take you more than ten minutes."

"Right," said Mr. Caversham. "Where's the parcel?"

Mr. Trembling had the grace to look embarrassed.

"I'm afraid I assumed you'd say yes. The parcel's in the trunk of your car already. It's quite a big one."

"That's all right," said Mr. Caversham. He was placid and obliging—qualities which, in the few weeks he had been there, had already endeared him to his employer.

His ancient Standard was in the corner of the yard, outside the garage (in which, when they were not speeding down the motorways of Europe, the Trembling forty-seater touring coaches were housed). Mr. Caversham glanced into the trunk compartment of his car. In it was a large square parcel wrapped in brown paper and well corded. It would, he guessed, be books. Henry Trembling, Arthur's brother, was a secondhand bookseller.

Mr. Caversham drove slowly and carefully. He was not sorry to be out of the office. His course took him along the quays, outside the ramparts of the old town and into the modern area of shops clustered round the railway station. Henry, a stouter, whiter, more paunchy version of his brother, helped him take out the parcel. It was surprisingly heavy—but books always weigh a lot. Henry pressed a pound note into Mr. Caversham's hand.

"For your trouble and your petrol," he said. It seemed generous payment for a quarter-mile run, but Mr. Caversham said nothing. As he drove back to the office he whistled softly between his teeth.

He was thinking of Lucilla.

Lucilla was something of a mystery in the office. She was Arthur Trembling's secretary. She had been there longer than any other member of the staff—which was not saying a great deal, for Trembling's paid their employees badly and parted with them rapidly. But it made Lucilla all the more inexplicable, for she was not only competent, she was positively beautiful.

The only theory which made sense to the other employees of Trembling's was that she was Arthur's mistress. "Though what she can see in him," as Roger said to Mr. Caversham, "beats me. I should have said he had as much sex in him as a flat soda-water bottle." Mr. Caversham had agreed. He agreed with almost everybody.

When he got back, he found Lucilla in the front office dealing with a lady who wished to take four children and a Labrador to Ireland. He thought she looked worried and, for a girl of her remarkable poise, a little off balance.

When she had dealt with the customer, she came across to him.

"I suppose Roger wouldn't wait any longer for his lunch," said Mr. Caversham.

"The poor boy, yes. He was hungry. Where have you been?"

"Running errands for the boss," said Mr. Caversham. He was an observant man, and now that Lucilla was close to him he could read the signs quite clearly—the tightening round the mouth, the strained look in her eyes; he could even see the tiny beads of perspiration on her attractive, outward-curving upper lip.

"What's up?" he said.

"I can't talk now," she said. "I've got to go back—to him. Can you get out for half an hour at teatime?"

"Should be all right," said Mr. Caversham. "Four o'clock. Belton can carry things for half an hour. We'll go to the Orange Room."

Lucilla nodded, and disappeared. Mr. Caversham reflected that it was girls who were cool and collected most of the time who really went to pieces when trouble came. And trouble was coming. Of that he had been certain since the previous day when he had heard Lucilla screaming at Arthur Trembling in his office.

The Orange Room was one of those tea shops which shut out the sunlight with heavy curtains, and only partially dispel the gloom with economy-size electric bulbs. A table in the far corner was as safe a place for the confessional as could have been devised.

Lucilla said, "He's a beast—a vile beast. And speaking for myself, I've stood it long enough. For over a year he's been stringing me along, promising to marry me. First he was ill. Then his mother was ill. His mother! I ask you. What's she got to do with whether he gets married or not?"

Mr. Caversham grunted sympathetically. It was all he felt that was expected of him.

"If he thinks he's going to get off scot-free, he can think again," said Lucilla. "He's up to something, something criminal, and I'm going to put the police on to him."

Mr. Caversham leaned forward with heightened interest and said, "Now what makes you think that?"

"It's something to do with the tours. Every time a tour comes back, there's a big parcel in his office. It's something he pays the tour drivers to bring back for him."

"All of them?"

"I don't expect all of them. Maybe there're some he can't bribe. But Roger's one of them. There's a secret compartment in each of the coaches."

"Did Roger tell you that?"

"No. Basil told me."

Mr. Caversham remembered Basil—a black-haired boy with buck teeth, who had been very fond of Lucilla.

"What is it? Watches? Drugs? Perfume?"

"Basil doesn't know. It was just a big heavy parcel. But I'm going to find out this evening. He's leaving early—there's a Rotarian meeting."

"The parcel isn't in his office now. I took it down to his brother's bookshop."

"Yes, but he took something out of it first. I came in when he was packing it up again. And if it's something valuable, it'll be in his private safe."

"To which," said Mr. Caversham, with a ghost of a smile, "you have, no doubt, a duplicate key."

"No, I haven't. But I know where he keeps his key. It's in a stupid little so-called secret drawer in the desk. I found out about it months ago."

"Few things remain hidden from an observant woman," said Mr. Caversham. "Are you asking me to help you?"

"That's just what I am asking."

"I agree. Two heads are better than one. What I suggest is this—I'll go down this evening and keep an eye on the bookshop. You have a look in the safe. I shouldn't take anything—just look. We'll meet later and add up what we've got. If it's enough to put old Trembling away, we'll let the police have it."

"Could we talk out at your place?"

"It's a bit off the beaten track."

"All the better. I've got a car."

"Eight o'clock, then," said Mr. Caversham. "Nip back now. We don't want to be seen together."

He gave her two minutes' start, paid the bill and walked back thoughtfully. Possibly he was wondering how Lucilla knew where he lived. He could not recollect that he had ever told her.

At twenty past five Arthur Trembling walked through the front office, scattering a general "Good night" as he went. Mr. Caversham thought that he, too, looked preoccupied. Perhaps his Rotarian speech was weighing on his mind.

Mr. Caversham helped Mr. Belton to close down the front office, got out his car and drove it toward the station, parking it in the yard. The last bit, he thought, would be better done on foot. He had noticed a sidewalk café nearly opposite the bookshop. He took a seat in the bow window, ordered plaice and chips, opened an evening paper and settled down to watch.

In the first half hour one old lady and one schoolboy entered the bookshop. Neither stayed more than three minutes. Shortly after six Henry Trembling emerged, put the shutters up, padlocked an iron arm into place across the door and departed.

"And that," said Mr. Caversham, "would appear to be that." Nevertheless he remained where he was. His interest had shifted to the office building next to the bookshop. This was a building with an entrance opening on the street, inside which he could see a board with names on it and a staircase which no doubt served the several offices in the building.

Mr. Caversham noted a number of men and women coming out. He also noted quite a few middle-aged and elderly men going in—a fact which seemed a little odd at that time of night. But what was odder still—none of them seemed to reappear.

Mr. Caversham scribbled a rough tally on the edge of his paper. "White hair, horn-rims, 6:18." "Fat, red carnation, 6:35." "Tall, thin, checked ulster, 6:50." By half-past seven he had a list of eleven people, and had exhausted the patience of his waitress. He paid his bill and left. As he came out of the café, a twelfth man was disappearing into the office building.

Farther down the street, on the other side, a red-faced man was sitting at the wheel of an old gray Buick. There was nothing odd about him except that Mr. Caversham, who missed little, had noticed him there when he went into the café nearly two hours earlier.

He walked back to his car and drove home.

The furnished cottage he had rented lay at the end of a short straight lane, rutted and dusty in summer, barely passable in winter. Some people might have found it lonely, but Mr. Caversham was fond of solitude. Now, in late spring, the trees were in full leaf and the approach to the cottage was a tunnel of shadow.

He touched on his headlights as he swung in off the main road, and braked just in time. The smart two-seater Fiat was parked in the middle of the drive, and not more than two yards in.

"Women!" said Mr. Caversham. He got out and approached the car cautiously. Lucilla was in the passenger seat. She did not turn her head as he came up. Mr. Caversham opened the door on the driver's side. The opening of the door operated the interior light, which came on and showed him Lucilla more clearly.

She was dead, and had been dead, he guessed, for some time. Her face was already livid. She had been strangled, and the cord which had strangled her was still round her neck, cut so deep into the flesh that only the ends could be seen dangling at the front like a parody of a necktie.

Mr. Caversham got out of the car and closed the door softly. He stood in the drive, balanced squarely on his legs, his thick body bent forward, his arms hanging loosely. His head turned slowly, left and right. He looked like a western gunfighter at the moment of the draw.

Abruptly he swung round, returned to his own car, jumped in, backed it out into the road, and drove it a couple of hundred yards before turning through an open field gate and running in under the trees. He had switched off all the lights before he started. Now he locked the car, and ambled back at a gentle trot by the way he had come. At the corner of the lane he stopped again to look and listen. Dusk was giving way to dark. Nothing disturbed the stillness of the evening.

Mr. Caversham allowed a slow minute to elapse. Then he walked up to the car, opened the door and climbed in without a second glance at the dead girl. The ignition key, as he had noted, was in the lock. The engine, which was still warm, started at first touch. He backed the car out into the road. From the direction of Southampton a car was coming, fast. He could see the headlights as it roared over the humpback bridge beside Shotton.

Mr. Caversham grinned to himself unpleasantly, swung the little car away from Southampton and drove off.

Half a mile down the road he turned into a drive and got out. It took him five minutes to shift the body into the back seat and then cover it with a rug. After that he switched on his sidelights and took to the road again. He drove quickly and surely, handling the strange car as though he had been driving it for months. A fast circuit of Southampton's sprawling suburbs brought him into the town again from the west. A few minutes later he was examining the road signs in a large development, which seemed to have been laid out by a naval architect.

Beyond Hawke Road and Frobisher Drive he found Howe Crescent. Number 17 was a pleasant, detached house, with a neat garden and a separate entrance to a fair-sized garage. Mr. Caversham drove straight in. The owners were, as he well knew, in Venice. He had himself sold them their tickets a fortnight before, and had helped them make arrangements for the boarding-out of their cat.

A bus ride and a few minutes' walk brought Mr. Caversham back to the place where he had left his own car. He climbed in and drove it sedately toward Southampton. As he entered the car park of the cinema he looked at his watch. It was just over three-quarters of an hour since he had found Lucilla. He seemed to have covered a lot of ground.

It was a cowboy film, and Mr. Caversham settled back to enjoy it.

The film finished at eleven o'clock and ten minutes later he was turning into the lane which led to his cottage. A police car was parked in front of his gate.

"Can I help you?" said Mr. Caversham. "Perhaps you have lost your way."

"Is your name Caversham? We'd like a word with you."

"Come in," said Mr. Caversham. He opened the front door, which was not locked, turned on the lights and led the way in. The last time he had seen the red-faced man he had been seated behind the wheel of an old gray Buick, on the opposite side of the road to Henry Trembling's bookshop.

The man said, "I'm Detective Sergeant Lowther of the Southampton Police. This is Detective Sergeant Pratt."

"Good evening," said Mr. Caversham. He managed to add a question mark at the end of it.

"We've come out here because we had a message that a girl's body had been found in a car."

"And had it?"

Sergeant Lowther looked at Mr. Caversham. It was not exactly a look of hostility, nor was it friendly. It was the sort of look that a boxer might give an opponent as he stepped into the ring.

He said, "Neither the body nor the car was here when we arrived."

"And had it been here?"

"According to a boy who came past the end of the road at half past seven, there was a car here. A Fiat. He happened to notice the number, too."

"Boys often do notice these things. I expect you'll be able to trace it."

"We have traced it. It belongs to a Miss Lucilla Davies." The sergeant paused. Mr. Caversham said nothing. "We contacted her lodging. She hasn't been home."

"The night," said Mr. Caversham, "is still young."

"Look—" said the sergeant. "I said—Lucilla Davies. Do you mean to say you don't know her?"

"Of course I know her. She works in the same place that I do. On a rather superior level. She is Mr. Trembling's secretary."

"Then why didn't you say so before?"

"Why should I?"

"Look," said the sergeant, "do you mind telling us where you've been?"

"I've been to the cinema. The Rialto. The film was called *Two-finger Knave.* And just in case you think I'm not being entirely truthful, I should mention that the film broke down after the third reel and we had to wait five minutes while it was being mended. The manager came on the stage and apologized."

"Look—" said the sergeant.

"And now, would you very much mind going away and letting me get to bed? If you will, I'll consider forgiving you for entering my house without a warrant in my absence."

"Entering—?"

"Well," said Mr. Caversham, "I'm quite certain I didn't make that muddy mark on the linoleum there. You can see it quite clearly. It looks to me like a boot, not a shoe."

"Look—" said the sergeant.

"However, you did at least have the delicacy not to search my bedroom."

Sergeant Lowther's face got a shade redder than before. "Assuming," he said, "for the sake of argument, but not admitting it—assuming that we had a look in here, just to see if you were at home, how would you know that we didn't go upstairs as well?"

"I don't think you could have." Mr. Caversham whistled softly, and the great dog rose from the pool of shadow at the top of the stairs and came padding down, his tail acock, his amber eyes gleaming.

"Well, I'm damned," said Sergeant Lowther. "Has he been lying there all the time?"

"All the time," said Mr. Caversham. "And when you're gone, I expect he'll tell me all about you. I understand a lot of what he says—and he understands everything that I say."

The dog's mouth half opened in a derisory smile, revealing white teeth.

"He's our man all right," said Sergeant Lowther to Inspector Hamish next morning. "I didn't like his attitude—not one little bit."

"That dog of his," said Sergeant Pratt. "Fair gives me the creeps to think he was lying there all the time, watching us, and never made a sound."

Inspector Hamish was tall, bald, and cynical, with the tired, empty cynicism of a life devoted to police duties.

"Have you checked at the cinema?"

"Yes, and there was a break in the film—just like he said."

"Then what makes you think he didn't go to the cinema?"

"He was too damned cool. Too ready with all the answers."

"You ask me," said Sergeant Pratt, "I wouldn't be surprised if you found he'd got a record."

"Do you think he's mixed up with Trembling's little game?"

"Could easily be. He was hanging round watching the bookshop last night, like I told you."

The telephone rang. Inspector Hamish answered it. His expression changed not at all. At the end he said, "All right, thank you." And to Sergeant Lowther, "We're going out to seventeen Howe Crescent. The car's there. The girl's in the back."

At about this time Mr. Caversham and Roger were opening up the front office at Trembling's. Roger seemed to be suffering from a hangover. Mr. Caversham appeared to be normal.

"It was some party," said Roger. "One of the old buffers who was on the first tour organized it. A reunion—can you imagine it?"

"I can," said Mr. Caversham with a slight shudder.

"The idea was, we had a bottle of booze from each of the countries we'd visited. All nine of them. We finished them, too. And that girl I was telling you about—the one on the first tour—"

The bell behind Mr. Caversham's desk rang.

"What does *he* want?" said Roger. "He's never been in before ten o'clock since I've been here."

The bell rang again. Mr. Caversham sighed, put down the three-color triptych advertising an economy tour in the Costa Brava and made his way along the passage.

Mr. Trembling was sitting behind his desk. His face was half hidden by his hand. When he spoke his voice was under careful control.

"Have you any idea where Miss Davies is?"

"Hasn't she got here yet?"

"No," said Mr. Trembling. "I telephoned her house. The lady there was most upset. Lucilla hadn't been back all night. They've just telephoned the police."

"How *very* worrying," said Mr. Caversham. "But I expect she'll turn up. Mr. Foster was saying how sorry the Rotarians were to miss your speech last night."

For a moment it seemed that Mr. Trembling hadn't heard. Then he raised his head slowly, and Mr. Caversham saw his face. If he had not known what he did, he might have felt sorry for him.

"Yes," said Mr. Trembling. "I was sorry to disappoint them. I felt unwell at the last moment. A touch of gastric trouble."

"You ought to have gone straight home. Not come back to the office," said Mr. Caversham severely. "There's only one place when your stomach's upset. In bed, with a hot water bottle."

What was left of the color in it had drained out of Mr. Trembling's face. The pouches under his eyes were livid. Mr. Caversham thought for a moment that he might be going to faint, and took half a step forward.

"What do you mean?" It was a croak, barely audible.

In his most reasonable voice Mr. Caversham said, "I left my wallet in my desk and had to come back for it. I happened to see your car in the yard and a light on in the office. Are you sure you're all right?"

"Yes," said Mr. Trembling, with an effort. "I'm all right. That'll be all."

It won't be all, Mr. Caversham thought to himself, as he walked back. Not by a long chalk, it won't. You set a trap for her, didn't you? Let her see where you kept the key. Let her see you take something out of that parcel and put it in the safe. Let her know you were going to be away at a Rotarian meeting. Came back and caught her. She must have told you she was meeting me. Perhaps she did it in an attempt to save her own life. So when you'd finished, when she was no longer your secretary, no longer anything but a lump of dead flesh, you put her in her own car and drove her out to my place. Not very friendly. Then, I suppose, you rang up the police. Lucky you didn't do it ten minutes earlier. *I* should have been in trouble.

By this time Mr. Caversham was back in the shop. Mr. Belton was talking to a girl with a ponytail about day trips to Boulogne, and a sour old man was waiting in front of Mr. Caversham's desk with a complaint about British Railways. Mr. Caversham dealt with him dexterously enough, but his mind was not entirely on his work.

Most of it was on the clock.

The police, he knew, worked to a fairly rigid pattern. Fingerprinting and photography came first, then the pathologist. Then the immediate inquiries. These would be at Lucilla's lodgings. How long would all that take? A couple of hours perhaps. Then they would come to the place where she worked. Then things would really start to happen. No doubt about that.

"Where's that Roger?" said Belton.

"He was here earlier this morning," said Mr. Caversham. "I expect he's somewhere about."

"He's not meant to be gadding about. He's meant to be helping me," said Mr. Belton. "I don't know what's come over this place lately. No organization."

It was nearly twelve o'clock before Roger reappeared. He was apologetic, but he did not explain where he had been. Mr. Caversham said, "Now that you *are* here, I'll go out and get lunch, if no one has any objections."

No one had any objections. Mr. Caversham hurried into the public house down the street and ordered sandwiches. He was back within twenty-five minutes, and found a worried Mr. Belton alone.

"I'm glad you've got back so quickly," he said.

"What's up?"

"I wish I knew. Mr. Trembling isn't answering his telephone. And Roger seems to have disappeared."

A prickle of apprehension touched the back of Mr. Caversham's neck.

"Which way?"

"What are you talking about?"

"I asked you," said Mr. Caversham in a new and very urgent voice, "which way Roger went. Did he go out of the front door into the street?"

"No. He went out down the passage. Into the back yard, I should guess. What's happening? What is it all about, Mr. Caversham? What's going on, for God's sake?"

People had sometimes accused Mr. Caversham of being hard to the point of insensitivity. He did, however, appreciate that he was dealing with a badly frightened man, and at that moment, when there was so much to be done, he paused to comfort him.

"There's nothing here which need bother you," he said. "I promise you that. Indeed, I should say that right now you were the only person in this whole outfit who had nothing to worry about. Just keep the customers happy."

He disappeared through the door behind the counter, leaving Mr. Belton staring after him.

The door of the Founder's Room was closed, but not locked. Mr. Caversham opened it without knocking and looked inside. Arthur Trembling was seated in his tall chair behind his desk. He looked quite natural until you went close and saw the small neat hole which the bullet had made under the left ear, and the rather larger, jagged hole which it had made coming out of the right-hand side of the head.

Mr. Caversham sat on the corner of the desk and dialed a number. A gruff voice answered at once.

"Southampton Police," said Mr. Caversham calmly. "I'm speaking from the offices of Trembling's Tours. Yes, Trembling's. In Fawcet Street. Mr. Trembling has been shot. About ten minutes ago."

The voice at the other end tried to say something, but Mr. Caversham overrode it.

"The man responsible for the killing is using the name of Roger Roche. He's thirty, looks much younger, has untidy, light hair, and is lodging at forty-five Alma Crescent. Have you got that?"

"Who's that speaking?"

"Never mind me. Have you got that information? Because you'll have to act on it at once. Send someone to his lodgings, have the trains watched and the roads blocked."

"What did you say your name was?"

"I didn't," said Mr. Caversham, "but I told you what to do to catch this murderer, and if you don't do it quickly you're going to be sorry."

He rang off and cast an eye round the office. There was no sign of any disturbance. A neat, cold, professional killing. If Mr. Belton had heard nothing, the gun must have been a silenced automatic.

The key was in the safe. Using a pencil, Mr. Caversham turned it, then carefully swung the safe door open. On the bottom shelf was a quarto-sized volume, in a plain gray binding, with no title.

He carried it to the desk and opened it. There was a blatant Teutonic crudity about the photographs inside which made even such an unimpressionable man as Mr. Caversham wrinkle his nose. He was still examining the book when a police car drew up in the yard, and Sergeant Lowther burst into the room.

"Ah," he said. "I might have known you'd be in on this one too. What's that you've got there? Yes, I see. *Very* pretty. Now, Mr. Caversham, perhaps you'll do some explaining."

"Not to you," said Mr. Caversham. He had heard another car draw up in the yard. A few seconds later Inspector Hamish came through the door. He looked coldly at Mr. Caversham.

"Have you picked him up yet?" asked Mr. Caversham.

"I got some garbled message," said the inspector, "about a man called Roger Roche. I thought I'd come and find out what it was all about before sounding a general alarm."

Mr. Caversham got to his feet. "Do you mean to say," he said, and there was a cold ferocity in his voice which made even the inspector stare, "that you have wasted ten whole minutes? If that's right, you're going to have something to answer for."

"Look here—"

"Would you ask the sergeant to leave the room, please."

Inspector Hamish hesitated, then said, "One minute, Sergeant—"

By the time he turned back, Mr. Caversham had taken something from his pocket. The inspector looked at it and said in quite a different tone of voice, "Well, Mr. Calder, if I'd only known—"

"That'll be the epitaph of the British Empire," said Mr. Calder. "Will you please, please, get the wheels turning."

"Yes, of course. I'd better use the telephone."

An hour later Mr. Calder and Inspector Hamish were sitting in the Founder's Room. The photographers and fingerprint men had come and gone. The pathologist had taken charge of the body;

and a police cordon, thrown round Southampton a good deal too late, had failed to catch Roger Roche.

"We'll pick him up," said the inspector.

"I doubt it," said Mr. Calder. "People like that aren't picked up easily. He'll be in France by this evening and God knows where by tomorrow."

"If someone had only told me—"

"There were faults on both sides," Mr. Calder admitted. "I expect I should have told you last night. There didn't seem any hurry at the time and I didn't know about Roger then."

"If you wouldn't mind explaining," said the inspector, "in words of one syllable. I am only a simple policeman, you know."

"Let's begin at the beginning then," said Mr. Calder. "You knew that Trembling was smuggling in pornographic books for his brother to sell?"

"Yes. We're on to that now. There's a side entrance into his shop, from the ground-floor office next door. The cash customers used to go in that way after the shop was shut, and out by a back entrance into the mews. You'd be surprised if I told you the names of some of his customers."

"I doubt it," said Mr. Calder. "However, it wasn't an easy secret to keep. Too many couriers were involved. Soviet Intelligence got on to it. They put in an angent—Lucilla Davies—to nurse it along. She blackmailed Trembling. He could go on bringing in his dirty books, as long as he agreed to take out letters—and other things as well—for them. Trembling's became the main south coast post office for the Russians."

"Neat," said the inspector.

"Then our side got to hear about it, too. And sent me down. What happened was that Trembling got tired of being blackmailed into treason, and decided to remove Lucilla. I don't blame him for that, but I do blame him for leaving her in my front drive.

I thought that was unnecessary. And very cramping for me. So I shifted her. However, I did ring up and tell you where to find her next morning."

"That was you, too, was it?"

"That was me. I thought if we played it properly, we'd be bound to provoke a countermove from the other side. They don't like their agents being bumped off. I guessed they'd send one of their best men down here—what I didn't realize was that he was *already* here. Roger fooled me completely."

"There's a moral to it somewhere, no doubt," said the inspector.

"The moral," said Mr. Calder, "is that if the various Intelligence departments and MI5 and the Special Branch and ninety-six different police forces didn't all try to work independently of each other, but cooperated for a change, we might get better results."

"You'd better put that in your report," said Inspector Hamish.

"I'll put it in," said Mr. Calder. "But it won't do a blind bit of good."

The Headmaster

The master spies at work in this country numbered, last year, four. They were known to Intelligence as the Language Master, the Science Master, the Games Master, and, in some undefined position of authority of all of them, the Headmaster.

Since the Portsmouth affair there have been but two. The Language Master was behind bars, and the Games Master had retired to Switzerland. The Science Master was still at his shadowy work in the Midlands, and the Headmaster was in the London area.

When it is said that Intelligence knew about these men, it must be understood that it was a matter of analysis and deduction rather than knowledge. A lot of confidential information was reaching the other side, much of it unimportant, but some of it highly important. Most of such items could be traced to their sources. And the lines drawn from these sources pointed inward and came together somewhere in the center of the metropolis.

"If I had to create the Headmaster," said Mr. Fortescue, "in the way that a scientist creates a megalosaurus from small fragments of tooth and bone, I should have to construct someone with the combined knowledge of a cabinet minister, a senior civil servant, and a don."

"An all-round man," said Mr. Calder. "Have we any hopeful line at all?"

"We have a line," said Mr. Fortescue. "I'm not sure if it's hopeful or not. Craven has disappeared."

"John Craven? I've seen nothing in the papers—"

"It will be there. Somewhat prominently, I'm afraid."

Since John Craven was a Queen's Counsel and Recorder of a Kentish borough, this seemed only too probable.

"He went down from his chambers by car on Saturday morning to his house at Charing. He was planning to return to town on Sunday night. The first time we knew anything was wrong was when he failed to turn up for a conference on Monday morning."

"Yesterday."

"Yes. We got busy at once, of course."

"Of course," said Mr. Calder. John Craven was one of his oldest friends. He was perfectly aware that he had another occupation besides his legal one.

"His car was still in the garage of his Charing house. The daily woman, who cooks for him and cleans the house, saw him start out for a walk after lunch on Sunday."

"He was a great walker," said Mr. Calder. He thought of his old friend, striding along a woodland path, red-cheeked, white-topped, head bent forward, stick swinging. "Have you any reason to connect it with the Headmaster?"

"Two reasons," said Mr. Fortescue. "First, Craven was one of three men who had been specially assigned to locating him. He had had, so far, absolutely no apparent success. Had he found out anything, he would of course have reported it at once."

"Of course," said Mr. Calder.

"However, the path that he was treading must have taken him unknowingly very close to the man. Too close for his comfort."

"You mentioned two reasons."

"It has the feel of a professional job," said Mr. Fortescue. "Carefully arranged, perfectly executed."

"I expect you're right," said Mr. Calder. He had never known Fortescue wrong in any important matter. "Just what would you like me to do?"

"The first thing must be to find Craven. I'd like it done, if possible, before the news is made public. I have informed our friends in the Special Branch. They can control ordinary police inquiry for a reasonable period. But I don't think we can keep the papers off it for more than forty-eight hours."

"I'll see what I can do," said Mr. Calder. "There was a sister, wasn't there? A widow. What was her name?"

"Mrs. Gordon. I have written down her address and telephone number. A very sensible woman. You should find her a great help."

So Mr. Calder and Mrs. Gordon traveled down to Charing together, and on Charing platform they found reinforcements.

"This is my friend, Mr. Behrens. He is a keen naturalist. I felt that four pairs of eyes would be better than two."

"It's very good of you to take so much trouble," said Mrs. Gordon. "Did you say four—?" She turned and found a great dog had moved up silently behind her. Its head came nearly up to her waist.

"Oh," she said. "He's beautiful."

Rasselas eyed her coldly. For Mr. Calder, who talked to him in his own tongue, he would do anything. He had become accustomed to Mr. Behrens, and even allowed himself to be taken by him in his car when he understood from Mr. Behrens' manner that the matter was urgent. But this was the limit of his tolerance.

"I spent a little time on the way down," said Mr. Calder, "working out, with Mrs. Gordon's help, the sort of walks her brother might have taken in the time available. Ah, you've got the maps—good."

Mrs. Gordon said, "Truscott, his head clerk, told me that he planned to be back in London well before dinner. He had some papers to read, and he hated reading after dinner. That would have meant leaving Charing at five at the latest—and he liked to get his own tea before starting back."

"Two hours, almost exactly," said Mr. Calder. "Less, if he wanted, but not more."

"He'd go as far as he could in the time. There were two walks I've been with him which would have fitted in almost exactly. There's not much to choose between them."

They spent a long morning, without result. What had taken the quick-striding barrister two hours to cover cost them nearly four. There were parts of it—along used roads and past houses—which they could ignore. But the rest had to be studied carefully.

After a quick lunch at a pub, they started on the second round. The path rose almost at once on a long slant, climbing the downs toward a wood.

"They could have watched him from up there—Mrs. Gordon, by the way, knows what we fear may have happened."

"I knew John did secret work. He didn't talk about it, of course."

"Of course not," said Mr. Calder. The path plunged into the wood—it turned out to be a mere screen of trees—then out again on to the downland.

Rasselas ran free ahead of them, his tail feathering in the breeze. Occasionally his nose dipped to the ground and rose again as he ran. He was like a great golden galleon answering to the first chops of the open sea.

"We won't waste much time here," said Mr. Calder. "It's lonely enough, but it's a lot too open. John had his wits about him. And he carried a gun."

The path turned now, and ran along the ridgeway. There were small coppices which were promising, and which they searched carefully but without success. Rasselas watched them, and from time to time Mr. Calder talked to him.

"He's not a bloodhound," he explained. "And there's no question of him acting as a tracker. What he's been trained to do is to notice when things are wrong—when they've been moved or altered. Anyone hiding in the bushes there, for instance, would have upset the pattern of the branches when he came out. If something which had been standing in the same place for some time had been shifted, it would leave a mark. That's the sort of thing he notices."

Rasselas sat on his haunches, grinning quietly as he watched Mr. Calder talking.

"He hasn't shown much interest yet," said Mr. Behrens.

"He'll tell us as soon as he sees anything."

They had already covered nearly fifteen miles that day, and were getting tired by the time they came to the deserted farm. The path skirted the farmyard. Under the collapsed Dutch barn, there still lay a few trusses of gray and moldy hay. The tiles were off the roof, daylight showed through the walls. The nettle was in command of the garden and yard.

Rasselas padded quietly round the back of the house, and when he did not reappear Mr. Calder went to look for him. He was sitting on his haunches, still as stone, looking at a rusty rain-water tank propped on its side against the broken brick wall.

In the tank, his knees to his chin, was John Craven.

"There were three men involved," said Mr. Calder to Mr. Fortescue. "And you were right. The planning was meticulous. As John reached the corner of the farm, one man directly ahead of him attracted his attention and made him stop. There were two other men, one on each side behind him and hidden. One hit him to stun him, the other caught his arms as he fell and held him while the first one hit him again, this time hard enough to break his neck."

"How do you know all this?"

"Rasselas worked it out for me," said Mr. Calder. And, after a pause, "What next?"

"The finding of the body will be given to the press. In the public version the body will be found by hikers, *behind* the tank, not in it. Craven's walking habits will be mentioned. It will be strongly suggested that Craven felt faint, sat down to rest and died of heart failure. There will be an inquest, of course. But the only evidence will be of identity. And an adjournment for—how long will you require?"

"It depends what I have to do," said Mr. Calder cautiously.

"The Headmaster took a grave risk in acting as he did. He must have felt that Craven represented a very real danger. And yet, curiously, Craven didn't know it. If he had suspected anything, he would have reported at once."

"Yes," said Mr. Calder.

"What you will have to do is to trace Craven's movements, his professional and social contacts, and try to discover why he should have become so dangerous without realizing it. Would a month be enough?"

Mr. Calder said, "I ought to know by the end of a month, if there is any chance of success . . ."

The first person he called on was Truscott. Craven's head clerk Truscott, and his sister Mrs. Gordon, were the only two people who knew that John Craven was more than a very successful barrister; and of the two, Truscott had been deeper in his confidence.

Mr. Calder sat in the barrister's neat room in Crown Office Row, overlooking the lawn of Middle Temple Gardens. It was a room walled with books. There were other books, marked with slips of paper, on a side table; a pile of briefs which would now have to be returned; a book diary with professional appointments; a flat desk diary with private engagements; and a locked cabinet of personal papers.

"He was a very methodical man," said Truscott.

"I hope it will make our job a bit easier," said Mr. Calder. He had explained to Truscott what he planned to do. "We'll start by listing everyone he saw privately in the last six months. The names will be in his private engagement book."

"I think this will help us, too," said Truscott. He produced, from the cabinet, a folder marked PERSONAL. "He kept all private letters here, and carbons of his replies. If he answered them by hand, he often made a spare copy."

"We'll use one as a check on the other. As a further cross-check, would you get your telephonist to give us a note of any numbers he called. If she doesn't keep a record, the post office could at least give us the toll calls."

"She keeps a record," said Truscott. "I'm not sure if it goes back six months, but I'll find out."

There followed a fortnight of work as hard and demanding as any that Mr. Calder could remember. He sat at John Craven's desk from nine o'clock in the morning until seven o'clock at night. He was introduced to the other members of the chambers as Craven's literary executor; Craven had been a considerable contributor to all sorts of journals, on legal and nonlegal topics, and had published two books of essay and reminiscence. Many of the friends whom Mr. Calder so patiently checked came from Fleet Street and New Fetter Lane.

The professional contacts caused little trouble. With Truscott's assistance he was able, in the first two days, to identify and put on one side the various solicitors who consulted Craven professionally.

This left a clutter of personal friends, relations, literary contacts, people he had met in the course of his political work, tradesmen, club acquaintances, and odd members of the public who will write to anyone whose name is known and who is foolish enough to have his address in the telephone book. A Christmas card list, with notes on some of the recipients, proved invaluable.

After a week of such work Mr. Calder felt so limp that he thought that he might be in for a bout of flu. But he was not dissatisfied with his results.

"There are three people," he said, "that I'd like to concentrate on. Any one of them could have access to secret information. And all three are new acquaintances."

Truscott looked over his shoulder at the names he had jotted down.

"Sir George Gould," he said. "He's something in the Treasury, I believe. Mr. Craven met him over his work with the Inns of Court Conservative Association. They were both concerned in the drafting of a new Rating Bill. General Hamish Fairside. He works in the War Office."

"Military Intelligence," said Mr. Calder.

"Freddie Lake. The name is familiar, but I don't think I ever met him."

"You're lucky," said Mr. Calder. "I have."

In the course of a long career, Sir Frederick Lake had held every conceivable post in the Foreign Service, had visited every known country in the world and had developed into the most compulsive bore of his generation.

"I'd better start with General Fairside," said Mr. Calder. "I have a nodding acquaintance with him. Let's have a look at *Who's Who.*

"Clubs. United Services, Naval and Military, and the Hambone." He turned the pages until he came to *Gould. George Anstruther, educated Winchester and New College, Oxford.* His clubs were the United University Club—and the Hambone.

"This is too true to be good," said Mr. Calder. With fumbling fingers he turned to the letter L.

Sir Frederick Lake belonged to no fewer than six clubs. The Hambone was fourth on the list.

Mr. Calder sat turning this odd coincidence over in his mind. A further thought struck him.

"Did Mr. Craven belong to any clubs?"

"He was a member of the Travelers', sir."

"No other ones?"

"Fairly recently, I remember, he was talking about joining the Hambone. But you know what these clubs are like, sir.

There was some opposition, somewhere, so of course he withdrew his candidature."

"I wonder," said Mr. Calder. "I wonder."

The Hambone Club in Carver Street is the offspring of that eccentric aristocrat, Sir Rawnsley Clayton. Having been turned out of the Athenæum for giving dinner there to a troupe of clowns, he had founded it as a place where he could meet his more Bohemian acquaintances. It was still much used by actors and writers, but had acquired a solid addition of politicians who found the Carlton too stuffy and of soldiers who found the Senior too exclusive.

It was to the Hambone Club that Mr. Calder was now making his way. Three weeks had passed since the death of John Craven. Mr. Calder had not hurried. The quarry he was hunting, if it existed at all, would await his coming.

He was conscious, as he walked through the misty lamplit streets, of a feeling close to guilt. He was breaking one of the oldest rules of the game. For so slight, so intangible, so elusive had been the clue upon which he had stumbled that he had not yet dared to record his suspicions. Possibly "suspicions" was too concrete a word altogether. It was a breath, a whisper, the first faint stirring of apprehension.

Yet when General Fairside, their acquaintanceship skilfully renewed, had invited him to dinner at the Hambone, and had mentioned casually that George Gould might be joining them for a drink afterward, he had paused to consider matters very carefully. In the end, he had slipped into the special pocket of his coat an automatic pistol. It had—like its owner—a short stout body; and it was equipped with a most efficient silencer. The moment he had put it into his pocket, he had felt the extravagance of the action. But he had allowed it to remain.

Mr. Calder found his host warming himself in front of a hospitable fire of logs.

"Nice of you to come out on a night like this," he boomed. "What are you drinking? Nonsense. Must have something before we start eating. Take away the taste of the food."

Over an excellent dinner they talked about the Service charity in which Mr. Calder was interested, and which was the ostensible reason for their meeting; and about old friends, in the Army and out of it. The General had been a subaltern in a rifle regiment, which had shared a particularly unpleasant section of the line with Mr. Calder's regiment in 1918.

"Sensible of you not to stay on in the Army," said the General. "No future in it."

"I wouldn't say that," said Mr. Calder.

"Oh, it suited someone like me. I meant for a brainy chap like you. By the way, what *did* you go in for?"

"Import and export," said Mr. Calder promptly. "What excellent Burgundy this is."

"I'm glad you like it. They know how to buy wine in this club. *And* how to look after it. Barlow! My guest likes the Corton."

Barlow, who was the doyen of the Hambone staff, smiled politely.

"I am glad you enjoyed it, sir," he said. "I had half a bottle with my own dinner." He sailed off down the room to attend to a black-haired man who had just come in.

"That's Sir George Gould, isn't it?" asked Mr. Calder.

"That's him. Doesn't look like a senior Treasury official, does he?"

"To be absolutely candid, I think he looks like a retired boxer."

"Not bad. Not bad at all. I fought him myself, in the first interregimental tournament after the war. He was in the Sixtieth.

A dirty fighter. We'll lure him along with a glass of brandy after dinner."

No lure was needed. Sir George came over as if drawn by a magnet, was introduced to Mr. Calder and was given a large brandy. Mr. Calder settled himself in one of the large leather armchairs which make the coffee room of the Hambone one of the best sitting-out places in London. Sir George, he reflected, would be a very difficult man to fool. His had been a lifetime of committees and desk work, a lifetime of watching the wheels go round, and occasionally of making them turn.

He was in an unbuttoned mood now, telling stories of undersecretaries and their ways, of experiences at the bar of the House of Commons, of the foibles of his own master. Another brandy, thought Mr. Calder, and he might become thunderingly indiscreet. Or would he? There was an inner wall of cold reserve in those gray eyes which were turned upon Mr. Calder from time to time.

It was quite late when the General said, "Hullo, Freddie, come and join us," and Mr. Calder looked up and saw the tall, spare figure of Sir Frederick Lake bearing down on them.

A sense of completion seized Mr. Calder. It was the feeling which assails a scientist when, at the end of a long and difficult series of calculations full of imponderables and unknown quantities, he feels the shifting ground hardening under his feet at last. It was a sense of satisfaction, but mingled with alarm.

He had known that Sir Frederick would come. His arrival had been part of a ritual. How often, he wondered, had these three men met together in this way, in this place, at this hour of night?

Mr. Calder shifted in his seat, and felt the weight of the silenced automatic pressing against his stomach.

"I think we could all do with another drink," said Sir Frederick. "What would you like? Port or brandy? George? General? And you, sir?"

"It's too late for formal introductions," said the General. "But this is Mr. Calder. He's an old friend of mine. And he knew John Craven very well indeed."

The diplomat bowed very slightly toward Mr. Calder and said, "A sad business. All the same, when it happens, it's not a bad way out, is it?"

Mr. Calder felt three pairs of eyes upon him, and his lips were dry. He said, "I suppose not, no."

"In the open air," said the General. "On a Sunday afternoon walk. Quite suddenly. I'd settle for that myself, eh?"

"If I am destined to die quite suddenly," said Sir George, "I think I should like it to be when I was in the box of the House of Commons at question time. Imagine the look on the Minister's face—"

The three men laughed.

Sir Frederick, still standing, said, "May I have your orders, gentlemen?"

Sir George and the General said, "Brandy," in perfect unison.

Mr. Calder said, "At this time of night, I'm very fond of a half pint of bitter."

"An excellent choice," said Sir Frederick, and rang the bell. "In certain circumstances, the grain and the grape go very well together. I can only suggest one amendment. You should have a pint, not a half pint."

"I will fall in with your suggestion," said Mr. Calder.

The benign figure of Barlow appeared out of the gloom. Sir Frederick gave the order.

"I sometimes wonder," said the General, "if Barlow ever goes to bed. If you want a drink at any time between ten o'clock and four in the morning, he always brings it himself."

"He sends the younger waiters home," said Sir George, "and sits, in solitary splendor, in a great padded chair in a sort of pantry next to the kitchen. On one occasion, when the electric bell was out of order, I penetrated to his lair."

"I picture him," said the General, "as leading a Regency life, going to bed at six in the morning and getting up at lunchtime—"

This speculation was cut short by the reappearance of Barlow. He was bearing, on a silver salver, three glasses of brandy and a half-pint tankard of beer.

"Barlow," said Sir Frederick, "that's the first time in twenty years I have known you make a mistake. I said a pint."

Even in the gloom Mr. Calder could see the man flush. He said hastily, "That's quite all right. Don't think of changing it. It'll do me very nicely."

In truth, he had only one idea now—to get the three men out of the club. Patience, patience and still more patience. Mr. Calder, who had played many waiting games in his life, had rarely been tried higher than he was that night.

But all things must have an end, even Sir Frederick Lake's anecdotes. Two o'clock was striking as Mr. Calder followed his three hosts down the steps of the Hambone Club, past the empty porter's hutch, through the great doors and out into the street.

There were three cars there. Mr. Calder said, "I won't trouble any of you for a lift. My flat is only ten minutes away, and I'd welcome the walk. And thank you, General, once more, for a most enjoyable evening."

As soon as he had turned the corner he paused, drew into a doorway and waited. He could hear the three voices; a laugh, a shouted good night; the slamming of car doors; three separate cars starting and driving away. Then silence returned.

While they had been sitting in the club, the mist had thickened. Since he had to move, and more quickly now, mist might be a useful ally.

He turned about and walked back the way he had come. The porter's hutch was still empty. One of Barlow's self-imposed duties would be locking up when the last member had taken himself home to bed.

The lights in the inner hall had been reduced to one reading lamp. From the walls the pictures of actors and actresses looked down from their heavy gold frames. Their incurious eyes followed Mr. Calder as he tiptoed across the floor.

A melodrama, thought Mr. Calder. In three acts. Act one, a deserted farmstead. Act two, a barrister's chambers. Act three, a London club.

He pulled on a pair of cotton gloves before opening the baize-covered door. His rubbersoled shoes hissed softly on the flagstones.

The club kitchen lay at the end of the passage. The door was open, and from a room leading off it a light showed. Mr. Calder drifted across, breath held, silent as thistledown. He pushed the door open with his gun.

Barlow was not sitting in the great padded chair which the General had described. He was standing beside it, working at the leather upholstery.

"Good evening, Headmaster," said Mr. Calder.

"I recognized you when you came here this evening." The voice was harsh. The tones of the well-bred club servant had disappeared with the deferential smile. The face was grinning. But it was the grin of a death mask. "I should have taken steps at once. First Craven, then you."

"I suppose it's no use me telling you that Craven suspected nothing. That you killed him to no purpose."

"I could not afford to take a chance."

Mr. Calder said, "I imagine there is some sort of concealed microphone in the coffee room, behind where the eminent gossips sit over their brandies? And a listening apparatus in this room?"

"You imagine correctly. The microphone and receiver are removable. Only the wiring is permanent."

"And the receiver is somewhere in that chair?"

"It was. I have removed it. In ten minutes, I should have had the whole apparatus dismantled."

"It is interesting to reflect," said Mr. Calder, "that had Sir Frederick Lake indulged in one more reminiscence, you would have got away with all this."

"I should like to know how you found out."

"Oh, it was a stupid thing," said Mr. Calder. "You brought me the half pint of beer which you *overheard* me asking for, instead of the pint which Sir Frederick actually told you to bring. An incredible mistake for an experienced club servant."

"Ah!" said the man. He raised his hand, without haste, to his mouth. The stench of cyanide filled the room. As Mr. Calder watched, the body arched, clung for a moment with hands braced to the chairback, then emptied itself into a black pool on the floor.

Before he left, Mr. Calder removed the microphone and the headset. The wiring he left. It would attract no notice. London clubs are full of aged and inexplicable wiring.

He was in bed by three, and asleep ten minutes later. His influenza seemed to be better.

Heilige Nacht

Squadron-Leader Leopold, late of the RAF, but now attached to the Foreign Office, took the early-morning flight from London Airport to Frankfurt on December 24th. This Christmas Eve flight had been totally booked for several weeks, and Leopold had to use his priority rating to get a passage. Technically this meant that he occupied the spare seat kept for such emergencies—the prerequisite of the off-duty air hostess. In fact, he spent most of his time on the flight deck talking to the pilot, an old friend of his.

Leopold was carrying his operational passport, which was made out in the name of James Bellingham and described him as an insurance broker. His complete luggage was a flight bag into which he had thrust a few overnight necessities when he had received the emergency call at eleven o'clock the night before.

At Frankfurt he transferred himself and his bag into the small two-seater craft which was waiting for him and which landed him, in a heavy shower of sleet, at an old Army airfield seven miles outside Bonn at eleven-thirty. Here he was met by Captain Massey, military attaché at the embassy. Massey hurried Squadron-Leader Leopold straight out to the car, which he was driving himself, and started off with him down the little-used secondary road which joins the airfield to the city.

These facts were all established beyond reasonable doubt and on the evidence of reliable witnesses, in the inquiry which followed. What was less certain is exactly what happened next.

The car was spotted by a farm worker at midday, upside down in a drainage culvert. There were long greasy skid-marks on the surface of the road and a gap had been torn in the fence guarding the fifteen-foot vertical drop over the culvert.

The sergeant of police, who was on the scene within ten minutes, was an intelligent man. He spotted the diplomatic badge on the car and telephoned the embassy to report that its two occupants had broken necks.

The first secretary himself took the call. Martin Seccombe was a diplomat of the old school. He was not fond of the military attaché, nor had he approved of the undercover activities which seemed to be part of his job. Nevertheless he had categorical instructions which came from too high up to be flouted and he knew precisely what steps had to be taken.

He therefore personally encoded and dispatched a message which was received in London at one o'clock and was passed immediately to DI6 with a copy to Mr. Fortescue, Controller of the External Branch of the Joint Services Standing Intelligence Committee.

At midday on that same day, Josef Bartz, a clerk in the dispatch section of the Bonn office of the Great Polish Electrical Combine, which was known throughout Eastern Europe simply as "PD" and was a world pioneer of electronic computers, closed his ledgers and locked them in his desk. The firm knocked off work at midday on Christmas Eve and it was customary, at this point, for the annual bonus to be handed out, with a personal good-will message to each of his workers from the head of the firm in Warsaw. It was gestures of this sort which inspired PD to describe themselves as "a happy family."

On this occasion the bonus was a large one, and the happy family atmosphere was particularly marked. Executives who had bought Christmas presents for their secretaries took this opportunity of presenting them personally; people called on friends in other departments; a sprig of mistletoe appeared over the door of the ladies' lavatory, and the whole interior of the PD building, which normally presented an appearance of smooth and decorous efficiency, bubbled over for the space of a single hour with life and high spirits.

Josef seemed to have a great many friends. He visited almost every department in the building.

One of these was in the basement and the notice on the door said HEAD OF MESSENGERS. A particularly riotous party was going on here and Josef was invited to join it. He was only in the room for five minutes but during this time he managed, unnoticed in the scrummage, to reach out with his foot and kick over a switch under the head messenger's desk.

When he left he took a lift straight up to the managerial floor and made for the office of the communications manager. He knocked on the door and receiving no answer looked into the room and found it empty. This can hardly have been a surprise to him since he had watched the communications manager, a quarter of an hour before, going into the board room.

Josef walked across quickly to the desk under the big turret window. It was a massive affair of steel, bolted to the floor, with a nest of small drawers on either side of the knee-hole. Josef said quietly to himself, like a child memorizing a lesson, "Fourth drawer from the top on the right-hand side."

The drawer was, as he had been told it would be, locked. He felt in his jacket pocket and pulled out a curious set of keys. Some had triangular shafts, some had a series of small wards no larger than pinheads, some had hollow shafts and no visible wards at all.

Josef was sweating now. A prickle of sweat stood out on his forehead and the palms of his hands were wet. In his haste he dropped the ring of keys and scrabbled for them on the carpet. It seemed to his strained senses to be an eternity before he knew that he had found the right one. It went easily into the tiny aperture and engaged the matrix of the lock with a reassuring click. Josef turned the key and the drawer slid open.

This was the crucial moment.

If anyone had discovered that the switch in the messengers' room was off and had switched it on again, an alarm would sound, emergency doors would close the staircases, the power in the lifts would be disconnected and the street doors would be locked. Everyone would be not only a prisoner in the building, but immobilized on the floor on which they happened to be when the alarm went off.

Josef ran to the door, opened it and listened. Life seemed to be continuing normally. He could hear the hum of the lifts going up and down and shouts of laughter from a room on the floor below. No alarm.

He ran back to the drawer and extracted from it a flat gray metal box, about the size of a book but much heavier. The box went into his briefcase which was already bulging with papers. He slammed the drawer shut, wiped the front of it with his handkerchief and remembered to wipe also the front edge of the desk, where his left hand had rested. A moment later he was out of the room and descending the staircase to the floor below. He was calmer now. The worst was over.

Controlling his impatience, he joined a party in the dispatch department and spent five minutes with them. Then he made his excuses, strolled to the cloakroom to pick up hat and coat and overshoes from his locker, wished the giant doorman a "Happy Christmas" and walked out into the street.

It was a quarter to one, and the sleet which had fallen earlier in the day had turned to snow.

At five minutes past one, Mr. Fortescue, in London, was talking on a private line to Mr. Calder's cottage in Kent. He said, "Get your car, and drive straight to London Airport. I'll meet you there. You'll be away for two or three days." At ten past one Mr. Calder's car was rolling out of its garage. At half-past two he was seated in the VIP lounge at London Airport.

"Fortunately," said Mr. Fortescue, "there's an extra mid-afternoon flight for Düsseldorf. I've booked you on it. It's about the only fortunate feature of the whole business. Behrens should be down here by this evening. I had to get him back from Leamington. I'll put him on the evening plane to Cologne-Bonn."

The loudspeakers were announcing the departure of the Düsseldorf flight, but Mr. Fortescue ignored them. There were things he had to tell Mr. Calder, even if the telling of them held up the plane.

When he had finished Mr. Calder said, "Do you think that the car crash was an accident?"

"I've no grounds yet for supposing anything else," said Mr. Fortescue. "We sent Leopold by a roundabout route via Frankfurt and private charter. I don't see how the opposition could possibly have anticipated this. Or how they could have made effective arrangements in time."

"I think you're right," said Mr. Calder. "Unfortunate that it should have happened when it did."

"You have a gift for understatement," said Mr. Fortescue. "I've arranged for Corrie to meet you. He'll give you the local picture. It isn't an entirely happy one, I'm afraid."

The loudspeaker made a third plaintive announcement of the departure of the Düsseldorf flight and Mr. Calder walked out onto the runway—a thick nondescript figure in a belted mackintosh, carrying a worn airplane flight satchel strapped to one shoulder and the lives of a number of people in his hands.

Josef Bartz reached the embassy at ten past one. It would have been quicker if he had taken some form of transport, but despite the weight of the briefcase he was carrying, he preferred to walk. He suffered his first shock when he found that the public office, the entrance to which was conveniently tucked away in a side street, was shut.

After a moment of indecision he walked round to the main door of the embassy. This was open, but guarded by a commissionaire who looked doubtfully at him.

"I have to see Captain Massey," said Josef. He spoke fair English.

The commissionaire said reluctantly, "In here, sir," and showed Josef into a waiting room furnished with four hard chairs, a table and a portrait of the Queen. Josef put the briefcase down along the front of the chair and sat with his legs over it. Twenty minutes passed. Outside, the snow fell softly.

The commissionaire returned, bringing with him a young man with a long, sad, horse-like face who introduced himself as Mr. Bear. Mr. Bear was, it appeared, a third secretary. He had come to Bonn almost directly from Oxford, and his recruitment to the Foreign Service was one of those things which sometimes happens, even in the best organizations.

Mr. Bear explained to Josef that Captain Massey had had an accident. Well, yes, quite a serious accident. His deputy was, unfortunately, in Greece. If Herr Bartz could come back after the holiday was over a temporary replacement for Captain Massey would no doubt have been found, and he could deal with whatever business it was that Herr Bartz might wish to discuss.

Josef, his face suddenly pinched and white, said, "Impossible. I must see someone. It is of the highest importance. It cannot conceivably wait."

When he had said this three times, Mr. Bear sighed, rose to his feet and said that he would have a word with the first secretary. As he went out he said to the commissionaire, "There's a loony in the waiting room. Better keep a careful eye on him, Forbes."

Martin Seccombe, disturbed at his lunch, listened briefly to what his junior had to report and said, "Sounds like one of

Massey's shady friends. He can wait till Monday," and returned to a consideration of the ginger pudding which was one of the specialities of the embassy chef.

Five minutes later Josef was out in the snow, still clutching his briefcase.

John Corrie met Mr. Calder at Düsseldorf, and during the forty-mile drive Mr. Calder was happy to let Corrie do the talking. He knew of him as an agent of the modern school, better at languages than at judo, more adept with a cipher machine and a computer than a gun or a knife—but a thoroughly reliable operator.

Corrie said, "It's not an easy setup here at the moment. I'm all right, personally. The office looks after me and backs me up. It's people like Massey I'm sorry for. The embassy is suffering from one of its holier-than-thou fits. It's not the ambassador's fault. He has his hands full doing his diplomatic work. I think the root of the trouble is the first secretary and some of the junior officials. Their policy is entirely negative. Don't stir up trouble. Don't give any cause for provocation. Suppose there is a microphone in the ambassador's drawing room, what does it matter? We're so bloody discreet that anything we say can safely be relayed to Moscow or Peking. It'd be all right if the other side would play, but the East German government has got a very strong and active organization right here in Bonn. It's not just an information-gathering outfit. It's equipped for strong-arm stuff as well. If ever there was a showdown, one of the first objectives would be to paralyze the government machinery in Bonn. The authorities here know it. They're not happy about it, and they'd like to take a strong line, but they don't know where to start. I've been getting a lot of cooperation from them lately. Lammerman, who's head of the Security police here, has been particularly helpful. He put me on to Josef Bartz and we worked this ploy together. Damn this snow. If it gets any thicker the roads will be blocked before morning."

"Tell me about the ploy," said Mr. Calder.

"We've had our eyes on the PD outfit for some time. Headquarters in Warsaw, a very elaborate communications setup, senior operatives all from the Eastern Zone. But we could never crack it. Its security was too good for us. Then Lammerman managed to get at Bartz, who was actually in the dispatch section. He handled him in the usual way. Paid him money for general information and copies of messages which were no earthly use to us because we couldn't decode them. Then he put the pressure on. Offered him a very large sum indeed for the coding-machine itself. Bartz reckoned that if we could supply him with the right keys, he could lift the machine during the jollifications which go on before closing-time on Christmas Eve. But he insisted that we give him sanctuary in England. Reasonable enough, really. He'd be a dead duck in Bonn. That's where Massey came in. He got the keys—it meant squaring the people who'd made the desk, but he did it—and when everything was set, he arranged for Leopold to come over to escort Bartz back to England. He had a private plane laid on for this evening. It may not be able to get off the ground now."

"Where's Bartz?" said Mr. Calder.

"Right now," said Corrie, "he's safe and sound in our embassy, waiting for *you* to chaperon him on his journey back to England."

Josef came cautiously round the corner of the road in which he lived. A man was standing in the doorway opposite his apartment house, and there were two more in a parked car twenty yards along the street. Josef turned in his tracks and stole back the way he had come. That escape was blocked. The manager must have checked on the coding-machine before leaving. He could imagine the flurry of orders. Any member of the dispatch department would be automatically suspect. Those who had left the building early, in particular. When they searched his desk they would find that the office carbons of all the messages he had sent in the past twelve months were gone too. That would have clinched the matter.

The briefcase weighed a ton. It was dragging his arm out of its socket. His first impulse was to throw it into someone's front garden. His second was that something might yet be salvaged from the mess. There were two things he had to do. He had to deposit the briefcase in safety. And he had to find somewhere to spend the night. The first, he thought, might be managed. There were private luggage lockers at all the rail and bus terminals. The second might not be so easy.

Mr. Calder said to Martin Seccombe, "You did *what?*"

"We had no instructions about him. The best we could do was to ask him to come back after the holiday, when someone would presumably have put us in the picture about him."

"And that was the *best* you could do, was it," said Mr. Calder. "What was the worst? Shoot him out of hand?"

The first secretary flushed. He did not like Mr. Calder. He disliked his appearance, and his tone. Above all he disliked his lack of respect for the acting head of Her Britannic Majesty's Embassy.

Before he could say anything, Mr. Calder added, "I suppose you realize that what Bartz was bringing us was not only this coding-machine. It was copies of all messages which had gone to Warsaw in the last year. When we'd decoded them we should have been able to identify the whole East German network, and the police would have cleaned it up, so that it would have stayed that way for a considerable time at least."

Martin Seccombe had got his breath back.

He said in what he hoped was an icily diplomatic voice, "I have no connection with Intelligence matters and no desire to know any details of them."

"Odd," said Mr. Calder. "Most people like to know *why* they've been sacked."

Martin Seccombe stared at him.

"When I report personally to the head of the Foreign Office, as I shall when I get back, that you and this young man"—he swiveled round for a moment to look at Bear, who shifted uncomfortably under that baleful glare—"have, by your pompous stupidity, jeopardized one of the finest Intelligence breakthroughs since the war—and probably cost the defector his life—you'll be out of a job." He paused, at the door and added, "Or maybe he'll move you to Saigon."

"What now?" said Corrie, as they climbed back into the car.

"We'll call on Lammerman," said Mr. Calder, "and see if he's got any ideas."

Colonel Lammerman, who was tall and thin and affected an eyeglass, said, "We originally got on to Josef Bartz through Mulbach. You know him, I expect."

"I've heard of him, of course," said Mr. Calder. "I've never had the pleasure of meeting him."

Franz Mulbach, who had been one of the prime movers in the German anti-Hitler movement, had saved his own life by luck and judgment after the July plot, and was now a senior member of the Bundeshaus. His name was respected in British Intelligence circles.

"If he has gone to anyone for help, he will have gone to Franz," said the colonel.

"Is there any reason why he shouldn't simply have booked in at a hotel?" Calder said. "Under another name, of course."

"On any other night of the year, perhaps. Not on Christmas Eve," the colonel replied. "The hotels will all be full. Families come in from the country to finish their shopping and look at the lights. The restaurants and beer cellars stay open until all hours. He might get a room in one of the not-very-reputable hotels in the red-light district, north of the river, but that would have its own perils.

"If he doesn't go to a hotel, what do you suppose he will do?" Corrie broke in.

"Walk the streets. Keep out of sight," Calder said.

"If he does that," said Colonel Lammerman, "he will be lucky to stay alive. Our Eastern friends are very strong among the taxi drivers and news vendors. They buy their allegiance, of course."

He turned to his second in command, a stocky Prussian of half his height and twice his girth, and said, "You will alert all forces—civil police, military police and our own special patrols—to the possibilities of the situation. Our patrols should be doubled, and the necessary extra arms issued."

"I've got a feeling," said Corrie, "that this might be a lively night. I see that it's stopped snowing."

At six o'clock Ernst Dorfinger, who specialized in daylight hotel robbery, stepped cautiously out of one of the little streets leading to the main line station and started to cross the square diagonally toward the station entrance. He had had an excellent afternoon and the bulging briefcase grasped in his right hand contained an assortment of transistors, cameras and personal jewelry.

When he was three-quarters of the way across the square a parked car flicked its spotlight full on to him. Ernst hesitated, turned and ran. The car started up. It caught him before he could reach the shelter of the back streets. Three men jumped out. One hit Ernst in the stomach. As he doubled up, the others caught him and hauled him into the car. The briefcase was thrown in on top of him. The car reversed and roared back across the square.

So quickly was it done that the policeman standing on the far pavement could hardly believe it had happened. As the car came toward him he jumped into the roadway and drew his revolver.

The car struck him squarely with its offside mudguard and bumper, skidded on the frozen snow, recovered and raced off down the Kaiser Allee toward the river.

Franz Mulbach lived in an old house on the Furstenberg Allee. He received Corrie and Mr. Calder in the first-floor living room overlooking the river. Mr. Calder noticed that although the house was old the fittings were not. The original fireplace, which must have been big enough for the traditional yule log, had been filled in and a monstrous imitation electric-log fire twinkled in front of it. There was concealed lighting in the old plaster cornices and an outsize television set filled one corner of the room.

Franz Mulbach himself was an outsize man—huge shoulders topping a barrel chest which rested shamelessly on a Falstaff of a stomach. Dressed in traditional white shirt, Lederhosen and shoulder harness he looked like an enormously inflated schoolboy.

He welcomed Corrie as a friend, pressed glasses of schnapps into their hands and said to Mr. Calder, "I know an old friend of yours. Mr. Behrens. We were together at one time during the war. A remarkable man."

"He should be here before midnight, unless all flights are grounded."

"So? A gathering of the eagles. Is there trouble expected?"

"We are in trouble," said Mr. Calder, and told him about it.

When he had finished, there was a short silence. Then Mulbach said, "Poor Josef. I have known him for nearly fifty years. We were at school together."

It seemed such an inadequate comment that Mr. Calder looked up in surprise. There was a hint of embarrassment in Mulbach's voice. But there was more than that. There was a note of reserve, and something else, almost the last thing he had expected to find in this stout, phlegmatic man: the tones of fear.

He sensed that a direct question at this point might lead to a rebuff. Instead, he said, "Who are these people who are hunting Bartz?"

"Scum," said Mulbach. "Professional criminals. Out-of-work bullies. In the days of Hitler they wore brown shirts and drew their pay for assaulting Jews and Communists. The state no longer pays for services of this nature. Therefore they are at the disposal of the Eastern network, who will pay them to hunt down anti-Communists."

"Mercenaries?"

"The trade of the mercenary was an honorable one," said Mulbach. "They insult it. They'd sell one employer to another for a few extra pfennigs. They mix private vendettas with business. They—they make me sick."

But they frighten you, too, thought Mr. Calder.

There was nothing more to be gained. As they rose to go, Mulbach said, in the manner of someone picking his words very carefully, "*If* Josef had come to me for advice, I think I should have told him that his best chance of safety was in the red-light district. The women there are rapacious, but they are an independent breed and not dishonorable."

As they drove back to police headquarters, Mr. Calder said to Corrie, "I think Josef did come to our friend for asylum. And I think he turned him away. Rather surprising, for someone with his record."

"Mulbach is getting old," said Corrie. "Too old to be troubled by hooligans. He doesn't want a bomb in the boot of his car next time he drives to the Bundeshaus."

* * *

The telephone rang in the penthouse flat of one of the leading dental surgeons in Bonn and a voice said, “I am afraid that the subject will not now return to his flat. It has been watched continuously since two o’clock this afternoon.”

“Keep one man there. Just in case.”

“Very well. You heard, perhaps, that we had a little trouble earlier in the evening.”

“I heard about it.”

“It was unfortunate. We got hold of the wrong man.”

“He is none the worse for it, I hope?”

“Not a bit. I’m afraid we hurt the policeman. He should not have got in the way. I think it will mean trouble.”

“If they want trouble,” said the dentist, “we can give them trouble. Plenty of it. Call out all our reserves. Their first job will be to comb through the brothel area. Understood?”

“Bed by bed,” said the voice at the other end of the telephone happily.

Since the war a new Bonn has arisen from the ashes of the old. It lies to the south of the river and contains the parliament house, the government buildings and the respectable homes of the functionaries who work in them. But north of the river the remains of the old town still cluster round the Electoral Palace and the shell of the Minster. This is a place of small cobbled streets ending in flights of steps, of dark courts and blind alleys.

The least respectable part of this disreputable quarter lies between the Stefanienstrasse and the Lichtentalerstrasse. The Hotel Wagram stands exactly halfway along the road joining these thoroughfares.

Red Maria was so called on account of her hair, not her politics. She dispensed her favors from a room on the first floor at the back of this hotel and was a woman of undoubted attractions but uncertain temper. When she heard the knocking, she climbed out of bed, padded across the floor in bare feet, opened the door six inches and said, "Go to hell, stinking little monkey. I am busy."

It was the proprietor of the hotel who had knocked. He said apologetically, "There are men downstairs, Maria. They insist on coming up."

Maria slammed the door and bolted it.

Five minutes later came a renewed knocking, this time heavier and more urgent. Maria ignored it. A body crashed into the door. This was too much. Maria got up, seized a bottle from the top of the chest of drawers and unbolted the door. As she did so the man outside charged again. This time the door gave way and he came in with it. Maria hit him with her bottle.

There was a scream from somewhere above them of "Police!" followed by a crash of broken china and a series of bumps as though a heavy body was being thrown down the stairs.

The man on the bedroom floor groaned and got up onto his knees. Maria, her flaming hair a red aureole above her bare shoulders, raised her bottle again. The man fumbled in his pocket, jerked out a gun and pulled the trigger.

The shot missed Maria and hit a looking-glass over the mantelpiece. Maria threw her bottle at the man and bolted out onto the landing.

Outside in the street the shot had been heard. Two men jumped from a waiting car and ran into the hotel. At that moment a police tender turned the corner of the Stefanienstrasse and came rocketing down the street, its spotlight playing on the front of the hotel. Three of the Feldengendarmerie tumbled out. A fusillade of bullets from the first story stopped them in their tracks. One man was hit and rolled back behind the car. The other two dived for shelter.

This was the beginning of the battle of the Hotel Wagram, which ultimately involved five carloads of the special patrols and more than forty policemen.

Mr. Calder, back at Headquarters, listened to the reports coming in. Colonel Lammerman, who was directing the police side of the battle by telephone from his desk, seemed unperturbed at the damage and casualties.

"Tonight," he said, "they show their hand. Good. They are forced out into the open. Better still." He spoke to the commandant of military police, to direct further reinforcements to the scene.

At one o'clock, when the shooting had died down, the casualties were being counted and the first batch of prisoners was being brought in, the door opened and Mr. Behrens walked through it. Considering that he had been lifted from the ninth tee on the Leamington Spa golf course by military helicopter, transported to London Airport, put on the night flight to Germany and driven by fast car into Bonn, he looked remarkably cheerful and unruffled.

Mr. Calder greeted him with relief. Mr. Behrens' knowledge of Germany and things German was a great deal more extensive than his own.

"You seem to be having quite a party," said Behrens.

"More like Walpurgis Night than Christmas Eve," agreed Mr. Calder. He sketched an outline of the proceedings so far.

At the end of it, Mr. Behrens said, "Do I understand that when you visited Franz Mulbach, you got the impression that Bartz had asked him for asylum and been refused?"

"He didn't actually say so, but that was the implication."

"And you thought he had turned him away because he was afraid of retaliation."

"That's the general idea," said Mr. Calder, looking curiously at his old friend. "Could I have been wrong?"

"I've heard a lot of odd stories tonight, but that tops the lot. Franz Mulbach, afraid! He hasn't a nerve in his fat body. He's been a fighter all his life. Do you remember what Schiller made old Wallenstein say? '*Ein ruheloser Marsch war unser Leben*'—'our life was a restless march.' People like that don't change, you know."

"If he wasn't afraid, he was acting."

"Very likely," said Mr. Behrens. "But I wonder why. Do you think we could venture out into the streets without getting shot?"

"The police could lend us a car."

"I'd rather walk," said Mr. Behrens. "I've spent the last twelve hours being driven by other people. I'd like to stretch my legs."

The snow underfoot had frozen and it squeaked as they walked on it. They avoided the main roads and went by quiet residential streets. There were still lights in a few of the windows, and the sound of singing and music as families sat together to welcome once again the dawn of the Christ-child's birthday. In the half mile between the police station and Franz Mulbach's house they met no one.

There were lights in the Mulbach house, too, and it was Franz himself who opened the door. He had changed out of his Lederhosen, and looked a great deal more businesslike in roll-necked sweater, dark trousers and short leather coat. He had one hand under the flap of the coat and Mr. Calder noticed that he only half opened the heavy front door, in such a manner that it shielded him but left him a free field of fire. He peered at them for a moment, then swung the door wide open, jumped out and started pump-handling Mr. Behrens' right arm.

"All right, Franz, all right," said Mr. Behrens. "I'm glad to see you, too, but there's no need to break my arm off."

"What a Christmas present," said Mulbach. "My old friend. Your colleague said that you were coming to Germany. What a surprise!"

"It surprised me, too," said Mr. Behrens.

"Come in, come in." Mulbach led the way to the first-floor living room, and switched on the lights. Mr. Calder saw that the windows were shuttered. "The occasion demands brandy."

Whilst their host was pouring out the drinks Mr. Behrens peered curiously around the room, as if weighing up its possibilities. Then he accepted the bulbous glass from Franz Mulbach, sniffed the contents with appreciation, and said, "Where have you put poor Josef Bartz?"

Mulbach did not even blink. He sniffed at his own brandy, said, "This came from Strohe at Klagenfurt. I should be good. Poor Josef. Yes, he was very upset."

"I can understand that."

"I wonder if you can? He was frightened for his own skin. That was natural. He was also bewildered. When the emissaries of a country that has a reputation for keeping its word say to a man, 'Steal this for us. Come straight to our embassy and we will guarantee your safety . . .' When they say this, and then turn him away from the doors of the embassy—"

"It was partly our fault," said Mr. Calder. "And partly our misfortune. If Captain Massey had not been killed—"

"Killed! I heard nothing of that."

"An accident, we think."

Mr. Calder told him. When he had finished, Mulbach swiveled round to look directly at Mr. Behrens. "Is this true?" he said. "When I heard Josef's story I concluded that there had been a change of plan. That it now suited your book, for some deep reason, that he should be caught."

"It's one of the occupational hazards of Intelligence work," said Mr. Behrens, "that when you do something simple and straightforward, everyone suspects a double motive and a treble bluff. It happened just as Calder said."

"So. But there is one thing I do not yet see. Why should you suppose that I would have Josef here?"

"'*Ein ruheloser Marsch*—'" began Mr. Behrens.

"You remember that," said Mulbach, delighted. "Schiller is a great poet, yes?" He repeated the words under his breath, savoring them. Then he said, "I will give you back another quotation. From Goethe, this time. You know what he said was the greatest ordeal? '*Sich zu beschranken und zu isolieren*'—'to be small, and alone.' Allow me to present you—"

As he spoke, he must have pressed some sort of spring, for the side wall of the old fireplace pivoted back on itself, revealing a narrow opening. Just large enough to accommodate a man. Out of it stepped a still apprehensive Josef Bartz.

At six o'clock that morning Colonel Lammerman said to Mr. Calder, "A highly satisfactory night's work. I do not think that the sturm-gruppen of our Eastern friends will function properly again for many months. We have lost one man—the first, the one who was run down by the car. He died an hour ago. And we have six wounded, two quite severely, They have three dead and sixteen wounded. And we have thirty-three prisoners in our hands."

"Will this enable you to break them?" said Mr. Calder. "For good, I mean."

"That would be too much to hope. The central organization—the men at the very top—are still out of our reach. I doubt if any of the hired bullies who took part in tonight's maneuvers even know their names."

Mr. Behrens scribbled something on a piece of paper and passed it to the colonel. "Does this mean anything to you?" he said.

The colonel looked at what was written, then said sharply, "Where did you get that information?"

"From a very old friend," said Mr. Behrens. "But I don't think he'd like to be quoted."

"I imagine not," said the colonel. He tore the paper into small pieces and dropped the pieces into the fire. "You will appreciate that in his legitimate business this man has many powerful friends and allies. If I myself suggested anything against him and could not prove it to the hilt, I should stand in more danger than he would."

Mr. Behrens walked over to the window. The first gray light of morning was beginning to steal back into the sky. There had been no more snow.

He said, "I imagine it should be quite possible for a light plane to take off from the airport?"

"I would think so," said the colonel. "Why?"

"A thought had occurred to me. There will be no regular service. But suppose we asked the airline—suppose, in fact, we appealed personally to the chairman, as a favor to the State—to arrange for a transport craft to be available to fly, shall we say, *a valuable cargo* back to London?"

The colonel stared at Mr. Behrens for a long moment in complete silence. Then, for the first time that night, a smile creased his face, broke and dissolved into a harsh bellow of laughter. He rose to his feet and stamped across the floor, slapping his side as he did so. "Wunderbar!" he said. "Kolossal." Then he stopped laughing, swung round and said, "But dangerous."

"Oh, I don't know about that," said Behrens. "There's a little risk, certainly. They mightn't rise to the bait at all. But give them plenty of time. We shan't want the plane before nine o'clock at the earliest. If you're in any real difficulty, you can always get the Army to help you."

The favor to the State was an Army Transport Command medium-sized personnel carrier with removable seats, one of a number which had been sold to the airline in the late 'fifties, when it was replaced in service by the DC all-purpose model. The airline used them for transporting staff and spares.

Mr. Calder, as he climbed on board at ten o'clock that morning, noticed that four seats had been installed on either side of the gangway. He surmised that they were to have an escort.

Josef Bartz climbed in behind Mr. Calder. He had had an uneasy two hours' sleep in a cell at the police station and the white glare off the snow accentuated the grayness of his face. Behind him came Mr. Behrens, who was carrying a bulging briefcase.

Christmas and the snow had combined to empty the airstrip and its approaches. Mr. Carter was glad to see this. It left room for maneuver, he thought.

Two open Volkswagens appeared from the crew quarters. They carried six passengers. Two were clearly the pilot and co-pilot. The other four were less easy to place. Their overalls suggested airline mechanics; their build, professional wrestlers; their faces, policemen.

"They're doing us proud," said Mr. Behrens. "I think I recognize that pilot. Isn't it Merker?"

"The Luftwaffe ace?"

"I think so. His co-pilot looks like an ex-Luftwaffe man too. There's something quite unmistakable about them, you know."

"Agreed," said Mr. Calder. "You can't mistake them. Any more than you can mistake an English naval officer in plain clothes. Good morning, gentlemen."

The cabin crew were climbing on board. Smiles and greetings were exchanged. The largest of the four large men introduced himself as Major Osler.

"We have had special instructions," he said, "to see personally to the safety of you—and your cargo."

He glanced round at Josef, who had sunk back into his seat and was staring glumly out at the empty, snow-covered expanse of the airfield.

"I'm only sorry," said Mr. Calder, "that you should have been forced to work on Christmas Day."

"In an affair of national importance," said Major Osler, showing his strong teeth in a smile, "the loss of a Christmas holiday is a minor consideration." He closed the door and fastened the eccentric catches. The pilot had switched on now. They could hear the four motors starting up, one after the other, on their warming-up run. Josef was fiddling with his seat belt.

"No need to fasten yourself in yet," said Major Osler.

He explained: "We have to taxi out to the far runway. It is the clearest of the four. We shall be ten minutes or more before—"

He stopped as the pilot shouted something, revved up his engines and then, unexpectedly, switched them all off.

The nose of an armored car had appeared from behind the administration building. It drove deliberately out onto the runway. Behind it came three more. They fanned out, one coming to a halt immediately in front of the airplane, two of them flanking it and one behind it. Once in position they too switched off their engines.

Mr. Calder stood up. He ignored both the gun which had appeared in Major Osler's hand and the ugly look on his face. In the silence which had fallen, his voice was loud enough for everyone in the airplane to hear.

"It's no use, Major," he said. "You're outgunned." As if to underline his words, the turret of the nearest armored car swung directly toward them and they looked into the barrels of the twin Vickers. "You can't move the plane while those cars are there, and any one of them could blow your tail off with one burst. I suggest we relax."

"In case," added Mr. Behrens mildly, "you should think it worth some desperate move, do let me assure you that the property you were instructed to fly to Eastern Germany is not in this briefcase. It is in a safe in the airport, under armed guard. All I have here"—he opened the briefcase—"is two bottles of schnapps and a Christmas present for my aunt."

For a moment Mr. Calder thought that Major Osler was going to use his gun. Then the vicious light died in his eyes and his face resumed its look of stony indifference. The faint beginning of a smile lifted the corners of the thin mouth. The major said, in the tones of a fencer whose guard has been penetrated, "*In Ordnung, mein Herr.*"

"We had bad luck and good," said Mr. Behrens to Mr. Fortescue. "Bad luck about Massey, and that ass Martin Seccombe. I hope something *will* be done about getting rid of him, by the way. But good luck over Franz Mulbach. And the best bit of luck right at the end. I was quite sure that if we appealed to the airline to help us they would seize the God-sent opportunity to hijack the three of us, and the coding-machine, and fly us straight across to the Eastern Zone."

"It was a very feasible counterstroke," agreed Mr. Fortescue. "But how could you be sure?"

"The head of their organization," said Mr. Behrens, "whose name Mulbach gave us, happens to be chairman of the airline."

"Upon the King . . ."

Gough—who was eighteen and a half, weighed eleven stone and had dark red hair and a dark red temper—opened the door of his study and shouted "Fa-a-a-g" in a voice which would have done credit to a sergeant-major in the Brigade of Guards.

The sound floated along the corridor, descended the stairs and penetrated the day-room in the far corner of which a thin boy of indeterminate age, with a serious, coffee-colored face and wiry black hair, was sitting on the hot-water pipes reading, for the third time, an airmail letter with a foreign stamp on it.

He was so intent on what he was reading that the sound took a few fatal seconds to register. Then he stuffed the letter into his pocket and hurled himself out of the room.

"Last again, Thorn," said Gough. "You're a dozy kid. I want these boots buffed up for parade this afternoon. I want to be able to see my face in the toe caps. And you've only got half an hour to do it, so look slippy."

The boy addressed as Thorn took the boots without comment and scuttled off. ("Thorn" was a serviceable approximation of his name. No one had been able to get his tongue round the double "a" and diphthong when he first arrived.)

He didn't mind cleaning boots. It was a job, a job of definite proportions. You could start it and finish it and contemplate the results with satisfaction. There were jobs which were not like that. His long, sensitive fingers touched the letter in his pocket. Instead of the usual three, it had taken five days to arrive. He wondered if the delay was entirely accidental.

He had started on the second boot when Hepplewhite put his

sleek head round the door and said, "Hello, Nuri. I've been looking for you. Flathers wants you."

"Flathers must wait," said Nuri. "I have only got ten minutes to finish these for Gough."

"He said he wanted you at once."

"Gough will not like it if I do not finish these. I am in disfavor already."

It was a delicate problem. The Reverend Dudley Fletcher (or "Flathers") was a housemaster, and capable of being unpleasant if flouted. On the other hand, Gough was head of the house, and a beating from Gough was a thing to be avoided at all costs.

"Look here," said Hepplewhite. "Suppose I finish that other boot. You go and see what Flathers wants."

"Do it well," said Nuri. "Gough desires to see his reflection in the toe cap."

"If I had a face like Gough's," said Hepplewhite, "I wouldn't be so keen to look at it, would you?"

His housemaster was not alone. A second man was seated on the other side of the fireplace. Nuri, who was a quick judge of character, put him down as a senior civil servant or a retired schoolmaster. Both men got up as Nuri came in. His housemaster said, "This is Mr. Behrens. He's connected with the British Foreign Office. He has some news for you."

There was no need for them to say any more. Nuri could read the news in their faces. He had read it unmistakably in the labored cheerfulness of his father's letter.

Twenty minutes later he faced a wrathful Gough.

"This boot's all right—but this one's a mess. And anyway, who the hell said you could hand the job over to Hepplewhite? I told you to do it yourself."

"I am sorry, Gough," said Nuri, seriously. "Had the interruption not been of a vital nature, I should certainly have concluded the task you gave me."

"*What* interruption?"

"I have had news from home. My father died yesterday. I have to return at once."

"I'm sorry," said Gough. He added, being a perfect gentleman, "May I wish your Highness the best of luck."

"That I may need," said Nuri.

Mr. Behrens said the same thing to him in the car on the way to London Airport. "You realize," he said, "that it's not going to be plain sailing. It's unfortunate that you were out of the country when your father died. Everyone thought he was getting over his stroke, and then he had this second one."

"Was it a stroke?"

"Oh, I think so," said Mr. Behrens. He looked at the young man beside him and wondered what was going on behind that solemn face. "Your father was well liked, and well guarded."

"He had enemies, too."

"Powerful enemies, bitter enemies," agreed Mr. Behrens. Two years before, when the King was on a state visit to London, Mr. Behrens and his old friend and colleague Mr. Calder had both been involved in the Security arrangements; arrangements which had culminated in a suitcase bomb exploding prematurely while the intended assassin was still carrying it, blowing him to blood-stained rags.

"They would give a good deal," he said, "to delay or spoil your coronation."

The fog rolled up to meet them as they crossed the new bridge at Staines. Mr. Behrens cursed, switched on his fog lamp and joined the bumping, crawling line of traffic. It took them two hours to reach the airport.

In the VIP departure lounge they found a reception committee assembled. Mr. Absalom, senior councilor from the embassy, stout and agreeable; Mr. Moustaq, his assistant, thin and silent; and a small, worried man called Forbes, who apparently represented the Ministry of Civil Aviation. Mr. Absalom and Mr. Moustaq kissed Nuri formally, on both cheeks, and Forbes shook his hand and said, "I'm afraid, your Majesty, that there is no possibility of a flight before tomorrow morning. Gatwick is worse than we are, and conditions at Manchester are almost as bad. We have arranged accommodation at the airport hotel."

As he said this, he looked at Mr. Absalom. Mr. Behrens guessed that there had been a difference of opinion about this.

Mr. Absalom said, showing his teeth in a smile as he did so, "It seemed to us that if there was an entire evening to be passed, it could be passed more pleasantly in London than in the lounge of an airport hotel."

Everyone looked at Nuri.

He said, "We will go to London." It was his first pronouncement as Ruler, and deeply though he disapproved of the decision, Mr. Behrens could not help admiring the manner in which it had been promulgated.

He said to Forbes, "I shall have to advise our people about this change of plan. Can I use the telephone in your office?" And to the others, "I strongly suggest that we leave our cars here, and use official transport. The drivers here will be much quicker and safer in the fog than we should be. I expect Mr. Forbes can arrange it for us."

Mr. Forbes said he would be glad to do so. The thought of getting rid of the whole party had cheered him up considerably.

It was an evening to remember. One of the things about it had been the speed with which Nuri had grown up, a process which normally takes two or three years, compressed into hours.

They had gone first to the embassy, where clothes more suitable than the regulation school uniform had been found. The suit was dark, a little modern in its cut for Mr. Behrens' taste, but inoffensive.

"You will need money," said Mr. Absalom. He produced a wallet. "Some cigarettes"—this was a thin, but expensive-looking case of silver with black filigree work—"and a lighter."

Nuri seemed more pleased with the cigarettes than with the money. He offered them round and lit one himself. "It was the thing I missed most when I went to that school."

"When did you start smoking?" asked Mr. Behrens.

"Not until I was ten," said Nuri. "It is considered wrong in our country for young children to smoke." He exhaled luxuriantly, and slipped the cigarette case into the side pocket of his jacket, running his fingers over its smooth surface and machine-turned corners. "Where shall we eat?"

They ate at the Savoy Grill. Nuri's sophistication did not, Mr. Behrens was glad to see, go as far as drinking alcohol in public, but he made a very good meal. When the last flakes of a second helping of a sticky confection had disappeared he summoned the head waiter with a gesture which brought that dignitary scurrying across the room, and said, "Please congratulate the chef for me. It was an excellent meal." And to Mr. Absalom, "What shall we do next?"

"We have a long and tiring day tomorrow," said Mr. Behrens.

"I had reserved a table at a night club," said Mr. Absalom. "There is a first-class cabaret."

"Splendid," said Nuri. He added, "If you feel tired, Mr. Behrens, there would be no need for you to accompany us."

"I am not in the least tired," said Mr. Behrens, tartly. "I was thinking of your Highness." He was scribbling a note on a piece of paper, and as they went out he handed it to the restaurant manager who accepted it without comment.

The Krokodil was not quite the sort of place that Mr. Behrens had anticipated. The large embassy car, complete with chauffeur and assistant chauffeur, after threading its way with difficulty through Old Compton Street and Frith Street, had finally forced itself into a crowded cul-de-sac, from the dark end of which a green crocodile winked a red eye at them and thrashed its neon tail.

"It is not pretentious," agreed Mr. Absalom. "But they have a good band, and the girls are discreet."

With this last statement Mr. Behrens had so far found no reason to disagree. Angie, Eed, and May had attached themselves to the party as soon as they reached the table. Angie had unbelievably blonde shoulder-length hair, and was now dancing with Nuri. There was not much scope for finesse on the tiny crowded floor, but both danced well, touching, parting, approaching and recoiling in the stylized modern fashion. May, who had red hair, was engaged in a thoughtful flirtation with Mr. Absalom. Eed had given up trying to fathom Mr. Behrens, and was drinking her fourth glass of champagne. She had black hair and a sulky but intelligent face. Mr. Behrens thought that in a more promising milieu Eed might have demonstrated quite an attractive personality.

He said, "Where have all the pictures gone?"

Eed stared at him over the rim of her glass, and then giggled. "You've been here before, I can see that. They took 'em down this afternoon for cleaning."

"I noticed the faded patches on the walls. What are they?"

"Photographs. The usual sort of thing. They're a bit rude, actually."

"They must have heard that I was coming," said Mr. Behrens.

Eed looked at him curiously. She thought that he was a odd 'un. She had put him down at first as a sugar daddy, but now she was not sure. There was a curious hardness about his eyes and mouth, which contradicted his appearance of grumpy middle-aged benevolence.

"A doctor once told me," said Mr. Behrens, "that too much champagne is bad for the lining of the stomach. Let's have a change." He picked up the wine list, signaled to the waiter and said, "I should like a glass of this brandy." He indicated the most expensive drink on the list. "And I'm sure this young lady will join me."

"You can only die once," said Eed.

The waiter said, "I'm sorry, sir, we are out of stock of that brandy."

Mr. Behrens moved his finger up the wine list. "Armagnac, then," he said.

"I *think*," said the waiter, "that we are out of that too. I could find out."

"Don't bother," said Mr. Behrens. He seemed to have lost interest in the topic.

"A little more champagne, sir?"

"Not at the moment." He turned to Mr. Absalom, and said, "I hope that lovely car we came in isn't going to be stolen."

"How should it be?"

"Soho is a dishonest quarter. Or so I have always understood. I don't come here much, in the ordinary way."

"The men will look after it."

"They will find it difficult to do so," said Mr. Behrens. "Unless they have periscopic eyes. Both of them are drinking at that table in the corner."

Mr. Absalom uttered an angry exclamation, jumped up and went over to the table. Mr. Behrens saw him expostulating with the men, one of whom got up and walked out. Mr. Absalom rejoined them.

"It was right of you to point it out to me," he said. "I shall report the men to the head of Chancery. They had no right to come in together. One should certainly have stayed with the car."

"There is very little discipline among young men today," said Mr. Behrens sadly. "If you will excuse me for a moment—"

He got up and made his way into the foyer. A thickset man in a dinner jacket was standing there. He wasn't exactly guarding the exit, but he was within easy reach of it.

"I would like to use your telephone," said Mr. Behrens. "An urgent call."

The man considered the matter, running his hand down a chin which looked as if it had already been shaved twice that day and was about ready for a third scrape. He said, "There's a telephone up there." He pointed to stairs at the end of the passage.

Mr. Behrens thanked him, and walked along the passage, conscious of the man's eyes focused like twin gun barrels on the small of his back. The stairs were carpeted, and led up to a hallway which was on ground-floor level at the back of the building. There were three doors on either side of the passage, but no sign of a telephone.

As Mr. Behrens was hesitating, the middle door on the left-hand side of the passage opened and a man came out. He was a big man, bulky but not fat, with skin the color of *crême caramel* and black hair set in tight varnished waves.

Mr. Behrens said, "The man downstairs—um—told me I would find a telephone up here. I—um—see no telephone. A most important call—"

"You could use the telephone in my office if you wished, sir."

"That's very good of you," said Mr. Behrens. He followed him in. "You would be the manager, I take it? I hardly like to trouble you in the middle of such a busy evening."

"All evenings are busy here. That telephone is through to Exchange."

"But it's not every night that you have to anticipate a police raid, I imagine," said Mr. Behrens.

"What makes you think we're anticipating a raid, sir?"

"I noticed that you had removed all the—um—exciting pictures from the walls downstairs. And most of the exciting drinks, too. I suppose those are the sort of things that get damaged, or perhaps lost, when you have a lot of heavy-handed policemen about the place."

Mr. Behrens was holding the receiver in one hand as he spoke, and was watching the manager's face. He saw the calculating expression in his eyes, and that was all he did see before the ceiling fell on him and the room rolled slowly over, twice, and dissolved.

Mr. Calder was sitting on a hard chair in an almost unfurnished room next to the superintendent's office in Carver Street police station.

When Mr. Behrens had telephoned him from the airport, he had suggested West End Central police station as a rendezvous. They both knew Chief Superintendent Park, head of the CID there, and had worked with him on many occasions.

When Mr. Calder reached West End Central, after crawling for three hours through the fog, abandoning his car in a garage at New Cross and finishing the journey by train, he found a message from the Savoy waiting for him. It said that the party was apparently going on to a night club in Soho, and it suggested that Mr. Calder go to Carver Street, which is the sub-station directly concerned with this area.

When Mr. Carver arrived at Carver Street, he realized that the move had been a mistake. The superintendent in charge had behaved with perfect correctness. He had accepted Mr. Calder's credentials, backed as they were by a message from his own chief, but he had made it quite plain that he regarded the position with disfavor. He did not like any civilians, even official civilians, interfering in police matters. And he did not like his superiors passing such civilians on to him, particularly on a night when he had his hands full. He probably had gastritis and troubles about his allowances as well, thought Mr. Calder. But it didn't make the situation any easier.

The superintendent explained, as if he grudged every word dispensed, "We've got a big job on tonight. Large-scale traffic in hashish. Involves two or three clubs and a lot of boardinghouses. Well—they're brothels, really."

"It sounds exciting," said Mr. Calder. "Which particular clubs and brothels have you got your eye on?"

The superintendent hesitated and then rapped out a list of names, adding, so quickly that there wasn't even a full stop at the end of the sentence, "I'm afraid I can't ask you to accompany us."

"Of course not," said Mr. Calder. He continued to sit patiently on his chair. The minute hand of the clock crept down toward the half hour after midnight.

"I fear," said Mr. Absalom, "that Mr. Behrens has been called away. We should, I think, be leaving."

"Why slide off now?" said May. "The night's hardly started."

Mr. Absalom looked past her at the thickset, black-jowled man standing in the doorway. He came forward, smiling. The girls fell silent.

"I think," said Mr. Absalom, "that it is agreed we go. Yes?"

"Oh, sure," said May. "Sure. I'm not objecting." She swallowed half a glass of champagne quickly, as though it had been a prop that the stage manager was going to remove. "Come on, Angie. The party's over."

"Angela will be coming with us," said Mr. Absalom.

The blonde girl had one arm linked through Nuri's. She was smiling nervously. They were all looking at the boy. There was the briefest pause, a tiny hitch, a half-beat in the music, a trip in the heart's rhythm.

Then Nuri said, with a smile, "Time for bed, eh?"

"That's right," said Mr. Absalom. "Time we were all in bed."

The party moved, as a body, to the door, then out into the foyer. The thickset man said, "Pleasant dreams, your Highness."

Mr. Absalom gave him a sharp, unfriendly glance. Then they were in the car. One of the chauffeurs was driving. The other held the door and climbed into the car with them, occupying the seat previously occupied by Mr. Behrens.

"Where are we going?" said Nuri.

"Actually," said Angie, "you're coming back with me for the night."

Nuri opened his brown eyes a little wider. Then he said, "That's very kind of you. We hardly know each other."

The girl chuckled. "You're a good boy," she said. "I can see that. You behave yourself, and we'll have no trouble. Right?"

"Naturally there will be no trouble," said Mr. Absalom. "Our first care must be for his Highness' comfort."

Mr. Behrens rolled over, grunted and sat up. His fingers scrabbled on the carpet. He opened his eyes fractionally, and closed them again, as an unfriendly hand thrust a white-hot skewer through the top of his head. Keeping his eyes shut, he fumbled in his top waistcoat pocket and brought out a transparent capsule about the size of a cigarette stub. He snapped it between finger and thumb and held this under his nose.

Five deep breaths later he sat up cautiously, and opened his eyes. The pain had retreated into a dull, throbbing dough-nut at the top of his head. His neck felt as though it had been broken and inexpertly set. Otherwise he seemed to be functioning normally. He was in a cell-like room, with two round windows set high up in the wall, and two doors. It looked like the sort of place a man might squeeze a secretary into if the secretary wasn't too fussy about her working conditions. It was furnished with a cheap typing table and one of those curious chairs with spindly chromium legs and no proper back to it.

Mr. Behrens picked it up. It was a better weapon than an ordinary chair. Unfortunately there was no one to hit with it. He put it down again, and tried the doors. Both, as he had expected, were locked.

Mr. Behrens took out his key fold. Hanging among his car keys and door keys were two steel implements. One looked like a toothpick with a spatulate tip, the other like a thinner version of the implement with which boy scouts are supposed to extract stones from horses' hooves. Mr. Behrens moved the chair across to the inner door and sat down. It took him three patient minutes to locate the spring in the lock, and another minute to lift and slide the gate. Then he opened the door, and found himself, as he had already guessed he might, back in the office in which he had been knocked out. It was now empty.

Mr. Behrens sat down behind the desk and tried the drawers. None of them was locked. In one he found, under some papers, a Walther automatic pistol with a full magazine. He put this in his jacket pocket, walked across to the passage door and opened it.

There was no one in sight, but there seemed to be quite a lot of people about. There was a hum and clatter from the floor below, and he heard a door open and shut. Mr. Behrens was a man who liked to do things in the simplest and least troublesome way. He went back to the office, lifted the receiver from the telephone and started to dial.

At one o'clock Mr. Calder had strolled out into the charge room. Here he found the station sergeant, a friendly soul, who produced a cup of tea and a tin of biscuits which Mr. Calder attacked gratefully, having eaten nothing since lunchtime.

"How's the big clean-up going?" he asked.

"It's Operation Washout so far," said the Sergeant. "We get these tip-offs. Sometimes they're hot. Sometimes just the opposite."

"Nothing at the clubs?"

"We gave the Krokodil the once-over. Clean as a Baptist chapel. We're moving in on the Quart Pot and the Tableau next. We'll do the boardinghouses later. You know what we'll find there? A lot of business men, down from Manchester and Liverpool. Virile, these Midlands business men."

The telephone rang. The sergeant picked it up, listened and said, "It's for you."

"Take your coat off," said Angie. "Make yourself comfortable. We got a bit of time to put in before anything happens."

"What is going to happen?" enquired Nuri.

"Actually we're waiting here till the police come."

"The police? That will be embarrassing for you, I imagine."

"I'm used to 'em," said Angie. "Besides, confidentially, I'm prepared to put up with a bit of embarrassment, if the money's good enough. It's you who's supposed to be embarrassed."

"Suppose I walk out before they come."

"Well, first, you can't, because I've locked the door and put the key where you wouldn't find it, and even if you did find it and unlocked the door, there's someone watching outside, and he'd put you back in again, twice as quick as you went out. So let's relax. We'll have a cup of tea, shall we?"

Nuri looked round the bedroom with interest. It was so neat, and so compact, like a cabin on a ship—the long cupboards with shelves above and below, the bed which folded up into the wall, the tiny curtained annex into which Angie had disappeared, and which seemed from the glimpse he had had of it, to be bathroom, kitchen and scullery combined. It was not unlike his own cubicle at school. Frillier, of course.

"You wouldn't happen," said Angie, "to have such a thing as a cigarette on you? I'm right out of them."

"But of course." Nuri put his hand in his pocket, and then stood for a moment, unmoving. There was certainly a case there. He ran his fingers over it, then drew it out, holding it up under the light. There had been ten cigarettes left in the case Mr. Absalom had given him. There were ten in this one. He picked one out and sniffed it delicately.

"I hope you don't mind," he said. "These are Egyptian."

"I'm not fussy," said Angie, reappearing with a tray on which she had set cups, saucers, milk jug and sugar basin. "Light it for me, there's a dear."

Mr. Behrens had finished telephoning and, being a man who did not believe in wasting opportunities, was examining the contents of the desk drawers, when he heard footsteps in the passage. The door opened, and Mr. Absalom came in. When he saw Mr. Behrens, he started to retreat. When he saw the gun in Mr. Behrens' hand he abandoned the effort, and stood very still.

"Come in," said Mr. Behrens, "and shut the door. Sit down. I'm glad you've come along. It's saved me the trouble of coming to look for you. What have you done with the boy?"

"When you deserted us," said Mr. Absalom, "—I still do not understand why—we took him back to the embassy. He is there now. Asleep. I came back here to find out what had happened to you."

"Ingenious," said Mr. Behrens. "But not good enough. The police are planning to raid a number of brothels tonight. The boy has been planted in one of them. You've got thirty seconds to tell me which one it is."

Mr. Absalom's small black eyes shifted from Mr. Behrens' face to the gun in his hand, and then back again.

"If you fire that," he said, "a lot of people will hear it."

"Were you aware," said Mr. Behrens, "that there are twenty-six separate bones in the human foot. The astralagus, the calcaneum, the scaphoid, the cuboid, three different cuneiform bones, five metatarsals and no fewer than *fourteen* phalanges."

As he spoke the last word he fired. Mr. Absalom gave a little squeal of surprise. The bullet had carried away the heel of his shoe.

"That was a sighting shot," explained Mr. Behrens.

There were hurried footsteps in the passage. Mr. Behrens got up, picked up a heavy cylindrical ruler from the desk and stood behind the door. It was the coffee-colored manager who came in. Mr. Behrens hit him very hard, on the base of the skull, dragged him into the room, locked the door and turned his attention again to Mr. Absalom, who seemed pinned to his chair.

"The last time I shot a man in the foot," he said, "the bullet struck the entocuneiform bone—that's the large one on the left—and broke three of the five metatarsals. He was three months in hospital, and the surgeons then cut off the foot. It was the only way of relieving the agony."

He raised the pistol.

Mr. Absalom's face was gray and his lips were quivering. He said, "I will tell you."

"You'd better not tell any lies," said Mr. Behrens. "I know the addresses, and if you happen to mention one which isn't on my list—"

He fired again, and the bullet hit the leg of the chair Mr. Absalom was sitting on.

"Stop, stop," said Mr. Absalom. "I am telling you now. It is a house in Spencer Street. At the corner. Number eighteen, I think."

There was a rattling of the door handle, followed by a knocking. Mr. Behrens walked over and opened the door.

Mr. Calder was standing in the passage outside. From below came the sounds of shouting, crashing and the stamping of feet.

Mr. Behrens said, "I'm glad you managed to get here. What's happening down there?" As he spoke he was carefully wiping the gun on his handkerchief, and putting it away in the desk drawer.

"When I got your telephone call," said Mr. Calder, "I persuaded our friends at Carver Street to organize a second raid here. I think it's going to be more fruitful than the first. Have you found out where the boy is?"

"I have," said Mr. Behrens. "The next thing is to get him out without a fuss."

Mr. Absalom seemed to be trying to say something. His mouth was opening and shutting like an expiring frog's.

"You will be too late," he said. "Much too late."

Nuri looked at the girl. She was lying back on the bed, her mouth half open, a smile of drowsy contentment on her lips. Her left hand, hanging down beside the bed, held a cigarette.

She must be entirely ignorant of the properties of bhang, he thought, or she would have realized at once, from the taste, what it was she was smoking. It was her third cigarette. The first had made her amorous. The second, fortunately, drowsy. The third was going to put her right out.

As Nuri watched her, her fingers parted and the half-smoked cigarette fell onto the carpet. Nuri picked it up and put it on the ash tray. Then he tiptoed across to the hanging curtains, and into the bathroom. Behind him, the girl stirred and said, "Where are you going?"

"Back in a moment," said Nuri.

He was standing on the end of the bath, working at the catch of the window. It was a very small window, but Nuri was as thin as an eel, and nearly as slippery. He went through feet first and found himself on a sloping roof of slates, which led up to a ridge-way. This was a highway, threading among the chimney stacks, and stretching the whole length of the block. Halfway along it, Nuri paused.

Something was happening in the street below. He could see the lights of cars and hear the slamming of doors, followed by knocking and voices shouting. Nuri smiled. For the first time that night he felt happy, by himself, up among the sooty chimneys. The last of the fog had gone and from above his head the stars winked back at him in friendly conspiracy.

He made his way as far as the end house, and found a promising-looking window. It was fastened, but he broke one of the panes of glass with the heel of his shoe, put his hand in and slipped the catch. It was an attic, and empty. He went out into the passage, made his way down three flights of stairs, first bare boards, then linoleum, then carpet, and out into a front hall. He got the front door unlocked and unbolted, and opened it a few inches.

There was a good deal of activity in the street, but most of it seemed to be happening at the far end. He slipped out, pulled the door shut behind him and ran.

As he turned the first corner, he saw a car parked, its lights out, and two men standing beside it. One he did not recognize. The other was Mr. Behrens.

On the way to the airport and the early-morning flight which was being held for them, Nuri told Mr. Behrens and the stranger, who turned out to be a Mr. Calder, something of his adventures.

"I can feel things with my fingers," he said, holding out a thin brown hand, "things which I could not see with my eyes. All our family have that facility. I knew, as soon as I touched it, that it was *not* the cigarette case which that fat pig Absalom gave me earlier. He had changed it for another. Probably in the car, when we were sitting squeezed together. Then it was clear that there would be something wrong with the cigarettes. Bhang, I guessed. What do you call it?"

"Hashish."

"It is against the law to smoke it."

"It's against the law even to possess it," said Mr. Calder. "If you had been found in that girl's room with a case of reefers in your pocket, you really would have been for it."

"It would not have been sufficient simply that I was in her room? She is a prostitute."

"It wouldn't have been good for your reputation, but it's not illegal."

"Curious," said Nuri, "that the law should punish the lesser sin."

"A lot of our laws are like that," said Mr. Behrens. "Here's the hotel. You've just time for a bath and breakfast."

Three days later, several thousand miles away from the soot of Soho and the fogs of London Airport, Mr. Calder and Mr. Behrens were standing on the first-floor balcony of the Hotel Continentale. The town had been en fête since dawn. The streets were packed with the outlandish crowds that had poured in overnight from the country districts. Houses and shop-fronts still blazed with electric lights, now paled by the morning sun. Every roof and window showed a flag, or a portrait, or bunch of flowers or paper streamers.

In the distance a band struck up.

"They'll be here soon," said Mr. Calder. And added, "I hope so. I want my breakfast."

"By the way," said Mr. Behrens. "Did they catch that fellow Absalom?"

"No. He and Moustaq both got out by plane that morning. Fortescue thinks they're in Cairo."

"If they know what's good for them," said Mr. Behrens, looking down at the crowd below, "they'll stay in Cairo. I hope they've made trouble for that club." His head was still sore.

"The second raid was a *great* success. They found a lot of unduitied liquor and a very interesting collection of blue films. Here they come."

A burst of cheering heralded the head of the procession. First came a company of boy scouts, older than their English counterparts, some of them sporting quite impressive black mustaches, but all bare-kneed and serious. Behind them, the Red Cross and the St. John's Ambulance. Then the massed bands. The municipalities. The fire brigade. The heroes of the Revolution, and the foreign diplomats. Mr. Behrens was glad to see that the procession had been organized to play down the military side. It was essentially a civilian jamboree. After the diplomats came several more bands, all playing vigorously, and all playing different tunes, followed by senior members of the government, and every male relative of the Royal House, each in a more gorgeous motorcar than the last.

Then came the mounted troops of the police, ceremonial lances at the carry, useful-looking carbines slung from their shoulders.

Then came the mounted troops of the police, ceremonial checks for a moment, and crashes down onto the shingle, came the roar of the crowd as the open, pale-blue-and-silver Rolls-Royce turned the corner.

In the back, upright, serious and straight as a blade, sat Nuri.

"'Upon the King,'" Mr. Behrens quoted softly, to himself. "'Let us our lives, our souls, our debts, our careful wives, our children and our sins lay on the King.'"

In the last four days Mr. Behrens had grown very fond of Nuri. The boy had shown himself brave and resourceful. He knew what he wanted to do and would, if given time, learn how to do it. If he could escape the sudden bullet, and the planted bomb. If he could answer propaganda with deeds. He had captured their hearts. Now he would have to capture their minds as well.

Mr. Behrens thought there was a chance, an outside chance, that he might do it.

MICHAEL GILBERT

Cross-Over

Mr. Calder sat behind the wheel of his old Ford Zodiac and stared out at the sodden world. It was four o'clock on a February afternoon and visibility was down to a hundred yards. It would decrease still further as afternoon fell away into evening.

Ahead of him, a length of white road crawled up toward the skyline, running with water in all its ruts. To left and right stretched unfenced moorland. The rain covered everything in a slowly moving pall.

A high-pitched whistling noise made him look down.

Headphones hung over the back of the passenger seat, the cushion of which had been taken out. In the open space where the seat should have been was a black, ebonite-fronted box. It had two tuning knobs and a single large dial graduated in degrees, on which a needle was rotating slowly.

The whistling stopped. The needle on the dial steadied and the voice of Mr. Behrens, distorted but clearly recognizable, spoke from the headset.

"Seventeen, eighteen, nineteen. Back to eighteen. Steady on eighteen. Over to you."

Mr. Calder put his thumb on the "speak" switch of the microphone and said, "Two hundred and thirteen. I shall have to re-plot. Out for a moment."

The map on his knees was mounted on plywood and covered with isinglass. He took a protractor from the pocket of the car, aligned it carefully on the isinglass and marked four points Then he picked up a graduated ruler and joined the points so that they formed two intersecting lines. He peered down at the map. It was now so dark that he needed a torch, and it took a minute to get it out of the car locker and focus it.

Then he picked up the microphone and said, "He's on the Nettlefold byroad, going north."

The ghostly voice of Mr. Behrens answered, "I agree. We'd better get moving. We'll take another cross-bearing ten minutes from now. If we keep on as we are, one of us ought to cut him off before he gets to Felshead. Out."

Mr. Calder started up the engine, engaged gear and splashed off up the road, his windshield wipers working busily . . .

It was nearly two hours later, and quite dark, when he turned out of the minor road which he had been following, into a rather larger road. Ahead of him, his lights picked out a signboard. "This looks like it," he said to himself. "And about time too."

The Bailiffs Arms was a dark crooked building, originally a posting-house, now a small residential hotel. Mr. Calder steered his car into the yard. There were two other cars parked there already. One was a Morris station wagon and belonged, he knew, to his friend, Mr. Behrens. The other was an old but solid-looking Mercedes.

Mr. Calder parked his own car, locked all the doors carefully and made his way through the back door of the hotel into the smoking room. A bright fire was blazing in the hearth. On one side of it Mr. Behrens was seated. On the other chair he recognized, with some surprise, the angular figure of Mr. Fortescue, who combined the offices of manager of the Westminster branch of the London and Home Counties Bank and of head of the Joint Services Standing Intelligence Committee.

Mr. Fortescue, who made few sartorial concessions, was dressed in the same black coat and striped trousers that he would have worn in his banker's parlor.

"I didn't know, sir, that it was you who was playing hare to our hounds," said Mr. Calder.

"It's the first time we've given the apparatus a field trial," said Mr. Fortescue. "I thought I might as well do it myself. Since you both arrived here within five minutes of me, I gather it was effective."

He put his hand into the side pocket of his coat, pulled out what seemed to be an ordinary cigarette lighter and placed it on the table.

"Extremely effective," said Mr. Behrens. "How does it work?"

"It's a transmitting set, which sends out a single VHF note. It's battery-powered, and will transmit for two hundred hours. It's tuned in to the receiving sets in your cars, which incorporate a direction finder. The whole thing's a development of the device which the Germans used for locating transmitting sets in Occupied France—only it's much more accurate, and it works over a much longer range."

"What sort of fix does it give you?"

"The makers say one mile at a hundred miles. That's under laboratory conditions. But you can't rely on that in practice."

"I'll say you can't," said Mr. Calder. "Every time your car passed under a power line, the beam jumped about like a performing flea. And another thing. You were doubling about—changing direction—going back on your tracks. If we were really after someone, and he didn't know we were there, presumably he'd get on to some route nationale, or autobahn, and go down it damned fast. Every time we stopped to plot his position, he'd get ten miles farther away from us."

"There's quite a simple solution to that," said Mr. Fortescue. "You must be given very fast cars. Anything else?"

"Can't they fit a cut-out to eliminate interference from power lines?"

"They're working on it now. It's the one big snag in the apparatus. But it's a difficult technical problem."

"Well, here's an easy one," said Mr. Calder. "I want a mapboard with an electric light built into it, so that I don't have to waste time messing about with a torch every time I plot."

"A good idea," said Mr. Fortescue. "What about you, Behrens?"

"I didn't experience any real snags," said Mr. Behrens. "We were helped by the fact that we were operating on a stretch of moor with very few roads. So, however roughly we plotted, there was never any real doubt where you were and which direction you were going. If there were a lot of little roads, it might be trickier. But I think it's a perfectly sound method of following a car without having to get within miles of it."

"Yes," said Mr. Fortescue. "I think the experiment can be said to have been successful."

"Was it just an experiment?" said Mr. Calder. "Or had you something practical in mind. Something you intended to use us on."

Mr. Fortescue said, "I've got something very practical in mind. We're going to use this device to uncover Route M."

For a long moment nobody spoke, and the only sound was the battering of the rain against the windows. Then Mr. Behrens said, "That's a very interesting idea. Which of us is going to be the hare on *that* run?"

"I'm afraid," said Mr. Fortescue, with a smile, "that you're both too well known to our friends on the other side to make convincing hares. You'll be acting as hounds, just as you did today. The hare's going to be Nichol. Do either of you know him?"

"David Nichol. Early thirties."

"That's right."

"I taught him German—that would have been just after the war. He must have been about fifteen. He was a good linguist, even then."

"He started learning European languages when he was eight. He speaks half a dozen, and is completely fluent in German and Russian."

"Unusual application for a boy of eight," said Mr. Calder.

"He was an unusual boy," said Mr. Fortescue. "With an unusual background. His father, John Nichol, was an ardent Communist. He was one of the first to join the anti-Franco forces in the field. He was very lucky. He survived for nearly a year."

"With that background," said Mr. Calder, "David should be a thoroughgoing Communist himself."

"And so he might have been. But some very odd stories got back to his mother, about the circumstances of his father's death. Very odd, indeed. According to his comrades, some of whom ultimately got back to England from internment, or prison camp, John Nichol wasn't an ordinary battle casualty. There was a mystery about his death. One story, which was widely believed, was that he had been betrayed to a Franco patrol by the orders of the commissar of his battalion. The Russians were becoming alarmed by his growing influence in the group, and came to the conclusion that he ought to be liquidated before he became canonized."

"There's a ring of probability about that," agreed Mr. Calder.

"It was probable enough to convince his mother. She decided to dedicate David—then aged eight, mind you—to the anti-Communist front. She was a woman of considerable imagination, and great persistence. She had her son trained in such a way that he was bound to go into Intelligence, which he did. Of course, we realized as soon as we set eyes on him that we'd got a man in a million. Single-minded, dedicated, with all the basic skills already learned. The difficulty was to know how to use him best."

Mr. Fortescue stopped to tap out his pipe, and said, "In the end, we sold him to the Russians."

"With a return ticket, I presume."

"We hoped so. We sent him to Korea, and arranged for him to be captured. He was an exceptionally intelligent and docile prisoner. They sent him to the Hwei Pé Camp School where he was thoroughly indoctrinated. When Soviet Intelligence were completely happy about him, they arranged for him to be returned to this country on exchange."

"Nice," said Mr. Behrens.

"He's been invaluable," agreed Mr. Fortescue. "But he can't keep it up forever. That's why we're going to use him to uncover Route M. A final fling."

"It seems almost a waste," said Mr. Calder. "I don't mean that as a criticism," he added hastily. "You'd be able to judge best. But a well-placed double agent—"

"Discovering how Route M works—where it starts—what the stations are en route—is becoming more important than anything else in our program. In the last ten years they've taken a constant stream of people out by it. Their agents, our agents, scientists, diplomats, all sorts. It's got to be shut down."

"If we shut it down, won't they simply open another route?"

"Oh, certainly. But it'll take time. It's the next six months that are important."

"Who do we think we're going to lose in the next six months?" said Mr. Calder. "Or is that an indiscreet question?"

"Extremely indiscreet," said Mr. Fortescue. "But I think I'd better tell you."

And he did.

When he had finished, Mr. Calder said, "If that's even on the cards, sir, I agree, of course. It's worth three of Nichol to put the ROAD CLOSED signs up. How soon will things start moving?"

"The first steps have been taken. Nichol has let his Russian masters know that he is under suspicion. He has asked for asylum, in the USSR, and they've promised to get him out. If we suspect him, it follows we won't allow him out of England by any normal route. He'd be stopped at the port or the airfield. Therefore he's got to go unofficially. And that means Route M. As soon as he gets his marching orders he'll tip us off, and we'll let you know. After that, I can give you very few instructions. You'll have to deal with each situation as it arises. If you can locate the route without the other side realizing what you're doing, so much the better. If you have to get rough and close it permanently it can't be helped."

"It seems to me," said Mr. Calder thoughtfully, "that there's one point where things are bound to get a mite complicated. And that's when we come to the actual cross-over. A lot's going to depend on Nichol, then."

"I recall him quite clearly, now," said Mr. Behrens. "A shock of thick black hair. A white, rather serious face. Very solemn and self-contained. A person who had elevated self-control to a moral principle."

"He has never touched alcohol in his life," said Mr. Fortescue, "and has never had other than a brotherly regard for a woman. Although," he added, "to judge from modern trends in fiction, even that is not an entirely safe simile these days."

"He sounds a bit of a prig," said Mr. Calder.

"Not a prig," said Mr. Behrens. "A puritan."

On a day in late April, David Nichol walked along the west bank of Hamble River and out onto the jetty. Ahead of him stretched the estuary, flat and placid. He looked very different from the smart young man in conventional clothes who had caught the train from Waterloo.

His journey had taken him to a room in a small hotel in a back street in Southampton, where he had stripped to the skin and put on the seaman's rig carefully laid out for him on the bed: corduroy trousers, rubber-soled shoes, and thick gray stockings into which the trouser ends were tucked; a string vest, a collarless shirt, a thick, blue, roll-necked jersey and a duffle coat.

Most of his own clothes went into the wall cupboard. A few personal belongings went into pockets or were squeezed into the top of an already bulging kit bag. Twenty minutes after entering the hotel, he had left it by the back door. From beginning to end he had spoken no word to anyone in the hotel.

His next stop was at a small bicycle shop. Here also he was expected. The owner of the shop—a long man with a squint—had a bicycle ready for him, and helped him to lash the kit bag onto the carrier. He also was a man of few words.

Nichol had stopped at a pull-in for motorists at Botley, and had eaten a meal of eggs and chips, with two mugs of teak-colored tea and several wedges of bread and butter, after which he had pedaled slowly on his way.

Just short of the jetty which he was making for stood a bungalow with a derelict strip of garden in front, and an overgrown lawn running down to the river behind. After examining the name on the gate, Nichol had wheeled his bicycle boldly into the garden, propped it against the wall, unstrapped the kit bag, shouldered it and walked away up the path to the gate. As he did so he saw, out of the corner of his eye, a curtain in one of the front windows of the bungalow twitch apart and close again.

At the far end of the jetty a thickset man with a beard was sitting on one of the iron mooring-bollards smoking a pipe, and watching the herring gulls fighting for galley scraps. He turned his head as Nichol approached.

"Nichol?"

"That's right, sir."

"You made good time. No hitches?"

"Smooth as clockwork."

"We shall be sailing in an hour. Can you handle a dinghy?"

"I've done most of my rowing at Windsor," said Nichol, "but as long as it's calm I shall make out all right."

"I could easily row you myself," said the man. "But it might look a bit odd if the owner took the sculls and the latest-joined member of the crew sat in the stern. I don't think we're being watched. But I don't believe in taking any chances."

"I'll manage," said Nichol.

In fact, he rowed very competently, and they were soon tying up under the stem of the ten-ton Hillyard Bermuda fore-and-aft-rigged sloop which was swinging in the tideway.

"You get below and lie down," said the owner. "I've declared a crew of two. One's ashore now. The other's below. They're both dressed exactly like you. All we've got to be careful not to do is to let the three of you appear on deck at the same time."

Nichol nodded, and disappeared down the orlop ladder. The owner cast a slow glance up the Middle Reach of Hamble River. No one appeared to be the least interested in him or his boat. He extracted a cigar from a case in his breast pocket, and lit it.

Almost exactly fourteen hours later, he said, "Slow ahead. Dead slow. Cut the engine."

It was an hour before daylight, and the sloop lay a quarter of a mile southwest of the Nez de Jobourg, rising and falling on a gentle swell. A thick white blanket of early-morning mist lay over the water.

"Couldn't have had better weather if we'd booked it in advance," said the owner. He had been up all night, his eyes were red-rimmed and his voice was hoarse, but he sounded happy.

"Looks all right to me," said Nichol. "What next?"

"Bertrand will row you ashore in the dinghy. I'm not sure, to within a mile, exactly where you are. But it's not important. All you have to do is to scramble up the cliff—there are half a dozen paths—and you'll find yourself on quite a good road. It runs parallel to the top of the cliff, about half a mile inland. It's got kilometers stones marked Auderville on one side and Beaumont-Hague on the other. You want the stone which shows Auderville—four and Beaumont—six. That's where the car will be waiting. Clear?"

"Quite clear," said Nichol. "As I don't even know your name, I'm afraid I can't write you a bread and butter letter—but thanks for a lovely trip."

"Don't mention it," said the bearded man. "Your kit bag is already in the boat, I see. Good-bye."

An hour later the sun was rising, red and glorious, out of the mist. The cutter had rounded the Nez de Jobourg and was out of sight, and Nichol was walking along the grass verge of the road, counting the little white hundred-meter stones—seven, eight, nine. The next kilometer stone must be in the dip ahead. No sign of a car.

Nichol perched on the stone and lowered his kit bag to the ground. It was a quarter to seven. Soon farm traffic would be passing. He would have to make a plan.

Someone came through a gap in the hedge and walked slowly toward him. It was a girl.

His first impressions were of size and color. She was big and she was blonde. As she came closer, he took in other details. She had a peasant's nose with no bridge to it, eyes which were pulled fractionally upward at the outer corners, and a generous mouth. She was wearing trousers which looked like jodhpurs but were more generously cut, a polo-necked sweater, and a wind-cheater. She had a businesslike look about her, Nichol thought. The sort of girl who could ride a horse, drive a car or plough a field.

She said, "Mr. Nichol? Put out your right hand. Press the tip of your index finger onto this black stuff. It'll wash off, I assure you. Now onto this pad. Fine."

She had taken out a small card which she compared carefully with the fingerprint which Nichol had made on her pad. Then she said, "The car is in a field, two hundred meters down the road. Give me your bag."

"It's a bit heavy," said Nichol. "I'd better take it—"

Before he could say any more she had swung the kit bag onto her shoulder and was walking off down the road.

The car, a dark green Citroën convertible tourer, had been skilfully tucked away in a dip among bushes.

"It is time that you ceased to be a sailor," said the girl. She spoke in the clear unaccented English of a foreigner who has been very carefully coached in a language, but mostly out of books. "Your traveling clothes are in the kit bag. You had better take off everything you are wearing. Even the underclothes are English."

"All right," said Nichol. The new clothes fitted him well. Gray worsted sports trousers, a heavy silk shirt with open neck and a silk scarf; a gray sports jacket, tighter at the waist than an English tailor would have cut it, and with padded shoulders.

As he took his old clothes off, the girl rolled them up and stowed them in the empty kit bag. Since the girl herself seemed to regard the operation as a matter of routine, Nichol tried to convey the impression that, so far as he was concerned, there was nothing out of the ordinary in stripping to the skin in front of a girl.

When he was dressed, she said, almost as though the operation they had just concluded had effected an introduction between them, "My name, by the way, is Shura."

"I had better know your second name, too."

She looked surprised. "The same as yours, of course," she said. "Shura Nichol. We are man and wife. That is how our papers are made out."

Nichol said, "Oh, I see. Yes. I suppose that's a sensible sort of arrangement."

"We are on a camping holiday. The kit is all in the back of the car. There are many camp sites in France and Germany. If we went to hotels, there would be registration forms to fill in—"

"An excellent idea," said Nichol. "Do I drive the car, or do you?"

"We take it in turns. It will be a long day's run. More than three hundred miles. We had better get started."

She threw the kit bag into the bushes.

"Isn't that a bit risky?"

"In England, perhaps. In France, no. The peasant who finds it will not report it. He will think it good luck."

The tip of Nichol's fingers touched the cigarette lighter, which he had transferred to his new clothes along with his personal possessions. Luck, he said to himself, that's what I'm going to need, too. Any goddamned amount of it.

Eighty miles away, in a wood south of Bolbec, the sensitive needle on the dial of Mr. Calder's car began to quiver. He picked up the microphone.

"He's off, I think," he said.

"Moving southeast," agreed the voice of Mr. Behrens.

The thing which David Nichol admired most in that long day's run was his companion's driving. He himself was a good driver. A part of his training had been the proper handling of cars, and a course at the Police Driving School had added technique to a natural aptitude. But he was not as good as Shura. She drove as safely as he did, and nearly five miles an hour faster.

There were other things to admire about her. Every move she made had the unconscious economy and control which is only achieved by an athlete at the height of training. Muscle was there under the flesh, but it was in the right place and was not obtrusive.

A ballet dancer at the peak of her career, an Olympic runner or jumper would have carried her subjugated body and limbs in just such a fashion.

As she drove down the long straight road from Bayeux to Caen, he looked at her out of the corner of his eye and found himself wondering about her past. She was clearly a Slav; a South Russian, he thought. Perhaps a Georgian. She could not have attained her perfection in English—which was matched, as he soon noted, by a nearly equal perfection in French—without at least twelve years' training. Yet she did not look more than twenty-four.

Could a totalitarian regime select boys and girls at twelve, as a breeder might select promising foals, and train them solely for its purposes? Teach them the requisite languages, train them in judo, and the use of poisons, teach them how to shoot, how to drive a car, how to operate a wireless set? There was nothing impossible about it. Sparta had selected her soldiers at the age of seven.

It would dehumanize them, of course. The only thing that Shura had not learned to do was to smile. Or could she do that too? Or make love? If the job demanded it, she could probably do that just as efficiently as she drove a car.

They had a picnic lunch in a wood south of Montargis. There was hot soup in a vacuum flask, and pâté and fruit. Shura served him first and then herself. She produced a bottle of wine and when he shook his head put it away, unopened, and substituted citronate.

"I fancy they've stopped for lunch," said Mr. Behrens. "We'll have time to work out an accurate fix on them now."

"We might have time for lunch ourselves," said Mr. Calder, sourly.

All that afternoon they drove on, east and south. Sometimes they talked. Nichol knew very well that if he asked her questions about herself they would be politely blocked, and she seemed as disinterested in him as an air hostess in a passenger.

There were maps in the glove compartment, but she seemed to know the route and never asked for directions. He tried to estimate where they would be likely to spend the night. If they kept up their present speed and general direction they would be somewhere south of Dijon. She had talked about camping. He knew that France was well ahead of other countries in this respect and had numerous camps, some of them run by national motoring and cycling organizations, others by the local syndicat d'initiative.

They were well-organized places with numbered tent sites, running water on tap and good sanitary arrangements. During the summer months a camp superintendent would live permanently on the site, in his own caravan.

They had crossed the Saône a few kilometers south of Beaune and were now running up the heavily wooded valley of one of its tributaries. Nichol, who was driving, glimpsed the giant pylons of the recently completed Saône-et-Loire hydroelectric project, striding up the hillside on the right of the road. It was half-past seven. There was perhaps an hour of daylight left.

"Not far now," said Shura. "The camp lies up this side road. It is a beautiful site."

"You have been there before."

"Once or twice. We turn left here. The road leads only to the camp site. We shall see it in a moment."

The road climbed gently round the contours of the hill. They swung round the final bend, under a wooden arch which said CAMP DE LOUVATANGE, and came to rest in the graveled space which formed the car park.

Despite the earliness of the season, three or four caravans were parked round the opening, and the flysheets of more than one tent could be seen among the trees beyond.

The door of the nearest caravan opened, and a man came out. He had a gingery mustache, thin gingery hair and a face the color of smoked salmon. He said, in very bad French, "Welcome to the camp. My name's Horton. Major Horton. I'm in charge here. If there's anything I can do for you, you must let me know."

His bulbous eyes frankly appraised the girl's face and figure, and he said with increased warmth, "Anything at all. As soon as you've settled down, come and have a drink and a chat in my caravan, and I'll put you wise to the camp routine."

Ex-public school, ex-Army, thought Nichol. Ex-Kenya, pro-segregation and anti- any sort of hard work as long as someone would pay him gin money.

"It would give us great pleasure to do that," he said in formal French.

"Hullo," said the major. "Here comes another of 'em. Wonder who *he* is. Wasn't told about this one. Unusual rush of business for the time of year."

"These damned power lines are playing Old Harry with my set," said Mr. Calder. "Over."

"Not much better here," said Mr. Behrens. "I think he's crossed the river. We shall have to keep pretty close behind him if we don't want to lose him."

"Why not let him settle down for the night? Then we can fix him accurately."

"Suppose he doesn't stop?"

"Drive all night, you mean?"

"Why not? There must be at least two of them."

"If they drive all night," said Mr. Calder, "we shall have to do the same. I'll take the Besançon road, you cross the river lower down and keep on his tail. I'll be able to give you some sort of cross-bearing when I get to the top."

Mr. Behrens said nothing. He was beginning to feel the strain. He could, if necessary, go on all night. But what he wanted at that moment, more than anything else in the world, was a hot bath and a good dinner.

He swung the car round the bend, saw too late the notice ahead of him, braked and came to a halt in a graveled forecourt.

Three people were walking toward him. One was a girl, the second a man in a bush jacket, with a reddish mustache. The third was David Nichol . . .

He had time to drop the earphones onto the floor and slide the seat cushion back over the set, before the man caught up with him. He glanced at Mr. Behrens' GB plate.

"My name's Horton," he said. "Major Horton. You wouldn't be a Modern Romany, I suppose?"

"That's right," said Mr. Behrens.

Nichol and the girl were moving off toward their own car.

"Your organizing secretary was here last week. He told me I should be seeing some of you chaps soon. I must say, I take my hat off to you. Straight out from your desks and offices. You won't have had much experience of this sort of thing, I take it?"

Nichol and the girl had got into the car, and were bumping off up one of the paths into the wood.

"I'm an accountant," said Mr. Behrens boldly. "I spend my life among balance sheets, and profit and loss accounts. It was only last week that I decided I *must* revert to a simpler method of existence. I haven't got much kit with me. A ground sheet, a couple of blankets."

"You're a real Romany," said the major admiringly. "I can see that. Prepared to rough it." Mr. Behrens shuddered. "I'm an old campaigner myself. I can probably give you a few tips. Let's find a nice sheltered place for you."

The major pointed at the taillight of the green Citroën.

"Better give them a bit of elbow room," he said with a chuckle. "They look to me like a honeymoon couple. Don't want to intrude on their privacy, eh?"

"Certainly not," agreed Mr. Behrens.

"Now you'll find quite a snug little berth here, under the roots of this tree. Spread the ground sheet over you, and peg it down each side. What about grub?"

"I've got some cold food with me, and a flask of coffee. I wasn't thinking of doing any actual cooking. Not yet."

"We could have a twig fire going in no time," said the major. "And I've got a few old safari pots and pans I could lend you."

"Thank you, no," said Mr. Behrens. "I've had a long and tiring day. I'll just rig up my—er—bivvy." The bitter thought was of Mr. Calder, at that very moment drawing up before some snug hostelry. "I'll be quite happy with a packet of sandwiches and a hot drink."

"The great thing," said the major, "when you're sleeping on mother earth is to dig a hole for your hip."

A hundred yards away, Shura had finished erecting the safari-model combined dwelling and sleeping tent and had plugged in the electric light from a spare battery in the car. It looked, Nichol thought, extremely inviting, a tiny refuge of light and shelter in a darkening world.

"Can I help?" he asked.

"It is really easier for me to do it. I know where everything is. Perhaps you could unroll the beds, while I set the table."

There were, Nichol saw, two sleeping bags, each with an inflatable mattress and pillow.

"All you have to do," said the girl, "is to blow them up. You will have to find what degree of inflation suits you best. I like mine quite soft. Just enough to keep my body off the ground. Will you have an aperitif before we eat?"

"Thank you," said Nichol. "I think I should enjoy that."

"Tournedos Rossini will do very nicely," said Mr. Calder. "Followed, I think, by a Sorbet, and a bottle of Clos des Lambrays, 1955."

Outside, it had started to rain.

David Nichol heard the rain pattering on the flysheet of the tent, and turned over in his sleeping bag. He was tired, but sleep seemed far away. There was something wrong with his mattress. He had inflated it too hard, and was rolling and bouncing like a small boat on a choppy sea. Also he was too hot.

He threw back the down-lined coverlet, and lay for a moment with his arms outside. A warm hand came out from the sleeping bag beside him. It touched his hand, then moved down to the mattress. There was a hiss of escaping air. Nichol felt himself sinking.

"Better?" asked Shura.

"Much better," he said.

Mr. Behrens was first up. He shaved under a cold tap, repacked his belongings, and ten minutes later was freewheeling out of the car park and down the hill. He felt it wiser not to disturb Major Horton. If there was indeed a fee to pay for one of the most excruciating nights he had ever spent, it could be collected, in due course, from the Modern Romanies.

In fact, he had not been unobserved. A pair of cold and protuberant eyes under projecting ginger eyebrows had watched his unobtrusive departure.

There was a telephone in Major Horton's caravan, connected to the exchange at Besançon. He asked for a number and when connected spoke rapidly. His French seemed to have improved.

Mr. Behrens stopped at the first café which he found open, and had breakfast and a more satisfactory wash and shave. He then drove his car into a side turning and switched on his set.

It was still only seven o'clock.

Mr. Calder answered at once.

"I hope you had a good night," said Mr. Behrens.

"Excellent," said Mr. Calder. "And you—?"

"Unspeakable."

"When you went off the air so suddenly, I assumed you'd run into our friend."

"You assumed correctly. My right hip is still paralyzed. I'll tell you all about it one day. I think he's off again."

It was a false alarm. It was after eight before the needle flickered, and started to creep across the dial.

"Due east," said Mr. Behrens.

"There are only two roads to Belfort," said Mr. Calder, who had been devoting his attention to the map. "The southern looks the natural one for them. I'll take it myself, and keep ahead. You can take the northern route through Vesoul. And keep out of trouble."

"I'll do my best," snapped Mr. Behrens. "Out."

It was at eleven o'clock, on the long climb up to Altkirch, that he ran into the road block. It was a single whitewashed pole on trestles across the road. In the split second when he spotted it as he came round the corner, he wondered if his car was heavy enough to crash it. The German frontier was about twenty miles ahead. He braked and came to a halt.

One of the policemen advanced toward the car. The other remained seated on his chair beside the road. They were oldish men, police reservists, Mr. Behrens thought. He was uncomfortably aware that he had had no time to cover up the apparatus on the seat beside him.

"What's all this about?" he said.

"Routine check," said the man. But he had seen the wireless set. His eyes jerked down to the number plate on the car, and Mr. Behrens saw him glance back at his companion, who got quickly off his chair.

Mr. Behrens opened the door of the car and slid out. They were on an upland plateau, with a long view of the road in both directions. There was no other car in sight.

On his left, twenty yards down the track, was a small hay barn. He could see the policemen's bicycles propped up against it.

"This apparatus—you have a license for it?"

Mr. Behrens sighed deeply.

"Of course," he said. He dipped his hand inside his coat and pulled out an automatic pistol. "If you do not do what I say, I shall be forced to shoot you both. I have already killed three men. I should not advise you to touch your own guns."

The two men backed away. There was no fight in them.

"Into that barn," he said.

The windows of the barn were mere slits, and the bar across the double doors looked stout. They would break out, but it would take them time.

He wheeled the two bicycles back to the road, and threw them down the ravine on the other side. Then he drove off.

Forty minutes later he was in Germany. There was no trouble at the frontier, where he joined a stream of cars passing the checkpost. His English passport and GB plate took him through without a hitch.

As soon as he had got clear of the traffic, he switched on his set again.

The earphones crackled angrily.

"Where the devil have you been?" said Mr. Calder.

"A bit of a holdup," said Mr. Behrens. "The police."

"You've been held up by the police?"

"On the contrary," said Mr. Behrens, pleased by his own wit.

"What are you talking about?"

"I'll tell you later. Where's our friend?"

"Ahead of us," said Mr. Calder. "East by northeast. I hope he stops for lunch soon."

The afternoon run was uneventful. Shura drove and Nichol kept his eyes on the map. They were turning slowly north, and he saw now that their long detour had been designed to avoid the barrier of Cologne, the Ruhr and the Lower Rhine where the NATO and West German defenses were thickest.

By teatime they were running into the southern part of the Black Forest, a region of dumpy hills, thick woodland and occasional lakes. They passed through empty holiday resorts. By August they would be packed with stout fathers in Lederhosen, white-faced Haus-fraus, and a Pied Piper's horde of flaxen-haired children.

At six o'clock they stopped at one of those lakeside villages and found a café open. They were the only customers.

"Where do you plan to spend the night?" asked Nichol.

"It is a Gast-haus in the forest, near Adelsheim. We shall have no company. It is not yet open for the season."

Now that they had left France behind, she seemed more relaxed, a little more sure of herself, a little readier to talk.

"You know the proprietor then? He allows you to stay there out of season?"

"Certainly. His name is Bauer. He was a member of Goering's personal bodyguard. The Reichsmarschall was an interesting man. Did you know that he was fond of birds?"

"Yes," said Nichol, cautiously. "So I had heard."

"Each of his country retreats was named after a different bird."

"A romantic idea."

"He was hightly romantic," agreed Shura. "This one was the retreat of the nightingale. Die Nachtigall."

It took them two hours, by tortuous roads which zigzagged up hills, twisted into hidden valleys, crossed streams brown with the local iron-ore and climbed again through pine forest cut into geometrical patterns. It was too dark to read the map and some of the roads they used would not, he felt certain, have been marked on any map at all. The last fifteen minutes were spent bumping along a sandy track.

"It is a private road," said Shura.

"It feels like one," agreed Nichol.

The Gast-haus der Nachtigall was a three-story, shingle-roofed building, with a deep balcony along the second-floor frontage, and a wide door leading under the balcony into an interior courtyard. There were no lights in the windows, but Shura drove confidently into the courtyard and sounded her horn.

A door serving the kitchen quarters opened and a man came out.

"Good evening, Herr Bauer," said Shura, in German.

"Good evening, Fraulein. You have made good time."

Horn-rimmed glasses set on a long, thin nose. The hair gray, running back from the brown, seamed expanse of the forehead. The mouth prim.

He said, "My boy will take your things up to your room. A fire has been lit in the Gast-zimmer. Come."

He led the way into the front room. It was paneled in pitch pine, and from the walls the creatures of the Schwartzwald looked down at them: squirrels, badgers, roebuck, blue hare, and ruffed capercaillie.

Herr Bauer had brought them, unasked, a tall bottle of white wine and a squat bottle of brandy. He filled two large glasses with wine and two small ones with brandy.

"After a journey," he said, "it is kinder to the stomach to take a small amount of fortified spirits before you drink a natural wine."

Nichol swallowed the brandy. It was aromatic. The glass of wine followed it more slowly. Herr Bauer refilled the wine glasses, said, "Dinner in half an hour," and withdrew.

Nichol said, "He doesn't look much like an S.S. man, does he?"

Shura said shortly, "I imagine that even in S.S. units there must have been administrative people—clerks, and quartermasters." She seemed to be regretting her earlier confidence.

Nichol nodded. The warmth from the tiled stove was welcome. Being locked away alone with Shura in this house in the middle of a forest gave him a delusive feeling of security. Tomorrow there would be trouble. Tonight was tonight.

"The luggage will be in our room by now," she said. "I will go and change. Give me a quarter of an hour.

Nichol sipped the second glass of wine. Somewhere at the back of his consciousness a very faint alarm had sounded. He took a moment to track it down. Two days before, when they had first met, the girl had shown no embarrassment when he had stripped to the skin in front of her. Why should she mind taking off all *her* clothes in front of him. And above all, why had she said something so entirely out of character, so miss-ish, as "I'll go and change. Give me a quarter of an hour." It made no sense.

Nichol put down his wine glass, got up and went across to the door. The place was quiet as a tomb.

He went out. There was a staircase ahead of him, leading to a landing running the length of the buildings. He guessed that the main bedrooms would face south.

There was a light under the door of one of them, and after a moment's hesitation he turned the handle and went in.

It was their room. Shura's suitcase was on one side of the double bed, open, and her windcheater, sweater and trousers were lying beside it. Evidently she had changed, but she had done so very quickly.

There was a newish suitcase on the other side of the bed. Nichol opened it and found shirts and underclothes, a pair of flannel trousers, a dark blue pullover and a jacket, all new and neatly packed. He took off his shirt and tie, ran some hot water into the basin and started to clean himself up.

Herr Bauer said, "A car has just come into the southwest driveway. It has pulled off the road."

He and Shura were in a basement room. They were watching a map of the estate on the wall, covered by glass. In the bottom left-hand corner two pinpoints of light glared red. "It could be a casual trespasser, a pair of lovers in a car. But if you are being followed—"

"I think we are being followed," said Shura. "There was a man in a dark blue Saab who came into camp after us last night. He left before we got up, and I have not seen him at all today."

"Martin is patroling now. If there is a dark blue Saab, we should take no risks. The driver will have to be attended to."

As he spoke, the lights on the panel flicked and changed pattern.

"Possibly I was wrong," said Herr Bauer. "The car is going. Nevertheless, I think we will take all precautions tonight. If there should be trouble—I hope your passenger is a sound sleeper?"

"I will make certain," said Shura seriously, "that he sleeps very well indeed."

It was, in fact, Mr. Behrens who had driven his car into the edge of the Nachtigall domain. He had backed out again in answer to a call on the wireless from Mr. Calder, who had come to a halt half a mile farther down the road. It was the first time they had set eyes on each other since leaving England.

Mr. Behrens pulled up, walked across and climbed into the back of Mr. Calder's car. In the darkness beside him something stirred.

He put out his hand and a cold nose was pushed into it.

"I didn't know you were bringing Rasselas with you," he said.

"He refused to be left behind." When Mr. Calder spoke, the great dog turned his head, and his amber eyes reflected the light from the dashboard.

"How are you going to get him back again?"

"We'll think about that when the time comes," said Mr. Calder. "I want to hear about your adventures last night. Tell me more about that chap at the camp."

"He called himself Major Horton. Leathery skin, baldish, with a halo of reddish hair, thick gingery eyebrows, poached-egg eyes."

"Sounds an unpleasant character. Do you think he rumbled you?"

"I wondered," said Mr. Behrens. "He did seem to accept me rather easily. If I really had been a Modern Romany, or whatever it was he called me, presumably I'd have had some sort of card or papers. And if he did suspect me, that would account for the trouble I had near Altkirch." He told Mr. Calder about it.

Mr. Calder said, "We shall have to sort that out with the Department when we get back. The important point at the moment is, *were you followed?*"

"I'm quite certain I wasn't."

"Did it occur to you that they might have put a midget transmitter in your car, during the night?"

"Certainly it occurred to me," said Mr. Behrens coldly. "I spent half an hour after breakfast turning my car out. Nothing had been tampered with."

"In that case," said Mr. Calder, "I wonder why we have already aroused such interest."

"Interest?"

"Before you arrived, a man walked up to the edge of the trees over there and kept me under observation for several minutes. He has gone now."

"You saw him?"

"No. But Rasselas told me about him. Never mind. The first thing is to find somewhere to eat. I passed a nice little place in the outskirts of Ringheim."

They were finishing dinner when Mr. Calder suddenly said, "Got it."

"Got what?"

"Nachtigall—the nightingale. It was one of Goering's hide-outs. He had five or six of them, all in remote areas, all top secret. When life at the center got too much for him he used to lie up in one of them. He called them his 'nests.' They were all named after birds, you see. The lark's nest, the heron's nest, the nightingale's nest."

"I wonder if he had one called the cuckoo's nest."

"I remember being shown round one of them by an American Intelligence officer in 1945. It had a very elaborate approach warning system, operated by crossing beams of infrared light. And one or two rather nasty booby traps for the benefit of unwanted visitors."

"A highly suitable staging point for our friends."

"Just what I thought," said Mr. Calder. "A bit later on I'll go and take a look at it. You'd better stop here and catch up on the sleep you didn't have last night."

"Are you sure you'll be all right by yourself?"

"I shan't be by myself," said Mr. Calder.

A tail thumped against the floorboards.

It was past midnight when Mr. Calder switched off the engine of his car, let it coast quietly down the last hundred yards of road and came to a halt under a clump of trees. It was a clear night, with a full moon marbling the sky. He had been driving without lights.

Now he climbed out of the car and stood for a moment. Rasselas sat beside him, head cocked, the tip of his right ear an inch from Mr. Calder's left shoulder. His nose gave a thrust, as if to say, "Go on—what are we waiting for?" Mr. Calder crossed the road and climbed through the boundary wire.

It was tidy woodland with most of the undergrowth cleared, and man and dog advanced steadily on a long slant toward the house.

They were halfway across one of the open glades when Rasselas stopped. He had heard something, away to the right. There was a thick patch of bushes on the far side of the glade, with a slight depression in the middle, which made an admirable hiding-place.

From watching Rasselas, Mr. Calder could chart, with great exactness, he progress of his enemies. He saw the ears prick, the amber eyes swivel slowly as they followed something invisible to him. Then the lip lifted in a silent snarl as two men stepped out into the glade.

They were dressed in foresters' uniform with leather leggings, and both carried, slung across their backs, short, double-barrelled rifles. Mr. Calder recognized them as the weapons issued during the war to guards in charge of working parties. They threw a spread of heavy buckshot, and were weapons for stopping and crippling, rather than for killing. One of the men carried a stick, which seemed to have some sort of spike on the end of it. The other had a heavy leather whip.

Mr. Calder slid his right hand gently inside his coat, until his fingers rested on the warm butt of his automatic.

The men walked slowly across the glade, heads turning to right and left, passed within six paces of where Mr. Calder was lying, seemed to hesitate for an instant and then were gone.

It was fully ten minutes before Rasselas stirred. Then he edged his way, silently, out of the thicket. Mr. Calder followed even more slowly. He was a professional himself and he recognized professional opposition when he saw it.

He moved slowly forward, Rasselas drifting beside him like a gray shadow. Now there was only a single line of trees between him and the house, since he was approaching it from the southwest corner and had a clear view of the long southern frontage. He noticed that a light still showed in one of the bedroom windows.

The space between the treeline and the house was dotted with bushes and shrubs, and Mr. Calder reckoned that if he went on his stomach, commando-fashion, it would be an easy matter to keep out of sight until he reached the house. If he could find a window open, he had a mind to explore further. As he started to move forward, Rasselas gave out a very soft, rumbling growl. Mr. Calder paused. When nothing happened, he moved again. Rasselas caught his ankle in his teeth.

At that moment the ground under Mr. Calder's hands gave way. At one moment he had his palms on solid earth. The next, his fingers were slithering over the lip of a cavity which had opened in front of him. If he had been moving forward, nothing could have stopped him falling into it.

It was a deep trench, with sheer walls cut into the chalk soil. It had been masked by a thin net of Hessian, on which sand and leaves had been sprinkled.

Mr. Calder extracted the pencil torch from his pocket, and directed its pinhead of light downward. Set into balks of timber at the bottom of the trench was a treble row of steel spikes, needle-thin, needle-sharp and fully twelve inches long.

He thought about an intruder, animal or human, falling on to them. The weight of his fall would drive the spikes through an arm or a leg.

He drew back slowly from the lip of the trench. It extended, so far as he could see, right along the front edge of the tree belt. As he was looking, the single light in the Gast-haus went out.

"There might have been some way round," he said to Mr. Behrens next morning. "But quite frankly, I didn't try. I could *feel* those spikes, all the way home."

"They were expecting you?"

"I think they must have been," said Mr. Calder. "It would take some time to uncover that trench. They daren't leave it open. I could feel a sort of ledge cut inside the lip, so I imagine it's boarded over by day and covered with loose sand. It's the sort of job that'd take a couple of hours to do properly. And whatever the size of the staff, I don't see that they could afford to keep two men patroling all night, and every night."

Mr. Behrens considered the matter.

"The girl might have been suspicious," he said, "when I practically bumped into her at the camp site. But surely—after a full day's drive—with no glimpse of a pursuer—"

"What about the trouble you had near Altkirch? It must have been a pretty definite tip-off to get the French police moving so quickly."

"I had the impression it was my car they were looking for," agreed Mr. Behrens. "The first thing the man spotted was the wireless. But it was only when he saw the number plate that he started to get excited. But if they were tipped off, who do you suggest did it? That man at the camp? Or the girl?"

"Or Nichol," said Mr. Calder.

Mr. Behrens did not sound surprised or horrified at the suggestion. He said, "It's a possibility that has to be borne in mind, of course. I hope it's not true. It suggests one precaution to me, however. The only car they know about is mine. The sensible thing now will be for me to keep close behind him. You keep right out on the wing."

Mr. Calder thought about this for a bit, and then grunted. "Yes," he said. "That seems right."

It was half-past six that morning when Shura slipped quietly out of bed. She put a raincoat over her pyjamas, and tiptoed from the room.

Herr Bauer was in the control room talking to two men. He looked up as she came in. He said, "We had a visitor last night."

"What have you done with him?"

"We have done nothing with him. He came, looked at us and went away." Herr Bauer glanced sourly at the two men, who shuffled and look at their feet.

"There are traces, too, of a car having driven in. It might all be nothing. It might be something."

Shura said, "If the car was a dark blue Saab, then we have been followed across Europe. And I have not the least idea how."

Herr Bauer said, "There are not more than four ways out of the Odenwald. I can have them watched. When you stop for your midday meal, telephone back to me here. I shall be able to tell you then . . ."

Nichol woke up at eight o'clock. He stretched out an arm, found the bed empty and sat up.

Shura was outside, on the balcony.

"I overslept," he said. "Are we late?"

"No hurry this morning. We need not start before eleven. Breakfast is being brought up to us here."

They took the morning's run at a much slower pace. Nichol had the impression that the clock had become more important than the map. They skirted Wurzburg and Bamberg to the south and stopped for their lunch in a tiny village called Plankenfels, ten miles short of Bayreuth.

Shura slipped away while the food was being cooked. When she came back Nichol thought he detected a change in her manner. It was very slight, and if he had not got to know her so well in the three days he had been with her, he might not have noticed it. Something seemed to have put her on her mettle.

During the afternoon Shura did the driving, while Nichol kept his eye on the map. They avoided Bayreuth, making a detour to the south, and climbed into the Fichtelgebirge. Gradually the country became more desolate, the farms fewer, the houses farther apart. Ahead of them, on the map, right across their track and slowly drawing nearer, sprawled the irregular green line which marked the farthest advance of the Russian Army in 1945 and now formed the boundary between the eastern and western worlds.

At this particular point the line joined the national boundary of Czechoslovakia, and ran almost due west, forming a right angle with it. It was into the neck of this sack that they were driving. They had been avoiding main roads for some time and Nichol was hard put to it to map their twisting progress, but in the fading light he glimpsed a board with the name QUELLENREUTH, and knew they were not more than ten kilometers from the frontier.

In the next village they turned left. A moment later, right again. They were now heading straight up into the angle itself, an area where his map was blank. He soon saw the reason. It was thick woodland. As they dived in among the trees, they switched on their headlights.

They were running north, and climbing. After about three miles, Shura seemed to hesitate for the first time. She slowed to a crawl, her eyes on the roadside. She saw what she was looking for, swung the wheel and put the car down a sandy track.

The track seemed to go on interminably, diving into the very heart of the forest, a tunnel of darkness among the trees. Then they were in a clearing. Nichol caught a glimpse of a log hut as Shura swung the car round, brought it to a halt and switched off all the lights.

Nichol stirred, but the girl put a hand on his arm. They sat in the darkness and waited. Then the car door was opened from outside, and a man gestured them out. They stumbled across the clearing to the hut; the door was opened and they went into darkness.

A torch came on. By its reflected light Nichol saw the face of its holder. He had never met him, but he recognized him at once from many photographs carefully studied. Colonel Tyschenko had been military attaché in Ottawa and Washington and in neither case had his hosts been under any illusions as to his real interests.

"I am sorry," he said, speaking in Russian, "to receive you in this melodramatic way. But we are waiting for the man who has been following you."

"The man in the Saab?" said the girl.

"Yes. He should be here any moment now. We will keep silent, if you please."

It seemed to Nichol like an hour, but was in fact only twelve minutes by the illuminated hand on his watch before there were footsteps outside. The door opened, and three men came in. As soon as the door was shut, Colonel Tyschenko snapped on the light, and the six occupants of the hut blinked at each other.

Two of the newcomers were Russian Security men, soldiers in plain clothes. They both carried machine pistols. The third was Mr. Behrens, his hands in his pockets, and a look of distaste on his leathery face.

"He parked his car a quarter of a mile down the track," said one of the men, "and was walking toward the hut when we stopped him. He had a gun. We have taken it."

Colonel Tyschenko had been staring in some surprise at the scholarly figure in the raincoat. Then his face broke into a smile. “Why,” he said, “it is Mr. Behrens. This *is* an unexpected pleasure. Where is your friend—the fat little man—Calder?”

“He’ll be here in a moment,” said Mr. Behrens. “And he’s got six men with him.”

The colonel chuckled. “No doubt,” he said. “No doubt. The six invisible men. It would be a good title for a film. I should be interested to know how you followed our car.”

“It’s Nichol’s suit,” said Mr. Behrens. “It has been impregnated with a particularly potent smell. When in doubt as to which way he had gone, I had only to get out of the car and sniff.”

“Remarkable,” said the colonel. “Particularly since he will have changed his clothes at least three times since leaving London.”

“We found a wireless set in the car,” said one of the men.

“I see,” said the colonel. “That opens up an interesting field of speculation.” He turned to Nichol. “*What* are you carrying that you had on you, *when you left London*?”

Nichol said slowly, “Fountain pen, silver pencil, notecase, wristwatch, and signet ring.”

He hoped that the cigarette lighter, which he dropped as they got out of the car, had fallen into an inconspicuous place.

“The details are not important,” said the colonel. “We shall be able to work them all out when we get you and Mr. Behrens, and the contents of his car, safely into our own territory.”

He turned to the Security men and said, “One stays here. One to go and check the arrangements for the crossing. We are using the normal route. Hurry.”

The man nearest the door turned and went out.

Shura spoke for the first time, “I hope, Colonel, that you do not blame me for this. I should, perhaps, have thought that some electrical device might be used.”

There was a pleading note in her voice that Nichol had never heard before; he had not imagined that such a girl could ever be humble.

The colonel said, "No, Shura. I don't think anyone could blame you too much. Indeed, you did well to take notice of the Saab and call Herr Bauer's attention to it."

The girl actually blushed.

"Thank you," she said . . .

Mr. Behrens, standing against the far wall of the hut where the guard had left him, considered the position. Even now that one of the guards had departed it was almost entirely unsatisfactory. Colonel Tyschenko was carrying a Vostok MU-2 pistol in a shoulder holster. He could see the light wooden butt as the colonel leaned forward to speak to Shura. The guard had a German-type Schmeisser machine pistol across his shoulders, carried in such a way that he could swing it round to the front and fire without unslinging it. The girl had a gun, but it was probably in her shoulder satchel on the table. He and Nichol were unarmed.

The door handle turned very gently, round, and back again.

Mr. Behrens took a deep breath, and let it out slowly. He was not fond of violence.

He said, "If you don't mind, I have to go outside for a moment."

Colonel Tyschenko looked at him, then said, "Of course. But I should warn you that this man can put a burst of six shots into a moving target at fifty yards."

"I wasn't thinking of making a dash for it," said Mr. Behrens, sourly. He started toward the door. The colonel signaled to the guard, who slipped back the bolt of the door and swung his gun round to the ready.

Mr. Behrens did not hurry. He wanted to be in one particuliar spot, next to the girl. The guard put a hand on the handle of the door and turned it. The door came open fast, as if kicked, and

Rasselas came through in a smooth golden curve, his teeth bared, making straight for Colonel Tyschenko's throat.

Behind the dog waddled the squat figure of Mr. Calder. He shot the guard twice, at close quarters, through the chest, before he could get his hand to the trigger of his machine pistol.

The colonel twisted as Rasselas struck him, and the dog catapulted over his shoulder, onto the floor. In the same moment, the colonel pulled out his Vostok and shot Nichol, who was jumping at him, through the right side of the body.

Rasselas buried his teeth in the colonel's leg.

Mr. Behrens had wrapped his arms round Shura from behind. It was a temporary advantage only. She was twice as strong as he, and better trained. She pried apart his fingers, grabbed his forearm and threw him across her outstretched leg. Then she stooped to grab her satchel, which Mr. Behrens had managed to knock onto the floor.

Mr. Calder crouched, steadied himself and shot Colonel Tyschenko. The bullet went through the colonel's mouth and out at the back of his head. As he fell, his Vostok dropped within a few inches of Nichol's hand. He rolled over and picked it up.

Shura's hand was already inside her satchel, when Nichol shot her. He was lying on the ground, and the bullet went upward, through her chest and into the top of her spine. The impact lifted her onto her toes. For a moment she looked as though she were poised for a dive. Then her knees buckled. As she fell, she struck the edge of the table, and slid off it. She was dead before she hit the floor beside Nichol.

After the last shot, there was a moment of complete silence.

Rasselas crouched over the colonel's body, motionless except for the angry twitching of his tail. The smell of the blood had excited him. His ancestors had hunted wolves and had fed on their entrails.

Mr. Behrens was the first to move. He groped for his glasses, put them on and climbed to his feet. He said, "We've got precious little time. That other guard will be here any moment."

"He won't be coming back," said Mr. Calder. He was breathing heavily, as though the death he had dealt out had been a physical exertion. "I can promise you that."

"In that case—" said Mr. Behrens.

"In that case," said Mr. Calder, "we've still got a hell of a lot to do. And the fact that we've now got all night to do it in doesn't make it any easier. I think the bodies will have to be buried."

"Yes," said Mr. Behrens.

"It's sandy soil, and we've spades in the car. We shall have to put them four feet down."

"Yes," said Mr. Behrens again. It would mean hours of digging. But he could see the sense in it. It was the rule. If you made a mess, you cleared it up. But there was more to it than that. If Colonel Tyschenko, his courier and his two personal bodyguards disappeared, the first idea would be that they had defected. And the mere suspicion of this would cause their opponents the maximum of trouble and uncertainty.

"Any blood there is, is on the matting. We'll bury that with them. We can use the girl's car for transport. After that I'll drive it off and leave it in the thickest part of the forest. This isn't a part of the world where intruders are encouraged. It could stand there until it falls to pieces."

"There's one other thing," said Mr. Behrens. "We ought to get Nichol to a doctor before morning. The nearest one I know of, who won't ask a lot of questions, is a hundred miles away."

Mr. Calder considered the problem.

He said, "Give me a hand with the first part, getting the bodies moved. Then leave me to do the rest."

"Will you be able to finish before the morning?"

"Almost certainly not. But I can lie up by day, and finish the job tomorrow night. I'll see you in Cologne, at our usual place, the day after tomorrow."

And so at four o'clock that morning Mr. Behrens was driving his car once more. His head was singing with the Benzedrine he had inhaled to keep himself awake. Beside him, Nichol was propped in the passenger seat. He had been delirious for some time and was now dozing. Mr. Behrens could only pray that they were not stopped. They would neither of them stand up to much inspection. And unless he could get Nichol into a doctor's hands in time to save his life, they were going to lose half the results of their efforts.

The continental side of Route M they now knew about and could deal with. But the English side—how it worked, who operated it—that was all locked away inside the white face and under the tangled head of black hair that lolled on the seat beside him.

A red light sprang out of the night. Mr. Behrens cursed, and slowed. But it was only the warning light for a level-crossing gate on the main line from Cologne to Basle.

Mr. Behrens coasted up to the barrier and switched off the engine. Nichol turned his head, and looked at him. The sudden silence and cessation of movement had wakened him.

"Where are we?" he said.

"Nearly there," said Mr. Behrens.

"There's something," said Nichol, "that I ought to tell you."

"Don't talk more than you must," said Mr. Behrens.

Nichol hardly seemed to hear him. His body was in the present, but his mind was in the past. He went on in a conversational voice.

"Last night, at that hotel, I made love to Shura. She seemed to want it. It was the most wonderful thing I have ever done. It was the first time in my life. I've been rather strictly brought up.

You appreciate that. I'd never imagined it could be such a perfect thing. And then I shot her. I had to shoot her." He sounded serious, and puzzled. "That can't be right, you know."

"In this job," said Mr. Behrens, "there is neither right nor wrong. Only expediency."

The night express thundered past, and the gates rose and Mr. Behrens engaged gear and drove on.

Prometheus Unbound

Mr. Fortescue was the manager of the Westminster branch of the London and Home Counties Bank. He was also head of the External Branch of the Joint Services Standing Intelligence Committee. In his first capacity, he welcomed Mr. Behrens into his office one fine morning in May; in his second, he turned to business as soon as the heavy mahogany door had sighed shut.

"I'm worried," he said, "about Calder."

"I'm not too happy about him myself," said Mr. Behrens. "We're neighbors as well as friends, you know, and when a neighbor starts cutting you—"

"It's come to that, has it?"

"I used to go up to play backgammon with him—at least once a week, sometimes more. For the last three or four weeks he's been making excuses. And they've become such feeble excuses that I gathered the impression that what he really wanted was to be left-alone."

"He leads a somewhat solitary life, doesn't he?"

"Entirely solitary. Apart from myself, the visiting tradespeople and an occasional hiker, I doubt if he sees anyone from year's end to year's end."

"Do you think," said Mr. Fortescue, "that he might be going mad?"

There was regret in his voice, but no surprise. Professional agents usually did come to an untimely end. The curious, involute, secretive, occasionally dangerous and always responsible way of life took its sure toll of them. A few were killed by the enemy; others took their own lives; half a dozen, as Mr. Fortescue knew, were living in quiet country houses where the furniture was fixed to the floors and the inmates ate with plastic knives and forks and were shaved by a resident barber.

"I should have thought," said Mr. Behrens, "that Calder was the very last man to go that way."

"It's the strongest," said Mr. Fortescue, "who break the most unexpectedly. If it wasn't for Operation Prometheus this wouldn't be so serious. I mean," he added, as he saw the look of pain in Mr. Behrens' eyes, "I should, of course, be desperately sorry if something like that did happen to Calder. He's deserved well of his country. And I know that he's a very old and dear friend of yours."

"I quite understand," said Mr. Behrens. "How deeply involved is he?"

"He is one of three men—the other two are myself and Dick Harcourt—who know *all* the details. Prometheus is an immense operation, and a great many people have to know a bit about it—you know a bit about it yourself—but we are the only three who know it all. We have been in it from the beginning. Indeed, I recollect that it was Calder who christened it Operation Prometheus."

"Has the name any particular significance?" asked Mr. Behrens. He himself had been involved in an attempt to kidnap a Bulgarian general which had been known as Operation House Agent, and another, of such secrecy that the details cannot even now be discussed, called Operation Bubbles; and he had sometimes wondered who thought up the names, and on what principles, if any, they worked.

"There was a little more sense in this than in most," said Mr. Fortescue. "Prometheus was born of a union between the sea, in the form of a nymph called Clymene, and a mountain, represented by the Titan Iapetus. When we first seriously turned our minds to the liberation and advancement of Albania—a people whose original name, as you no doubt know, means 'Sons of the Eagle'—Operation Prometheus seemed quite an apt piece of nomenclature."

"Do I gather that these plans may be coming to a head?"

Mr. Fortescue placed the tips of his fingers together and said, "Albania is in a state of balance. Not the balance of tranquility, but the balance of strong opposing forces. In one direction, they are drawn to Russia—Enver Hoxha is an ardent Stalinist, even now that Stalinism has become unfashionable. In another direction, they have much in common with Yugoslavia—a union with Tito would please many. To the south they have strong, ancient and sentimental ties with Greece."

"Pull devil, pull baker," said Mr. Behrens. "Who do we think will win?"

"We know who we'd *like* to win," said Mr. Fortescue. "Our money is on Greece. If Georgiades Mikalos could be sure of our help—sure that it would be effective—then it's pretty certain he'd have a good shot at it. But our joint timing has got to be accurate—accurate to a hairsbreadth. The stakes are too high for error. Mikalos will not forget what happened to Xoxe."

"Where is Mikalos now?"

"In the hills behind Argyrokastron. Enver Hoxha has a fair idea where his hideout is, but he can't do much about it. Mikalos is well protected by his own partisans, and has, besides, a convenient back door into Greece. But if he is inaccessible to Enver, he is also inaccessible to us. And when the time comes we shall have to establish liaison with him. The idea was that Calder would go. He knows the country well—he was there with our mission in 1944. And he speaks the language."

"You say, the idea was that he should go. Do you now consider him too unreliable to send?"

"That is exactly what I want you to help me make my mind up about," said Mr. Fortescue.

* * *

Three days later Mr. Behrens trudged up the long winding hill, overhung with trees, which led to the hilltop on which Mr. Calder's solitary cottage stood.

He found the golden hound, Rasselas, lying on the front step. The dog seemed unhappy.

"Where is he?" said Mr. Behrens.

Rasselas thumped with his tail, and looked reproachfully over his shoulder toward the interior of the house.

At this moment Mr. Calder appeared in the hall. He was wearing what looked like a white nightgown. Combined with his bald and tonsured head, it gave him the appearance of a disreputable monk. He blinked and frowned into the sunlight, then seemed to recognize Mr. Behrens and said, "Come in. I'm very busy. But come in."

"If you're too busy to see me," said Mr. Behrens tartly, "I can always go back. After all, it's only two miles."

"No, no. Come in. You can probably help me."

Calder led the way into the sitting room.

"What on earth are you up to now?" said Mr. Behrens.

Across one end of the room was stretched an enormous piece of blank white paper pasted onto a backing of plywood. Coming closer, Mr. Behrens saw that six large pieces of lining paper had been joined together. Coming closer still, he saw that the paper was not, as he had supposed, blank. Considerable areas of it were covered with Mr. Calder's neat, crabbed writing, interspersed with curious symbols and pictures.

"I have been enagaged for some weeks," said Mr. Calder. After a pause he went on, "I fear it may have made me seem unsociable, but I have been engaged in one of the most curious and most important tasks that I have ever undertaken in my life."

"I can't understand a word of it."

"Some of it is in a special shorthand which I use for this particular purpose. Otherwise I couldn't hope to get it all in."

"But what is it?"

"I am tracing the genealogy of Prometheus—back to Adam, and down to myself."

"Down to you?"

"Down to me," said Mr. Calder. He seemed to be entirely serious.

"But how," said Mr. Behrens mildly, "can you be sure that you *are* descended from Prometheus? Of course, I know that if one goes back far enough everyone is descended from everyone else, approximately."

"There is nothing approximate about this. I have felt for some time that there was royal blood in my veins. But sometimes I have been aware that there is a higher plane than royalty. The plane of divinity."

Mr. Behrens looked at his old friend, and there was grief in his eyes. "Have you really come to believe this bosh?" he said.

Mr. Calder was not embarrassed.

"It is hard to grasp," he said, "but that is because you do not have the clue. Curiously enough, I was put on the track by Rasselas—"

The great dog, hearing its name, moved into the room and stood looking up at Mr. Calder. Mr. Calder patted his head absent-mindedly.

"When you consider a dog's pedigree," he said, "you realize that it is essential to follow both the male *and* female lines. The mistake we make in human genealogy is concentrating on the male. Prometheus was no ordinary divinity. He was the inventor of architecture and astronomy, of writing and the use of figures, of prophecy, medicine, navigation, and metalwork. He inherited strength and intelligence from his father, imagination and curiosity from his mother. He bestowed on mankind the gifts of fire—from his father. And from his mother, the gift of hope."

"His mother's was the greater gift," said Mr. Behrens.

"I'm afraid you're right," Mr. Behrens said to Mr. Fortescue on the following afternoon.

The meeting took place in one of the group of offices occupied by the Committee for European Coordination in Richmond Terrace, under the shadow of the hideous new Air Ministry building. The third man present was Commander Richard Harcourt, small, compact, dark, and energetic, and recognizable the length of St. James' as a product of the Royal Navy.

All Mr. Behrens knew about him was that he had had a Greek mother, and had made a big reputation for himself in submarines in the Adriatic during the war—two reasons, no doubt, for his presence on this particular committee.

"The last time I saw him myself," said Mr. Fortescue, "he spoke somewhat wildly on the subject of classical mythology."

"Do you think he's gone broody?" said Commander Harcourt.

Mr. Behrens was familiar enough with the jargon of the Security Service to know what he meant.

"I didn't detect any ideological slant in his conversation," he said. "It was quite a generalized form of eccentricity."

"Basically, I'm sure he's still sound," said Mr. Fortescue.

"He may be sound," said the commander, "but is he still a good Security risk?"

The same thought was troubling them all. The store of secrets inside Mr. Calder's dome-shaped head was such that even a casual overspill would be priceless gleaning for the enemy.

"You'll have to keep as close an eye on him as you can," said Mr. Fortescue.

Mr. Behrens traveled sadly back to Lamperdown.

When Mr. Calder and he had retired from active service in MI6 (as it was then called) and had joined Mr. Fortescue's organization, they had been encouraged to set up house within a few miles of each other. They would thus be able, as Mr. Fortescue had put it, to give each other covering fire. It was a sensible precaution which had already stood them in good stead more than once.

Mr. Behrens felt the defection of his ally very keenly. He was so silent at dinner that night that even his aunt, who was not given to small talk, noticed it. She supposed, since he had been up twice already that week to see his bank manager, that his troubles must be financial.

In the early hours of the following morning Mr. Behrens got quietly out of bed, put on a pair of flannel trousers that were hanging ready behind the door and pulled a sweater over his head. As an afterthought he opened the drawer of his bedside table and extracted a gun, which he dropped into his trouser pocket.

As he stood in silence in the front hall, he heard again the noise that had summoned him from sleep. It was a scratching—gentle but persistent, as if someone were making repeated but unsuccessful attempts to strike a match.

He walked across and opened the front door. The great dog Rasselas was standing in the misty moonlight. He made no attempt to come in, but when Mr. Behrens moved toward him, the animal sighed and backed away.

"Understood," said Mr. Behrens. "I'll have to get some shoes and a coat. Wait here."

It took them half an hour to climb the hill to Mr. Calder's cottage. The door was closed but unlatched, and Mr. Behrens went through the place carefully. There was no sign of disturbance. There had been a wood fire in the grate and Mr. Behrens felt the ashes; there was still heat in them.

He went up to Mr. Calder's bedroom and opened one or two of the drawers. Nothing seemed to have been disturbed. He returned to the sitting room, and here he noticed something.

The framed genealogy of Prometheus had disappeared.

Mr. Behrens was at Richmond Terrace by ten o'clock that morning, and since he had telephoned ahead, Mr. Fortescue and Commander Harcourt were waiting for him.

"I've shut the cottage up," said Mr. Behrens, "and told all the tradesmen that he's been called to the bedside of a sick cousin. His dog is with me for the time being. I thought I should have the devil of a job persuading Rasselas, but oddly enough he came quite quietly."

Mr. Fortescue nodded. It was the tradition of the Service. When a disaster occurred, you concentrated first on covering up. And this was black disaster.

"He'll have to be found," said Commander Harcourt. "Even if he's just had a brainstorm and wandered off somewhere, we can't leave him loose."

"No," said Mr. Fortescue. That was clear, too. "Is there any indication where he can have gone?"

"I had a word with the stationmaster at the junction. There's a very early train for London—it leaves about five in the morning. Takes the milk up and brings the newspapers back. There was a man on it who might easily have been Calder."

"I have a feeling that London is the place to start," said Mr. Fortescue. "I'll get the department onto it. Keep in touch."

The summons came three days later, after breakfast. It was a glorious morning of high summer, and Mr. Behrens was contemplating a quiet day among his hives when the telephone rang.

"Tottenham Court Road police station," said Mr. Fortescue. "And bring the dog with you."

Mr. Behrens found three men in shirt-sleeves in the superintendent's baking oven of an office—the superintendent himself,

Detective Inspector Inskip, and Commander Harcourt. They were studying a large-scale street map as Mr. Behrens came in. The heat, which had been so pleasant in the country, was a heavy burden in London.

"One of our men spotted him in Charlotte Street yesterday evening," said the Commander. "He lost him, but as Calder seemed to be shopping, it seems likely that he's hiding out somewhere in the area. That's the idea we're working on, anyway."

The superintendent nodded, even though the whole affair seemed to him to be quite irregular. The man they were looking for had apparently committed no offense, and there was no warrant in existence for his apprehension. Nevertheless his instructions, which he had received personally from the assistant commissioner in the early hours of that morning, were too specific to admit of argument or even of discussion.

"I've got men blocking the roads—" he demonstrated on the map. "I gather you're going in to look for him. Inskip will be with you. He knows the area well, but it won't be easy to search."

"We're hoping the dog will help us," said the commander.

"Rather you than me," said the superintendent. "Best get going."

Mr. Behrens recollected having visited Mr. Calder, some years before, when his old friend had been lying in a private ward of the Woolavington Wing of the Middlesex Hospital suffering from what was described on his medical sheet as "multiple gunshot wounds" (and was, in fact, the aftereffects of a nearly successful attempt by a German student to exterminate him with a home-made bomb). On these visits Mr. Behrens had walked to the hospital from the Tottenham Court Road, through the maze of courts and alleys which lies to the north of Oxford Street. And he had noticed what a curious chunk of Central Europe had settled itself into this small area—a sort of Quartier Latin whose existence was unsuspected by Londoners who kept to the main roads.

The larger shops were mostly tailors, furriers and boot-makers, but there were smaller and more curious trades: wig-makers and button-molders, gilders, glass polishers, key cutters and bead-stringers. There were shops which sold bath chairs and perambulators, shops which sold harps and shops which sold trusses; bakers, butchers, cut-price wine shops, delicatessen stores; and hundreds of cafés—tiny flyblown places devoted to the fellow nationals of the proprietor—Greeks, Cypriots, Poles, Danzigers.

The heat wave had brought the women out onto the rickety, first-story balconies where they sat in frowsy housecoats and dressing gowns, surveying life as it passed up and down the steaming street in front of their dispassionate eyes; men in cotton singlets and tight trousers, lounging in the cafés or basking in the sun; and, of course, swarms of children.

It was the children who attached themselves to Rasselas. A chattering, expectant covey of them followed him everywhere.

"What's the point of it?" growled Inspector Inskip. "Are they waiting for the dog to do tricks, or what?"

"Children have always loved Rasselas," said Mr. Behrens. Where the other two were hot and cross, he was perversely cheerful. He found the gaudy streets, with their dirty shop fronts and exciting smells, stimulating.

"It seems to me," said Commander Harcourt, "that we're on a wild-goose chase. The finest bloodhound in England couldn't smell out his owner in—this." He waved his hand at the street ahead.

They had been quartering the area systematically, taking each road in turn, walking down it on one side and up it on the other. Now they had reached the end of Surrey Street, and a choice of two narrow passages lay ahead of them.

"Oh, I think he'll tell us if Mr. Calder is anywhere about," said Mr. Behrens. "He doesn't do it by smell. He does it by instinct."

"He must have a hell of an instinct to work in these conditions," said the inspector.

"Let's take the left-hand one first," said the commander. "It looks a bit cleaner."

At the end of the passage Rasselas paused for the first time of his own accord. He was staring up at the back of the building which lay between them and the parallel passage. Then he swung round and padded off down the pavement. The men followed.

His objective was the other passage, and the house at the end of it. It was a lonely relic of the Blitz, standing like a surviving tooth in an ancient head among the shored-up stumps of its fellows. The ground floor was a shop, but the window was so grimy that it was impossible to tell what merchandise it dealt in. The name above the door was Margolis.

Rasselas sank onto his haunches outside the door, and stared upward. It was a three-story house. The windows were curtained and uncommunicative.

"If he was a game dog," said the commander, "I should say he was pointing. Do you know anything about this place?"

The inspector said, "An old woman keeps it—a Greek, I think. She's never given us any trouble."

Rasselas' tail had begun to thump gently against the pavement. The children had fallen silent. They looked hopeful. Whatever it was they had come to see was clearly about to happen.

"If we all go in," said Mr. Behrens, "the lady'll have a fit. Why don't you go, Inspector?"

The inspector nodded, pushed the door open and disappeared into the gloomy interior.

Five hot minutes trickled by. Mr. Behrens wiped the perspiration from his forehead. The crowd, he noticed, had grown.

The inspector reappeared. He came up to the other two and said very quietly, “I think it’s our man. He’s got a room on the top story. I got the old girl to go up and speak to him, but he’s locked his door and he won’t come out.”

“He might come out for me,” said Mr. Behrens. “He’ll know my voice, anyway.”

“Worth a try,” said the commander. “Where the hell did this crowd come from?” There were older people with the children now—dark faces, flashing teeth, bright eyes—all silent, expectant.

“I think it’s the combination of the dog and the Inspector,” said Mr. Behrens. “I’d better go up and see if I can’t settle it quietly. We don’t want to start a riot.”

Inside the shop, which was so dark that Mr. Behrens was still unable to see exactly what it sold, he found a large lady, dressed in black.

She gestured upward. “Poor man. He is, I think, touched.”

“I’m afraid he is,” said Mr. Behrens. “We’ll try to get him out with as little trouble as possible. Is this the way?”

There was a door at the back of the shop leading to a flight of linoleum-covered stairs. Mr. Behrens trudged up. His heart was heavy. When he got to the top landing he saw that the door, directly opposite the head of the stairs, was ajar.

He called out, “It’s me, Behrens. Are you in there, Calder?”

From inside the room a voice, which Mr. Behrens barely recognized, said, “Come no nearer, son of Jupiter. Prometheus stands at bay.”

Mr. Behrens walked forward and slowly opened the door. Mr. Calder, his chin fringed with a three-day beard, was sitting in his shirt-sleeves on the edge of the bed. The framed genealogy of Prometheus filled the two walls behind him.

But it was not this that caught and held Mr. Behrens’ eye.

Mr. Calder had an automatic pistol in his hand. Before Mr. Behrens could say another word, Mr. Calder had raised it and pointed it. As the gun went off with a deafening roar, Mr. Behrens went down. The bullet sang through the half-open doorway, exploded a pane of glass in the landing window and whined out into the street.

The gun went off again.

Mr. Behrens, who had been crawling rapidly backward, found himself halfway down the top flight of stairs, his chin on a level with the landing floor. He turned his head, and saw Commander Harcourt and Inskip crouching below him.

Outside, the crowd was giving tongue.

"Damn and blast," said the commander. "This is just exactly what we *didn't* want to happen."

"What sort of gun?" said Inskip.

"A Colt automatic. Eight shots, if the clip's full."

"Six to come then," said the inspector gloomily. "Is he a good shot?"

"He's a marksman, with any sort of weapon."

"He missed you."

"I don't think he meant to hit me. It was meant as a sort of warning salvo."

"It's going to be impossible to rush him," said the inspector. "We might call out the fire brigade, put up a ladder, and lob a couple of tear-gas bombs through the window."

The commander said acidly, "Our instructions were to take him with a minimum of fuss. Not the maximum."

"Can you suggest any other way?"

"Yes," said the commander. "I can." They saw he had a gun in his hand. "From the top of the stairs, I think I could hit him in the leg before he could hit me."

"Hitting him in the leg won't stop him," said Mr. Behrens. "You'd have to hit him in the head to do that."

"That might be a solution," said the commander softly. The two men were lying on the stairs, their faces a few inches from each other.

Mr. Behrens said, "I couldn't agree to that."

"Kinder, really," said the commander. "In the long run."

Mr. Behrens hesitated.

At that moment something hit them in the back and there was a sudden flurry of movement. Rasselas had cleared their prostrate bodies, bounded along the short landing and disappeared through the door. From inside came a crash.

"Come *on!*" said Mr. Behrens.

They found Mr. Calder flat on his back, with Rasselas on top of him, trying to lick his face off.

The months that followed were the saddest that Mr. Behrens could remember. The newspapers splashed the story, and then forgot about the seige of Surry Street. Mr. Calder had been removed to an institution near Godalming. His condition had become steadily worse, and no one had been allowed to visit him. "He wouldn't know you," the doctor in charge had said to Mr. Behrens, when he made his third application. "And you wouldn't enjoy it."

Mr. Behrens had only seen Mr. Fortescue once. He gathered that Operation Prometheus was proceeding. Commander Harcourt was going in in place of Mr. Calder. Mr. Behrens was too well trained to ask any further questions.

Eventually his low spirits attracted the attention of his aunt, who suggested that he take a holiday. She said she had heard that the west coast of Italy was very pleasant in the autumn.

"How can I possibly go?" said Mr. Behrens. "I can't leave Rasselas. And he'd be too much for you."

"Put him in a kennel."

"A kennel, indeed. What an idea!"

"Other people put their dogs in kennels when they go abroad."

"Rasselas isn't an ordinary dog."

Every time his name was mentioned, the great golden creature looked at the speakers. During all that time he had shown no signs of restlessness. He had merely been passive. It was as if he was waiting for some event, and content to wait patiently.

"If you won't go," said his aunt, "I will. You're no pleasure to live with at the moment." And she packed her bags the very next morning and departed for Rapallo.

Late the following afternoon Mr. Behrens was sitting in his study contemplating an empty future, when the bell rang. There was a device in the front door through which Mr. Behrens could view his visitors before admitting them. Peering through it, he was astounded to find himself looking into the sagacious face of Mr. Fortescue.

In all the years he had known him, Mr. Behrens had rarely known Mr. Fortescue to leave the square mile of streets between Victoria Station and the Admiralty Arch. It was as great a shock as if, making his way through one of the leafy lanes near his house, Mr. Behrens had come face to face with a London omnibus.

He hastened to open the door.

When they were comfortably seated, and a drink had been offered, and refused, Mr. Fortescue said, "I had business at Dover this morning, and when I saw that my return journey brought me almost through Lamperdown, I thought I would look you up. I had one or two things to tell you, which could not very easily have been said on the telephone."

Low though they were, Mr. Behrens' spirits sank still lower.

He said, "It was very good of you to take the trouble."

"I know that you have been interested in our—" Mr. Fortescue permitted himself a very slight smile—"in our Operation Prometheus. Calder was, of course, to have been our emissary to

Mikalos. When it became perfectly clear that he could not undertake the assignment, we had to find a substitute. The only other available candidate was Commander Harcourt."

Mr. Behrens found himself thinking of the last occasion on which he had met the commander. He had clearly intended, if no other solution had presented itself, to kill Mr. Calder; and thinking matters over afterward, Mr. Behrens could not find it in his heart to criticize the decision. It is true that the commander had not been thinking of Mr. Calder as a man. He had been thinking of him as an abstract problem in security. But on any grounds, would not Calder have been better dead than in a padded cell?

Mr. Behrens became aware that some comment was expected of him, and said, "Yes. I imagine Commander Harcourt will do the job excellently. He was obviously the man for the job."

"Unfortunately," said Mr. Fortescue, "it was just as obvious to the other side."

Mr. Behrens looked up sharply.

"Has something gone wrong?" he said.

"They must have reasoned that we would surely send Harcourt—we have so few people who know the area and can speak the language. They were obviously on the lookout for him, and picked him up soon after he landed. Unfortunately, before he could talk to Mikalos."

"Is he dead?"

"Oh, yes," said Mr. Fortescue. "His body was found. His throat had been cut. It was put down as the work of brigands—Harcourt was traveling as a Greek businessman. No one has officially connected him with us. And we shall, of course, deny all knowledge of him."

"Of course," said Mr. Behrens. "You'll have to find someone else to do the job now, I suppose."

"Yes—we'll find a substitute."

Outside, the autumn afternoon was turning into evening. A group of boys were kicking a soccer ball on the green, being careful to keep off the mown cricket square. A little red mail truck flashed past in a cloud of dust. Mr. Behrens sighed. Six months ago it had seemed to him that the Old Rectory, the village of Lamperdown, and the County of Kent were all that he needed to keep him happy for the rest of his life.

But now something had happened. A subtle piece of scene changing had been worked. There was a different backdrop, a couple of flats had been whisked away, a change had been made in the lighting and Arcady had become a prison cell.

Rasselas seemed to feel it, too. Ever since Mr. Fortescue had arrived, the big dog had been restless. Now he was lying in a corner of the room, regarding Mr. Fortescue open-mouthed, as if he were the embodiment of the successive disasters which had befallen them.

"In all the time I've worked for you," said Mr. Behrens, "I've never yet asked you a favor."

"True," said Mr. Fortescue.

"I'm going to ask one now. I want to take over this mission. I have a good working knowledge of Greek and Italian—not enough to pass as a native, but enough, I think, to get over to Mikalos whatever you want him to know."

"I'm afraid—" said Mr. Fortescue.

"Before you turn it down, bear in mind that if you say no you're probably going to have two mental cases on your hands, instead of one. If I have to sit here much longer doing nothing, I shall go mad."

"I can certainly find you a job—"

"I want this particular job."

"It's impossible."

"Why is it impossible?"

"It's impossible," said Mr. Fortescue, "because the job no longer exists. It's been finished."

Mr. Behrens stared at him. Rasselas was on his feet, hackles up, amber eyes gleaming.

"What do you mean? Quiet, Rasselas. Lie down. I thought you said that you needed a substitute."

"We already have a substitute—we had him ready at the same time as Commander Harcourt. It's better to double up on these important jobs. The substitute actually left England the day before Harcourt. I picked up his report at Dover this morning. It crossed a few hours ahead of him. But he'll be in England now." Mr. Fortescue looked at his watch. "Indeed, he'll be on his way to London. I don't know a lot about dogs, but it seems to me that if you don't open either the door or the window, Rasselas will attempt to break out of his own accord."

"Rasselas!" said Mr. Behrens in his sternest voice, but the dog took not the slightest notice. The deerhound turned to Mr. Fortescue, exactly as if he were appealing to someone with more sense.

Mr. Fortescue raised the latch of the window, swung it open, and Rasselas went through it in one smooth golden arc, raced down the front drive like a driven duststorm, and threw himself at the stocky figure standing in the gateway.

"It would appear," said Mr. Fortescue, "that our substitute has got here a little quicker than I thought he would. I hope the dog doesn't kill him in his enthusiasm. A written report is one thing. A verbal report will be even more enlightening."

It was some hours later, after Mr. Fortescue had departed for London, that Mr. Behrens got round to saying, "But why?"

Mr. Calder, looking a little thinner, but remarkably brown and fit, leaned back in his chair, scratched the dome of Rasselas' head and said, "It was very difficult—very difficult, indeed. We found out—but a lot too late—that Harcourt had sold out."

"Commander Harcourt?" Mr. Behrens thought of the dark, clever, determined face. It seemed impossible, though not so impossible as some of the things that had happened in the past twenty years. Then as Mr. Behrens thought about it, a lot of facts fell into place.

"They got at him through his Greek relatives. He's been their man since the war. God knows what damage he did before we got on to him."

"And he was in Operation Prometheus from the start!"

"From the start. He knew it all—every detail. So we had only two options. Either drop the whole thing or try a sort of triple bluff. If I were groomed for the job, you see, and then went off my head, Harcourt became the obvious and natural substitute. Of course he had to say yes, meaning to make contact with his own friends just as soon as he got ashore in Albania. But Mikalos has plenty of friends, too. They got him first. Meanwhile, I'd landed fifty miles down the coast. I suppose I was about the last person the opposition expected to see, so I had quite an easy run. And a very interesting talk with Mikalos. Prometheus is more than a little tired of having his liver pecked out by the eagle. We may be seeing some action in that part of the world quite soon."

"I wish you'd told me!" said Mr. Behrens.

"I wanted to. Fortescue wouldn't hear of it. And I'm afraid he was right."

"What do you mean?"

"Think back to that time in Surrey Street. If Rasselas hadn't intervened, Harcourt was going to take a shot at me, wasn't he? If you had known what you know now, would you have behaved exactly as you did?"

"I suppose that's right," said Mr. Behrens. "So you and Fortescue were the only people in the know."

"Certainly not," said Mr. Calder. "Rasselas knew *all* about it."

A Prince of Abyssinia

Mr. Calder was silent, solitary and generous with everything, from a basket of cherries or mushrooms to efficient first aid to a child who had tumbled. The children liked him. But their admiration was reserved for his deerhound.

Rasselas had been born in the sunlight. His coat was the color of dry sherry, his nose was blue-black and his eyes shone like worked amber. From the neat tufts at his heels to the top of his dome-shaped head, there was a royalty about him. He had lived in courts and consorted on his own terms with other princes.

Mr. Calder's cottage stood at the top of a fold in the Kentish Downs. The road curled up to it from Lamperdown, in the valley. First it climbed slowly between woods, then forked sharply left and rose steeply, coming out onto the plateau, rounded and clear as a bald pate. The road served only the cottage, and stopped in front of its gate.

Beyond the house, there were paths which led through the home fields and into the woods beyond, woods full of primroses, bluebells, pheasant's eggs, chestnuts, hollow trees and ghosts. The woods did not belong to Mr. Calder. They belonged, in theory, to a syndicate of businessmen from the Medway towns who came at the week ends, in autumn and winter, to kill birds. When the sound of their station wagons announced their arrival, Mr. Calder would call Rasselas indoors. At all other times, the great dog roamed freely in the garden and in the three open fields which formed Mr. Calder's domain. But he never went out of sight of the house, nor beyond the sound of his master's voice.

The children said that the dog talked to the man, and this was perhaps not far from the truth. Before Mr. Calder came, the cottage had been inhabited by a bad-tempered oaf who had looked on himself as custodian for the Medway sportsmen, and had chased and harried the children who, in their turn, had become adept at avoiding him.

When Mr. Calder first came, they had spent a little time in trying him, before finding him harmless. Nor had it taken them long to find out something else. No one could cross the plateau unobserved, small though he might be and quietly though he might move. A pair of sensitive ears would have heard, a pair of amber eyes would have seen; and Rasselas would pad in at the open door and look enquiringly at Mr. Calder who would say, "Yes, it's the Lightfoot boys and their sister. I saw them, too." And Rasselas would stalk out and lie down again in his favorite day bed, on the sheltered side of the woodpile.

Apart from the children, visitors to the cottage were a rarity. The postman wheeled his bicycle up the hill once a day; delivery vans appeared at their appointed times; the fish man on Tuesdays, the grocer on Thursdays, the butcher on Fridays. In the summer, occasional hikers wandered past, unaware that their approach, their passing and their withdrawal had all been reported to the owner of the cottage.

Mr. Calder's only regular visitor was Mr. Behrens, the retired schoolmaster who lived in the neck of the valley, two hundred yards outside Lamperdown Village, in a house which had once been the Rectory. Mr. Behrens kept bees, and lived with his aunt. His forward-stooping head, his wrinkled brown skin, blinking eyes and cross expression made him look like a tortoise which has been roused untimely from its winter sleep.

Once or twice a week, summer and winter, Mr. Behrens would get out his curious tweed hat and his iron-tipped walking stick, and would go tip-tapping up the hill to have tea with Mr. Calder. The dog knew and tolerated Mr. Behrens, who would scratch his ears and say, "Rasselas. Silly name. *You* came from Persia, not Abyssinia." It was believed that the two old gentlemen played backgammon.

There were other peculiarities about Mr. Calder's menage which were not quite so very apparent to the casual onlooker.

When he first took over the house, some of the alterations he had asked for had caused Mr. Benskin, the builder, to scratch his head. Why, for instance, had he wanted one perfectly good southern-facing window filled in, and two more opened on the north side of the house?

Mr. Calder had been vague. He said that he liked an all-round view and plenty of fresh air. In which case, asked Mr. Benskin, why had he insisted on heavy shutters on all downstairs windows and a steel plate behind the woodwork of the front and back doors?

There had also been the curious matter of the telephone line. When Mr. Calder had mentioned that he was having the telephone installed, Mr. Benskin had laughed. The post office, overwhelmed as they were with post-war work, were hardly likely to carry their line of poles a full mile up the hill for one solitary cottage. But Mr. Benskin had been wrong, and on two counts. Not only had the post office installed a telephone with surprising promptness, but they had actually dug a trench and brought it in underground.

When this was reported to him, Mr. Benskin had told the public ear of the Golden Lion that he had always known there was something odd about Mr. Calder.

"He's an inventor," he said. "To my mind, there's no doubt that's what he is. An inventor. He's got government support. Otherwise, how'd he get a telephone line laid like that?"

Had Mr. Benskin been able to observe Mr. Calder getting out of bed in the morning, he would have been fortified in his opinion. For it is a well-known fact that inventors are odd, and Mr. Calder's routine on rising was very odd indeed.

Summer and winter, he would wake half an hour before dawn. He turned on no electric light. Instead, armed with a big torch, he would pad downstairs, the cold nose of Rasselas a few inches behind him, and make a minute inspection of the three ground-floor rooms. On the edges of the shutters were certain tiny thread-like wires, almost invisible to the naked eye. When he had satisfied himself that these were in order, Mr. Calder would return upstairs and get dressed.

By this time, day was coming up. The darkness had withdrawn across the bare meadows and chased the ghosts back into the surrounding woods. Mr. Calder would take a pair of heavy naval binoculars from his dressing table, and, sitting back from the window, would study with care the edges of his domain. Nothing escaped his attention: a wattle hurdle blocking a path; a bent sapling at the edge of the glade; a scut of fresh earth in the hedge. The inspection was repeated from the window on the opposite side.

Then, whistling softly to himself, Mr. Calder would walk downstairs to cook breakfast for himself and for Rasselas.

The postman, who arrived at eleven o'clock, brought the newspapers with the letters. Perhaps because he lived alone and saw so few people, Mr. Calder seemed particularly fond of his letters and papers. He opened them with a loving care which an observer might have found ludicrous. His fingers caressed the envelope or the wrapping paper very gently, as a man will squeeze a cigar. Often he would hold an envelope up to the light as if he could read, through the outer covering, the message inside. Sometimes he would even weigh an envelope in the delicate letter scales which he kept on top of his desk between a stuffed seagull and a night-scented jasmine in a pot.

On a fine morning in May, when the sun was fulfilling in majesty the promise of a misty dawn, Mr. Calder unfolded his copy of the *Times*, turned, as was his custom, to the foreign news pages and started to read.

He had stretched his hand out toward his coffee cup when he stopped. It was a tiny check, a break in the natural sequence of his actions, but it was enough to make Rasselas look up. Mr. Calder smiled reassuringly at the dog. His hand resumed its movement, picked up the cup, carried it to his mouth. But the dog was not easy.

Mr. Calder read once more the five-line item which had caught his attention. Then he glanced at his watch, went across to the telephone, dialed a Lamperdown number and spoke to Jack at the garage, which also ran a taxi service.

"Just do it if we hurry," said Jack. "No time to spare. I'll come right up."

While he waited for the taxi, Mr. Calder first telephoned Mr. Behrens, to warn him that they might have to postpone their game of backgammon. Then he spent a little time telling Rasselas that he was leaving him in charge of the cottage, but that he would be back before dark. Rasselas swept the carpet with his feathery tail, and made no attempt to follow Mr. Calder when Jack's Austin came charging up the hill and reversed in front of the cottage gate.

In the end, the train was ten minutes late at the junction, and Mr. Calder caught it with ease.

He got out at Victoria, walked down Victoria Street, turned to the right, opposite the open space where the Colonial office used to stand, and to the right again into the Square. In the southwest corner stands the Westminster branch of the London and Home Counties Bank.

Mr. Calder walked into the bank. The head cashier, Mr. Macleod, nodded gravely to him and said, "Mr. Fortescue is ready. You can go straight in."

"I'm afraid the train was late," said Mr. Calder. "We lost ten minutes at the junction, and never caught it up."

"Trains are not as reliable now as they used to be," agreed Mr. Macleod.

A young lady from a nearby office had just finished banking the previous day's takings. Mr. Macleod was watching her out of the corner of his eye until the door had shut behind her. Then he said, with exactly the same inflection, but more softly, "Will it be necessary to make any special arrangements for your departure?"

"Oh, no, thank you," said Mr. Calder. "I took all the necessary precautions."

"Fine," said Mr. Macleod.

He held open the heavy door, paneled in sham walnut in the style affected by pre-war bank designers, ushered Mr. Calder into the anteroom and left him there for a few moments, in contemplation of its only ornament, a reproduction in a massive gilt frame of Landseer's allegory "The Tug of War."

Then the head cashier reappeared and held open the door for Mr. Calder, and Mr. Fortescue came forward to greet him.

"Nice to see you," he said. "Grab a chair. Any trouble on the way up?"

"No trouble," said Mr. Calder. "I don't think anything can start for another two or three weeks."

"They might have post-dated the item to put you off your guard." He picked up his own copy of the *Times* and reread the four and a half lines of print which recorded that Colonel Josef Weinleben, the international expert on bacterial antibodies, had died in Klagenfurt as the result of an abdominal operation.

"No," said Calder. "He wanted me to read it, and sweat."

"It would be the established procedure to organize his own 'death' before setting out on a serious mission," Mr. Fortescue agreed. He picked up a heavy paper knife and tapped thoughtfully with it on the desk. "But it could be true, this time. Weinleben must be nearly sixty."

"He's coming," said Mr. Calder. "I can feel it in my bones. It may even be true that he's ill. If he was dying, he'd like to take me along with him."

"What makes you so sure?"

"I tortured him," said Mr. Calder. "And broke him. He'd never forget."

"No," said Mr. Fortescue. He held the point of the paper knife toward the window, sighting down it as if it had been a pistol. "No. I think very likely you're right. We'll try to pick him up at the port, and tag him. But we can't guarantee to stop him getting in. If he tries to operate, of course, he'll have to show his hand. You've got your permanent cover. Do you want anything extra?"

He might, thought Mr. Calder, have been speaking to a customer. You've got your normal overdraft. Do you want any extra accommodation, Mr. Calder? The bank is here to serve you. There was something at the same time ridiculous and comforting in treating life and death as though they were entries in the same balance sheet.

"I'm not at all sure that I want you to stop him," he said. "We aren't at war. You could only deport him. It might be more satisfactory to let him through."

"Do you know," said Mr. Fortescue, "the same thought had occurred to me."

Mrs. Farmer, who kept the Seven Gables Guest House, between Aylesford and Bearsted, considered Mr. Wendon a perfect guest. His passport and the card which he had duly filled in on arrival showed him to be a Dutchman; but his English, though accented in odd places, was colloquial and fluent. An upright, red-faced, gray-haired man, he was particularly nice with Mrs. Farmer's two young children. Moreover, he gave no trouble. He was—and this was a sovereign virtue in Mrs. Farmer's eyes—methodical and predictable.

Every morning, in the endless succession of the fine days which heralded that summer, he would go out walking, clad in aged but respectable tweed, field glass over one shoulder, a small knapsack on the other for camera, sandwiches and thermos flask. And in the evenings he would sit in the lounge, drinking a single glass of schnapps as an aperitif before dinner, and entertaining Tom and Rebecca with accounts of the birds he had observed that day. It was difficult to imagine, seeing him sitting there, gentle, placid, and upright, that he had killed men and women—and children, too—with his own well-kept hands. But then Mr. Wendon, or Weinleben, or Weber, was a remarkable man.

On the tenth day of his stay, he received a letter from Holland. Its contents seemed to cause him some satisfaction, and he read it twice before putting it away in his wallet. The stamps he tore off, giving them to Mrs. Farmer for Tom.

"I may be a little late this evening," he said. "I am meeting a friend at Maidstone. Don't keep dinner for me."

That morning he packed his knapsack with particular care and caught the Maidstone bus at Aylesford crossroads. He had said that he was going to Maidstone and he never told unnecessary lies.

After that his movements became somewhat complicated, but by four o'clock he was safely ensconced in a dry ditch to the north of the Old Rectory at Lamperdown. Here he consumed a biscuit, and observed the front drive of the house.

At a quarter past four, Jack arrived with his taxi and Mr. Behren's aunt came out, wearing, despite the heat of the day, coat and gloves and a rather saucy scarf, and was installed in the back seat. Mr. Behrens handed in her shopping basket, waved good-bye and retired into the house.

Five minutes later, Mr. Wendon was knocking at the front door. Mr. Behrens opened it, and blinked when he saw the gun in his visitor's hand.

"I must ask you to turn around and walk in front of me," said Mr. Wendon.

"Why should I?" said Mr. Behrens. He sounded more irritated than alarmed.

"If you don't, I shall shoot you," said Mr. Wendon. He said it exactly as if he meant it and pushed Mr. Behrens toward a door.

After a moment, Mr. Behrens wheeled about and asked, "Where now?"

"That looks the sort of place I had in mind," said Mr. Wendon. "Open the door and walk in. But quite slowly."

It was a small dark room, devoted to hats, coats, sticks, old tennis rackets, croquet mallets, bee veils and such.

"Excellent," said Mr. Wendon. He helped himself to the old-fashioned tweed hat and the iron-tipped walking stick which Mr. Behrens carried abroad with him on all his perambulations of the countryside. "A small window and a stout old door. What could be better?"

Still watching Mr. Behrens closely, he laid the hat and stick on the hall table, dipped his left hand into his own coat pocket and brought out a curious-looking metal object.

"You have not, perhaps, seen one of these before? It works on the same principle as a Mills grenade, but is six times as powerful and is incendiary as well as explosive. When I shut this door,

I shall bolt it and hang the grenade from the upturned bolt. The least disturbance will dislodge it. It is powerful enough to blow the door down."

"All right," said Mr. Behrens. "But get on with it. My sister will be back soon."

"Not until eight o'clock, if she adheres to last week's arrangements," said Mr. Wendon, quite knowingly.

He closed the door, shot the bolts, top and bottom, and suspended the grenade with artistic care from the top one.

Mr. Calder had finished his tea by five o'clock, and then shortly afterward strolled down to the end of the paddock, where he was repairing the fence. Rasselas lay quietly in the lee of the woodpile. The golden afternoon turned imperceptibly toward evening.

Rasselas wrinkled his velvet muzzle to dislodge a fly. On one side he could hear Mr. Calder digging with his mattock into the hilltop chalk and grunting as he dug. Behind, some four fields away, a horse, fly-plagued, was kicking its heels and bucking. Then, away to his left, he located a familiar sound. The clink of an iron-tipped walking stick on stone.

Rasselas liked to greet the arrival of this particular friend of his master, but he waited with dignity until the familiar tweed had come into view. Then he unfolded himself and trotted gently out into the road.

So strong was the force of custom, so disarming were the familiar and expected sight and sound, that even Rasselas' five senses were lulled. But his instinct was awake. The figure was still a dozen paces off and advancing confidently, when Rasselas stopped. His eyes searched the figure. Right appearance, right hat, right noises. But wrong gait. Quicker, and more purposeful than their old friend. And, above all, wrong smell.

The dog hackled, then crouched as if to jump. But it was the man who jumped. He leaped straight at the dog; his hand came out from under his coat and the loaded stick hissed through the air with brutal force. Rasselas was still moving, and the blow missed his head but struck him full on the back of the neck. He went down without a sound.

Mr. Calder finished digging the socket for the corner post he was planting, straightened his back and decided that he would fetch the brush and creosote from the house. As he came out of the paddock, he saw the great dog lying in the road.

He ran forward and knelt in the dust. There was no need to look twice.

He hardly troubled to raise his eyes when a voice which he recognized spoke from behind him.

"Keep your hands in sight," said Colonel Weinleben, "and try not to make any sudden or unexpected move."

Mr. Calder got up.

"I suggest we move back into the house," said the colonel. "We shall be more private there. I should like to devote at least as much attention to you as you did to me on the last occasion we met."

Mr. Calder seemed hardly to be listening. He was looking down at the crumpled, empty, tawny skin, incredibly changed by the triviality of life's departure. His eyes were full of tears.

"You killed him," he said.

"As I shall shortly kill you," said the colonel. And, as he spoke, he spun round like a startled marionette, took a stiff pace forward and fell, face downward.

Mr. Calder looked at him incuriously. From the shattered hole in the side of his head, dark blood ran out and mixed with the white dust. Rasselas had not bled at all. He was glad of that tiny distinction between the two deaths.

It was Mr. Behrens who had killed Colonel Weinleben, with a single shot from a .312 rifle fired from the edge of the wood. The rifle was fitted with a telescopic sight, but the shot was a fine one, even for an excellent marksman such as Mr. Behrens.

He'd run for nearly a quarter of a mile before firing it; he had to get into position very quickly, and he had only just been able to see the colonel's head over the top of an intervening hedge.

He burst through this hedge now, saw Rasselas and started to curse.

"It wasn't your fault," said Mr. Calder. He was sitting in the road, the dog's head in his lap.

"If I'm meant to look after you, I ought to look after you properly," said Mr. Behrens. "Not let myself be jumped by an amateur like that. I hadn't reckoned on him blocking the door with a grenade. I had to break out of the window, and it took me nearly half an hour."

"We've a lot to do," said Mr. Calder. He got stiffly to his feet and went to fetch a spade.

Between them they dug a deep grave behind the woodpile, and laid the dog in it and filled it in, and patted the earth into a mound. It was a fine resting place, looking out southward over the feathery tops of the trees, across the Weald of Kent. A resting place for a prince.

Colonel Weinleben they buried later, with a good deal more haste and less ceremony, in the wood.